PRAISE FOR HELEN HARDT

"I'm dead from the strongest book hangover ever. Helen exceeded every expectation I had for this book. It was heart pounding, heartbreaking, intense, full throttle genius."

~ Tina at Bookalicious Babes Blog

"Proving the masterful writer she is, Ms. Hardt continues to weave her beautifully constructed web of deceit, terror, disappointment, passion, love, and hope as if there was never a pause between releases. A true artist never reveals their secrets, and Ms. Hardt is definitely a true artist."

~ Bare Naked Words

"The love scenes are beautifully written and so scorching hot I'm fanning my face just thinking about them."

~ The Book Sirens

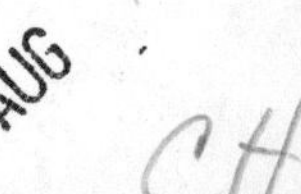

Surrender

STEEL BROTHERS SAGA
BOOK SIX

This book is an original publication of Helen Hardt

Cover Design by Waterhouse Press, LLC
Cover Photographs: Shutterstock

Paperback ISBN: 978-1-943893-22-5

Surrender

STEEL BROTHERS SAGA
BOOK SIX

For all the amazing members of Hardt and Soul!
And in memory of Lucy.

WARNING

This book contains adult language and scenes, including flashbacks of child physical and sexual abuse, which may cause trigger reactions. This story is meant only for adults as defined by the laws of the country where you made your purchase. Store your books and e-books carefully where they cannot be accessed by younger readers.

PROLOGUE

Jonah

Two hours later, I arrived in the small town near the New Mexico border. The address hadn't shown up on GPS, so I had to drive the roads of the town until I found what I was looking for. It was a cracker box house on the outskirts of town. A one-car detached garage sat off to the side.

Tom Simpson's hideout.

I parked a block away to hide my car and then walked stealthily to the small abode.

I didn't bother knocking, just turned the knob on the door. Oddly, it was open. I walked in. A nice enough home, sparsely furnished.

"Tom? Come out here, you sick son of a bitch."

No response. Not that I thought there would be. I walked through the living area, down a hall, to a couple of bedrooms. One was clearly being used, but no one was there. The door to what turned out to be a bathroom was also closed, but I opened it and walked in, not caring if I might catch Tom Simpson in the middle of a crap. But it was also vacant.

On the other side of the bedrooms was a small kitchen. Supplies had clearly been laid in. One more door. I opened it. It led to a dank basement surrounded by dark concrete walls. As I descended the stairs, eerie fingers seemed to crawl over my body.

The steps. The walls.

I inhaled, nearly gagging. Waste. Whether it was human or animal, I didn't know.

I looked around once I got to the bottom.

My heart nearly stopped. It was exactly how Talon had described it. I could almost see the phoenix on the dark-gray walls, taunting him.

I had just walked into the cave-like cellar where my brother had lived for two months when he was a child of ten.

My skin tightened around me. I could hardly catch my breath. Was there no oxygen in this place?

I suppressed my fears as best I could and looked around. No windows, which was odd, and the room was pitch black. I waited for my eyes to adjust, feeling the wall for guidance, and I checked out the space. The rough concrete walls scratched at my—

I jerked.

A groan had come from the corner. I inched forward slowly, and a heap of blankets emerged in my field of vision. More groaning.

Someone was here. Someone in this basement where those three psychos had kept my brother.

I didn't dare speak. I made my way slowly and quietly to the blanketed lump on the floor and removed the dirty covers.

The body, bound and gagged, recoiled away, whimpering.

My God.

It was alive.

"Hey, hey," I whispered. "I'm not going to hurt you."

It was a male, naked, his bony body streaked with blood and grime. His head had been shaved.

"I want to help you. I'm a friend. I'm going to take the gag off you, but don't scream. All right?"

The man whimpered and nodded.

I removed the gag carefully. "Who are you?"

He groaned, muttering unintelligible words.

"It's okay. You don't have to talk. I'm going to get you out of here." As quickly as I could, I unbound his ankles and wrists.

I startled when a sound like a board creaking came from somewhere upstairs. Tom must have come back. I threw the dirty blanket over the sickly man. "Shh," I said. "Don't let him know I've untied you. I'll take care of him. If I don't come back for you in half an hour, find something to use as a weapon, and get the fuck out of here."

I hated leaving him there, but he'd at least be safe while I was in the house. I'd told him to leave if I didn't return, but he was so bony and sickly looking, I wondered if he'd be able to get up the stairs.

But he would. Talon had gotten up those very same stairs.

"I'll be back for you. I promise."

I hoped I'd be able to keep that promise.

I walked toward the stairway, the dark walls seeming to pulse and close in.

My God, how had Talon survived this?

And who was the man in the cellar?

I willed myself to get a grip and ascended the stairs slowly. I had come here alone and unarmed. I hadn't thought about protecting myself. I could kick the shit out of Tom Simpson with a look, and if he had a knife, I could easily disarm him.

But if he had a gun...

The man was a killer. A cold-blooded killer. And God only knew what he'd done to this poor man in the cellar.

Bile nudged up my throat. That was a crock. I knew exactly what Tom had done. The same thing he'd done to my brother.

I shut the door of the basement quietly and walked through the small kitchen. The doorknob to the front door turned slowly.

A man entered, carrying a bag of groceries. As far as I could tell, he was unarmed. The hair on his head was dyed dark brown.

But the eyes...

A maniacal smile crossed my face. I had him.

Finally.

Finally, I would avenge my brother.

My smile became wider.

"Hello, Tom."

CHAPTER ONE

Melanie

I was determined to take my life back. Take myself back. I didn't for one moment think that Jonah and I were over. I could forgive him for ignoring my call that night. After all, I was the one who had left him, sneaked out of this house because I was too embarrassed to stay and talk with Talon and Jade after they caught us naked by Jonah's pool.

But one thing I knew more than anything else—I could no longer depend on Jonah for my safety, for my protection. I had to make peace with the ghosts of my past so they would no longer follow me and haunt me.

I drove to my loft in the city. I had gotten a voice mail earlier from my insurance agent, telling me that the police had gotten all the evidence they needed and that I could now go to the loft and take whatever I wanted without a police escort. I would start there. Once my insurance company paid and I got the place fixed up, it was going on the market. Yes, I wanted to take my life back, but I wouldn't do it in that loft. Too much history there. I would begin somewhere else.

I pulled into my parking spot and went into my building. I took the elevator to the fourth floor and walked toward my door. The police tape was gone, and a new lock had been installed. It was a touch-tone lock, and the police had given me the code and instructions on how to change it. I punched in the four digits and opened the door.

"Dr. Carmichael?"

I looked over my shoulder. Officer Ruby Lee, whom I had met while I was in the hospital and talked with several times, walked off the elevator toward me. I almost hadn't recognized her because she wasn't in uniform. She wore khaki pants and a white Oxford shirt buttoned almost all the way up. Her slick, dark hair was still pulled back and secured in a severe bun.

She had lovely features and searing blue eyes, yet she still dressed like a man when she wasn't in uniform. To each her own.

"Officer Lee, what are you doing here?"

She smiled broadly. "It's Detective Lee now."

"Oh. Congratulations. I was wondering why you weren't in uniform."

"I didn't expect to see you here tonight," she said.

"I didn't expect to be here either. But here I am. Why put this off, you know? It's not going to get any easier."

"Well, don't let me bother you. I was going to look around. I want to make sure the uniforms and the others didn't miss anything."

"Anything new on the case? Do you have any leads?"

"No. I'm afraid not. I've talked to just about everyone I can, even though this isn't officially my case anymore. In fact, I probably shouldn't even be here. I'm off duty. But something about this case..."

I startled. "What?"

She shook her head. "It's kind of...personal to me. Let's leave it at that."

I was a psychotherapist. I couldn't leave anything "at

that."

"Make yourself at home, such that it is. If you're here to help, you're certainly welcome."

"Thanks. I appreciate it." She followed me into the loft.

The place was still in shambles. Of course it was. The police department wasn't going to hire a cleaning service to clean up after a felon—or themselves, for that matter. I regarded the living room. My sofa had been ripped apart, and I darted my gaze to the floor. My book sat there, nearly hidden by the sofa's dust ruffle. I picked it up and turned it over to see the front cover.

Ice crept through my veins. "Bitch" had been scrawled across it in black marker.

"I'm sorry you had to see that," the other woman said, taking it from me.

"It's all right, Officer. I mean Detective."

She smiled. "How about we just settle on Ruby?"

I returned her smile. "Then you call me Melanie."

She held out her hand. "Deal." Then she took the book from me. "This should have been taken in as evidence. Damn. And I'm not wearing gloves."

"I guess it has both your prints and mine on it now. Sorry about that."

"Don't be sorry. None of this is your fault. The guys on this case will be hearing from me." She shook her head. "Morons."

I cocked my head at her.

"Sorry. They're overworked, just like we all are. And since you got away and aren't horribly hurt or dead, this case isn't a priority. I wish it were, but unfortunately, our resources are limited."

I sighed. Story of my life. Never a priority.

Stop it!

I'd made a promise to myself to stop thinking of myself as average, and damn it, I was going to keep that vow, no matter how neglectful my parents had been or how neglectful the police were being now.

"I think it's sad that my case isn't a big priority, but I guess I understand." I looked around the room again. "I don't think I want any of this stuff. I'll get some insurance money for what's been ruined. I'll use that to buy new stuff. I think I'll call a charity and have the rest of this shit picked up." I whipped out my cell phone and quickly searched for the number for the Salvation Army.

"Hold on," Ruby said. "I'd like to do some more investigating if it's okay. I mean, before you dump all this stuff."

"I thought the officers and detectives already got everything they needed," I said. "That's why I could come without an escort."

"So they said, but they obviously missed the book." She held it up to me. "Like I said, I'm off duty. This case is...personal to me."

The second time she'd said that. Surely she didn't expect me, a therapist, to let it go.

"Pardon me for prying," I began, "but why? Why is it personal?"

"I don't really want to talk about it."

"You opened that door, Ruby. This is my apartment, and you're not here officially. If anything you find can uncover the lunatic who kidnapped, drugged, and tried to kill me, I'm all for it. But I need to know why."

She sighed and looked around. "Not really any place to sit, huh?"

"Unfortunately, no. At least not in here. We can sit on the bed in the other room. Or here on the floor." I gestured.

"Works for me." Ruby sat down cross-legged.

I sat across from her. "Look, you don't have to talk about anything you don't want to talk about, but I need to have some clue as to why this is personal to you."

"All right." She cleared her throat. "Here goes. There's a reason why I was taken off the case when they promoted me."

"Yes?"

"This is difficult for me to talk about. It's a crazy sort of coincidence that is almost unreal."

My heart started beating faster. What was she getting at?

"I've been estranged from my family since I was fifteen. I ran away from home and never looked back."

Teenagers didn't usually run away unless they had a very good reason. "What happened? Why would you do that?"

"I ran from my father."

"What about your mother?"

"She's dead. At least I think she is. He always told me she was, but I've never been sure, you know?"

I nodded. "What does all of this have to do with my case?"

She inhaled a deep breath and let it out slowly, closing her eyes for a moment. When she opened them, they flamed a bright blue. "I know about your history with Gina Cates, and I know about her uncle who abused her."

This was all information I had given to the police when I was questioned, and surely they had heard it from Dr. Rodney Cates, Gina's father, as well, since he'd been the prime suspect in my abduction until he exonerated himself with an ironclad alibi.

"I hope you know I can't talk to you about any of that.

Even though Gina is dead, her psychotherapy notes are still protected under HIPAA."

"Yeah, I understand all of that. I'm not going to probe you for information on Gina. I know all I need to know about her. We were actually close once. A long time ago."

"You were?"

"Yes. She was my cousin. The man who raped her is my father."

CHAPTER TWO

Jonah

Tom was unfazed. His eyes didn't widen. His face didn't pale. Icy. Yup, an iceman. But I saw beneath the surface. Beads of sweat were emerging on his forehead. His hands trembled. Only slightly, but I noticed.

"Nice of you to bring groceries. Were you planning to feed your guest in the basement?" I stood, advancing toward him.

His trembling hands got the best of him, and he dropped the bag of groceries. Apples rolled toward me as he turned to flee.

Oh, hell, no.

I ran after him and tackled him on the lawn with a thud. If only it had been concrete, I could have hurt the psycho. "You motherfucking son of a bitch!"

"Who are you?" he yelled. "You've got the wrong guy!"

"You want to tell me you're not Tom Simpson? The fucking mayor of Snow Creek? One of the men who raped my brother? That bad dye job can't hide who you are."

"Let me go!"

I threw my body on top of him and clamped my hand over his mouth. "I'd recognize those eyes anywhere. My best friend has the same ones, and so does his baby son. And if I ever find out you touched one hair on that baby's head— Fuck!"

I removed my hand quickly. The fucker had bitten me hard enough to draw blood.

He moved quickly, but I was bigger and stronger. In a flash, I had my hand back over his mouth, pain be damned. My blood smeared crimson across his cheeks.

"You think you can get away from me, you stupid motherfucker? I'm not a ten-year-old little boy. I'm a grown man, and I can destroy you." I straddled his thighs, keeping his legs in place, and wrung his neck with my other hand. I looked around quickly. We were isolated enough that no one could see us, thank God. "I could break your neck. Right now as you lie here, struggling to get free. I could break your fucking neck, Tom."

He mumbled unintelligibly against my hand.

"Why did you do it? Are you just that sick? Or did somebody pay you off? Why did you take my brother? Was it to get back at my father for something? You're going to fucking tell me. When we go in the house, I'm going to duct tape your fucking arms and legs together, and you're going to start talking."

His lips moved beneath my palm, and I clamped my hand harder over his mouth. "No more biting, or I'll make this worse for you." I squeezed his neck harder. "Do we understand each other, Tom?"

He screamed against my hand, his voice vibrating against my palm.

"It's a yes or no question. You nod or you shake your head. Do we understand each other?"

His eyes seemed to calm. What the fuck?

Slowly, without releasing my hold on his mouth, I unclenched my thighs from around his. Quick as a jackrabbit, I stood and jumped, bringing him with me and into a chokehold. I led him back into the house and threw him onto a chair.

Among the apples and other groceries on the floor was, lo and behold, a roll of duct tape.

I picked it up. "You use a lot of this, don't you, Tom?"

He grunted, rubbing his neck.

Quickly, I opened the duct tape and bound his wrists and ankles. "Now we know you're not going anywhere."

"Who are you?" he asked.

I laughed out loud. "Do you really want to go there? Play the 'you've got the wrong guy' routine?"

"Help me! Help me!" His voice was forced and not very loud.

"Who the hell will hear you? That poor guy you have tied up downstairs? He's so weak from the abuse he can hardly move. And why would he help you if he could? You've used and abused him, just like you did my brother, just like you did your own nephew. Just like you did all those other kids and God knows who else."

He opened his mouth and then shut it.

"Got something else to say?"

"Joe..."

"So you do know who I am. Shocking."

"Joe, you don't understand."

"I think I understand just fine. You and your psycho friends have been doing this for a long time. It's over as of today. We caught Larry Wade, and now we've got you. But before I call the cops in here to drag your ass off to prison, I have a question for you. Who the hell is the third guy who abducted my brother?"

Tom pursed his lips into a line.

"Just like Larry. You're not talking. What the hell does this guy have on the two of you?"

His lips remained closed.

"You know, I wasn't in the Marines like Talon was. I don't have any experience torturing people. But I do have a very imaginative mind. I bet I could get you to talk."

He shook his head, his lips still pursed.

I was talking a big game. I had no idea if there was anything in the tiny house that I could torture him with, and I didn't really relish the idea of doing anything other than pummeling him into tomorrow. But I had to do something. Something that would hurt him enough to talk.

"Ever been fucked in the ass, Tom?"

Tom stiffened. He was trying to remain unfazed, but this got to him. I could tell. The sweat was meandering down the sides of his face now, and he inhaled a swift breath.

"Don't get too excited. I have no intention of doing the deed myself. Unlike you, I can only get a hard-on for women I feel something for. Not some poor soul down in the basement, and certainly not little boys and girls. And definitely not you. But I bet there's something around here that I could shove up your tight virgin ass. Something big. Something to make you feel what it felt like to my brother all those times."

"Joe, please..." Tom strained against his duct tape bindings.

"Begging? Really? You? The quintessential iceman?" I paced around the living room, eyeing everything, looking for something long and thick. "Do you really think I give a fuck? You're delusional. How many times did Talon beg you? How many, Tom? How about Luke? How about that poor guy in the basement?"

He opened his mouth again, but I slugged him with a right

hook.

"Not interested. Let's just say that every time you open your mouth, I'm going to torture you longer."

"You could never torture anyone, Joe." He lifted one corner of his mouth in a half smile. His face went stoic. The iceman had returned. "You don't have it in you."

Rage swelled within me. "You have no idea how mean I am. Part of me died that day when you took my brother. Part of my humanity...and it never fucking grew back."

That was a lie. Melanie had nurtured what was missing within me, and I had been on the road to becoming whole again.

But she was gone now.

And right now, I wasn't feeling real human. In front of me sat one of the monsters who had tortured my brother.

Payback time.

I walked into the kitchen and zeroed in on an old broom standing in the corner. Not thick enough, but it would have to do. I broke it over my knee and regarded the splintered ends.

Yeah. One of those would do it.

Weapon in hand, I returned to the living room, where Tom had hopped to the door. I grabbed him by the arm and yanked him back down onto the couch.

I held up the splintered piece of broom handle. "What do you think I can do with this?"

His eyes widened. Only slightly, but I noticed. Then his irises flicked to the right and back. The iceman was melting again.

"I see you're getting the picture. But first—" I channeled every bit of strength I had and whipped Tom across the cheek with the stick.

He grunted, but still, his countenance was unfazed.

"Enjoy that? We're just getting started." I whipped him again, this time on his shoulder.

He grunted again. "You won't do it, Joe."

"What did I say about talking? You just added more time to your torture, asshole. But you like fun. It's fun, what you do to others. All those innocent kids. I mean, why would you do it otherwise?"

He said nothing.

I raised my hand to whip him once more when the door crashed open.

I jerked toward the noise. A man in all black, including a ski mask, stood there, pointing a Glock at me.

Icy blue eyes glared. "Don't you fucking move, or I'll blow your head off."

CHAPTER THREE

Melanie

I stiffened. Had I heard Detective Lee—Ruby—right? "Gina's uncle is your father?"

She nodded. "I'm not proud of it. I didn't even know him until I was in my teens."

"Then you didn't grow up with him."

She shook her head. "No. My mom was a single mother. She died when I was fourteen. At least that's what I was told. I never saw a body. She didn't have any family that I knew of or that anyone could find, so the court sent me to the man whose name was on my birth certificate. My father."

"And what was his name?"

"My father? Who knows which one he's going by now? He went by a lot of different names. His real name is Theodore Mathias. He went by Theo—when he was using that name, that is."

I flashed back to a session I'd had with Gina.

"What was his name? What did you call him?"

"I called him Tio."

"Why did he want you to call him that?"

"I don't know."

"It's Spanish for uncle. Was your uncle Spanish?"

"No. He was my mother's brother. They were both born here."

Could Gina have meant Theo? She had been eight years old when the abuse started, younger when she got close to her uncle. Perhaps to her, Theo had sounded like Tio.

"When was the last time you saw your father?" I asked.

"I hadn't seen him since I left. He never came looking for me. But a couple months ago, he called me. I'm not sure why I agreed to see him. A glutton for punishment, I guess." She laughed nervously. "Maybe I thought I could get something on him. Anyway, he came to town with a girlfriend. Some ex-supermodel who hung on his every word. It was pretty sickening."

My stomach dropped. "Oh my God." Had Talon been right?

"What?"

"The model. Was her name Brooke Bailey?"

"Yeah. That was her. Gorgeous, but God, so full of herself."

Yes, that was Brooke Bailey to a T.

"She went on and on and on about my high cheekbones and my delicate features and how she wanted to do a makeover on me. Get me into some decent clothes that would flatter my body, do something with my hair. Pretty much made me want to vomit." Ruby rolled her eyes.

I was pretty close to vomiting myself, but not because Brooke had wanted to make Ruby over. This was crazy. Finally things were starting to add up. Talon had been right. Turned out that this was all too close for comfort for a reason.

Unbeknownst to her, Ruby had just given me the proof I needed. Proof that Gina's uncle was most likely also one of the men who'd abducted Talon. The third man. The one who had so far been elusive. I wasn't sure how much I could say to Ruby right now. It was still somewhat conjecture. All I knew for sure was that Brooke Bailey's boyfriend, Nico Kostas, was Ruby's father and the same man who had abused Gina. There was still no proof that he had abducted Talon, other than the circumstantial fact that someone named Milo Sanchez—another alias that Theodore Mathias had used, according to Rodney Cates—had the exact same tattoo as Nico Kostas and one of Talon's abductors.

"Does your father happen to have a tattoo?"

"Yeah, he has several."

"Any chance one is on his forearm?"

She nodded. "Yeah, he does have one there. On the left, I think."

Bingo.

"Let me guess. It's a phoenix."

"How did you know that?"

I had just identified the third abductor. I swallowed back the nausea that threatened to overtake me.

"You okay?" Ruby asked.

I nodded. "I'm sorry. My mind was racing there for a minute."

"You didn't answer my question. How did you know my dad had a phoenix tattoo on his forearm?"

"I'm not at liberty to say yet." I silently hoped she'd buy that. She was a cop. She understood keeping things under wraps. "So you haven't seen your father for a few months, you say?"

She shook her head. "Nope. And let me tell you, I have no desire to ever see him again."

"Why is that?"

"Why do you think? He's a horrible excuse for a human being. He raped and abused my cousin, leading to her suicide." She let out a huff. "Let me rephrase what I just said. I *do* want to see him again—behind bars."

Was it too soon for me to voice my theory that Gina had not committed suicide but instead had been murdered? Probably. Not before I talked to Jonah and Talon. And I certainly couldn't tell Ruby what else I suspected—no, what I *knew*—about her father. That he had been one of the three who abducted and molested Talon Steel.

"Ruby, he didn't ever..."

She sighed. "No. He tried once, but I got away. That's why I ran away when I was fifteen."

My heart went out to her. The therapist in me wanted to find out everything and help her. "What did you do? Where did you go?"

She stood. "You have any booze around here? If we're going to stroll down memory lane, I need a drink."

A drink didn't sound bad to me, either. "I might have a bottle of wine around. Maybe some gin. I'm not a huge drinker."

"Neither am I," Ruby said. "But if I'm going to talk about dear old Daddy, it's a necessity."

I rummaged through the kitchen and found a bottle of Pinot Noir. I foraged for my corkscrew and opened the bottle quickly, pouring two glasses. I handed one to Ruby.

"I wish I had a decent place to sit."

"Don't mind me. The floor is fine." She sat back down cross-legged.

"I'm really sorry," I said. "About what you went through with your father, I mean."

Ruby took a long sip of her wine. "That's not bad. Wine is my drink of choice, though I'm not usually a big Pinot Noir fan. I'd like to learn more about wine sometime."

Ryan Steel popped into my mind. Now there was a man who knew wine. I looked at Ruby. She did have a lovely face, and her hair, although pulled back, was clearly thick and a lush dark brown, nearly black. Her eyes were a startling clear blue. I smiled in spite of myself. This woman must have been a wet dream for Brooke Bailey. A blank canvas upon which she could work her makeover magic.

Certainly not Ryan Steel's type. But then, what did I know about his type? I hardly knew the man. He'd been absent from family stuff lately because it was his busy season. He was gorgeous, though. Model handsome, and Ruby Lee was far from a model. With a makeover though—

I stopped that thought. Now *I* sounded like Brooke Bailey. God forbid.

"I like wine myself too. Pretty much all red wine."

"Yeah, I prefer red as well. It has so much more complexity than white."

I wasn't really interested in talking about wine, but it was a way to open Ruby up. "What's your favorite? Red wine, I mean."

"That's a tough one. I love a good vintage Bordeaux, but sometimes a nice Barbera table wine from Italy is perfect. Depends on my mood, you know?"

Clearly, she already knew way more about wine than I did. I had never heard of Barbera. I'd have to ask Ryan about it. "Yeah, I get it."

"So you were asking about my father."

"Yeah. I don't want to pry, but you already know that Gina

was a patient of mine. Anything you can tell me that might shed light on the situation, even though she's gone now, would help me."

"I don't know that much about him, really. Or rather, I don't know that much about what he does. He's gone by many names in the past. Obviously, he's a child molester, and I can't even begin to imagine what other things he might be culpable of. Hence the need for all the aliases, I guess." She took another sip of wine.

I regarded her. Ruby was being nonchalant about this. Too nonchalant. It was a facade. Her facial muscles were tensed up. I wanted to tell her she could be herself with me. To be angry if she needed to be. That I understood. But it was too soon. We hardly knew each other, so I couldn't go into therapist mode yet. "Do you know which alias he was using when you saw him recently? When you met Brooke?"

"She called him Nico. That's a new one. I'd never heard him use it before."

"How do you know about all the others?"

"I've kept tabs on him over the years." She shook her head. "It's crazy, to be honest. I don't know how he gets away with the shit he does. He's never even been arrested."

"What was his relationship with your mother like?"

"It was nonexistent. I didn't even know who he was until my mom left." She cleared her throat. "She never told me anything about my father. Always refused to talk about it when I asked. Then, when she disappeared, my birth certificate was pulled, and there was his name and birth date."

"So you never knew the story between them?"

"Nope. According to my father, it was a one-night stand that went wrong."

"I'm so sorry."

"Don't be. The man is a psychopath. I'd just as soon not have his genes, but I wasn't given a choice in the matter."

"So what happened then? When you ran away? Did your father come looking for you?"

"Are you kidding me? He never wanted me in the first place. Sure, I was good enough for a fuck buddy, but he could find that easily anywhere else, as we both know."

"Where did you go?"

"It was summer when I left, and I lived on the streets for a few weeks. It wasn't that difficult. My mom and I had been pretty poor, and I'd been reduced to stealing to eat more than once. So this was nothing new, though I tried to avoid stealing as much as possible. I didn't want to be arrested and sent home. Once fall came, I knew I had to find other arrangements. I was afraid to go to social services, for fear they would send me back to him. So I got a job waiting tables, with the help of a fake ID, and within a few weeks, I had scraped together enough to move into this really shitty place on the wrong side of town. But I kept quiet, slid under the radar, and stayed safe for the next three years, until my eighteenth birthday. I also went to the police department and filed a complaint against my father. Then I applied to the police academy."

"Wow."

"My happy ending didn't start there, though. I found out I had to be twenty-one and a high school graduate to be accepted into the police academy. So I needed a new plan. I had worked my way up to night manager at the little diner where I waitressed, so I kept that job, moved into a slightly better place, got my GED, and waited another three years. During that time, the PD never did anything about my father. I contacted them every week for a while. Then I gave up."

"Wow," I said again.

"At that point, I didn't want to leave anything to chance, so I started working out voraciously. I was determined that in three years, I would be accepted at the academy and become the best police officer out there. I would put people like my father away."

"So why haven't you? Put your father away, I mean?"

"Because the dirty bastard never leaves a trail. I've never had probable cause to even have him arrested, let alone evidence that would stick through a trial and conviction."

"Really? What about Gina?"

"She refused to press charges. I stopped pestering her after a while. She was having a hard enough time as it was."

"And there was nothing else?"

Ruby shook her head. "He's one smart and sneaky son of a bitch. But he'll trip up sometime, and when he does, I will be there, handcuffs in hand."

Her blue eyes burned like hot fire. I had no doubt that Ruby would be there. And I had no doubt that she would see her father behind bars at some point in the future. The near future, if the Steels and I had anything to say about it.

CHAPTER FOUR

Jonah

In the back of my mind, I had always wondered how I would react if I had to stare down the barrel of a gun.

People always said your life flashed before your eyes.

Mine didn't.

Perhaps if I'd still had Melanie, or perhaps if I still felt needed by my family, I would've feared for my life.

But I didn't.

Melanie was gone because I had betrayed her. Let her down. And Talon had Jade now. Thanks to Melanie, he was healing, and he and Jade would have a beautiful life together.

Neither of them needed me anymore.

No one needed me.

Except for...

The man in the basement.

I could not leave him here to be further abused by these two degenerates.

So I decided to bluff.

"You think I'm scared of your fucking gun? I called the police five minutes ago. They'll be here anytime. So kill me if you want to, but the poor guy downstairs will rat you out if I'm not here. He's gone. I let him go." I looked to Tom. "He knows your name, Tom. I told him everything. And even if he's too weak to talk? Larry Wade told me everything. He rolled over on you two sick fucks, and they will find you eventually."

I knew from Talon that the third abductor had brown eyes, not blue like the masked man, but oddly, my comment got his attention. His blue eyes narrowed slightly, and I zeroed in on them.

Something sinister lurked behind those eyes. They were cold. Harsh. Unreal.

"Nice timing," Tom said to him, his voice icy and unwavering. It was an act, though. Sweat dripped from his hairline.

"I saw his car. A beamer parked a block or so away. Big red flag. That's why I put on the mask. What'd you do? Walk in without a mask or a gun? Without checking out your surroundings? Your overconfidence is going to get you killed. Dumb fuck." The man in black turned to me. "What'd you say about Larry Wade?"

"Don't listen to him," Tom said. "Larry would never roll over. I've made sure of it."

"Really?" I laughed. "How do you think I found *you*?" Another bluff, but one that worked.

Tom raised his eyebrows.

I turned to the man in the mask, the one with the gun, which was finally starting to fuel my fear. *Hold it together, Joe.*

"And you... What should I call you? You go by so many different names."

"You're bluffing," the masked man said.

I stood my ground, desperately hoping I wouldn't piss myself. "You want to take that chance? They'll be here before you can kill me and catch the guy in the basement. So go ahead. Shoot. Then you'll be arrested for my murder as well as for all the other vile shit you've done."

"Shit." The man turned to Tom. "I'm out of here."

Tom tried to stand but fell back onto the sofa. "You're going to fucking leave me here? To get caught? After all these years? All I've done for you?"

"Jesus fucking Christ." He yanked Tom off the sofa. "Hop out to the car, for God's sake. Let's get the fuck out of here."

They left quickly.

I gulped down relief as a blue car—a Mustang—skidded across the gravel, taking Tom and the masked man with it. Nausea swelled in my throat.

I had just bluffed my way out of being shot.

Damn, I had to take a shit.

But first, I had to call the cops. For real this time. I yanked my cell phone out of my back pocket, and then I heard some scratching behind me.

I turned.

The poor man had made his way up the stairs and was on his hands and knees, falling toward me.

I shoved my phone back in my pocket and ran to him. "My God. Here." I picked him up—he weighed no more than Melanie—and laid him on the couch. "Let me get you a glass of water."

I ran to the kitchen, found a cup, quickly filled it, and brought it back to him. I put a pillow under him to perch his head and shoulders up. I held the cup up to his lips. "Not too much at first. Your system needs to get used to it."

After he had taken a couple of sips, I set the cup on an end table.

"Can you tell me who you are?"

"Kahh..." His voice cracked and turned to a whisper.

"It's okay. You'll get your strength back, and then you'll be able to tell me." I ran into the bedroom and found a pair of sweatpants. I brought them back out to the man and helped him struggle into them. Now at least he didn't have to be ashamed of his nakedness.

Unfortunately, the odor of waste had ascended with the young man. He needed a shower badly, but right now, I wasn't sure he had the strength. I could at least get a warm cloth and wipe his face and hands for him.

"Hold tight. I'll be right back." I went quickly into the kitchen and soaked a dishrag in warm water. I returned and rubbed it over his face and hands.

"Can you tell me anything?"

"Kahh..." he said again.

"Yes, I'm going to call the cops." I reached to grab my phone out of my back pocket, but the man touched my forearm. I looked into his eyes. They were greenish brown.

"Kahh-lin."

CHAPTER FIVE

Melanie

I had a million more questions for Ruby—starting with the other names her father used, everything that Gina had told her, how she had escaped—but I wasn't sure where to begin.

Ruby picked up the bottle of wine sitting next to us on the floor and held it up. "You mind?"

"Please, help yourself." I held up my glass so she could top it off as well.

She took a sip of her now refilled glass. "Melanie..."

"Yeah?"

"I'd appreciate it if you...didn't tell anyone I was here. You know, since it's no longer technically my case and I'm off the clock."

"Of course. Except I would like your permission to talk to my..." My what? What was Jonah to me now? Until I knew, and until I had his and Talon's permission to discuss their situation with Ruby, I had better keep mum. "Never mind."

"You want to talk to someone else about this?"

"Not at the moment."

"Fair enough. But this isn't a secret as far as I'm concerned. I'm not out to protect my father."

I took a sip of wine. "Then there are a few people I'll need to tell, but I don't know when. In the meantime, do you mind talking a little bit about Gina?"

"No, I can talk about it. I've come to terms with what happened—well, as best as I can."

"What do you mean?"

"You have to remember that I didn't know Gina until I met my father. She was quite a bit younger than I was, by about eight years. And in case you're wondering, that makes me thirty-two." Ruby smiled. "I'm not one of those women who has problems telling people how old she is."

"I'm not either. I'm forty, if you want to know."

"You look great."

I laughed. "So do you." She truly did. Her skin was flawless. Even without makeup, she had a lovely natural blush to her complexion. Why she downplayed her looks, I didn't know, but I had my suspicions.

"Thanks. Anyway, when I ran away, I was fifteen, and Gina was seven. It wasn't until she found me as an adult that she told me what my father had done to her. I've always felt a lot of guilt about that. If I hadn't left, he would've done it to me, and perhaps she would have been spared."

Guilt. It emanated from Ruby like a black aura.

Seemed everyone I'd met lately was suffering with guilt... along with me.

"You can't take that on your shoulders," I said. "What your father did to Gina lies at his feet, not at yours. Not at anyone's except his."

"Yeah, I know all that. And I know you're a shrink— Oh, God. I'm sorry."

I let out a chuckle. "It's okay. We're all used to that."

"Oh, good. I guess. Anyway, I know that. I've actually gone through a few counseling sessions through work. But it's hard to shake, you know?"

How I did know. "Believe me, I understand. I've spent the better part of the last six months wondering where I went wrong with Gina. If she was suicidal, why didn't I see something in our sessions?" I shook my head. "Guilt is enough to kill you sometimes."

She nodded. "That's for sure. For what it's worth, I don't blame you for Gina's death."

"Thank you. That means a lot. Her parents do, though. They filed a grievance against me with the medical board, and now they're suing me for malpractice, as well."

"You're kidding me."

I took a sip of wine. "Nope."

Ruby shook her head. "That takes a lot of nerve."

"Why do you say that?"

She let out a sarcastic laugh. "Because they both knew exactly what was going on with my father."

CHAPTER SIX

Jonah

Colin?

"Not Colin Morse?"

He nodded.

I had only seen Colin Morse, Jade's ex-fiancé, once. One evening, and I had threatened him because he was threatening Talon. I'd been mad as hell, but I hadn't acted on it, thank God. Colin had been a nice enough looking young man, with dirty-blond hair and brownish-green eyes. Now his head was shaved clean, he must have weighed at least thirty pounds less, and he looked thoroughly drained.

He didn't appear to recognize me.

What had they done to him? And why?

I knew damned well *what* they had done, and the "why" was probably no more than because they were sick as fuck. But why Colin specifically?

He had disappeared sometime after our last meeting. His father had been looking for him for a couple of months now. Had he been here all that time?

"How long have you been here?" I asked.

"I don't know," he croaked.

"Who brought you here?"

"Don't know," he said again.

"What do you remember?"

He shook his head.

"I'm sorry. Try not to talk. I'm going to call the cops now, and an ambulance for you. I know you must be hungry, but we need to get you to a hospital. You're obviously dehydrated and malnourished."

And physically, emotionally, and sexually abused, but I didn't need to voice that. He knew that as well as I did. His body was battered and bruised, so he had most likely been beaten, too.

That fucking snake Tom Simpson. At least we had an eyewitness now.

Or maybe not. Tom and the other guy had probably used masks, like they always had with Talon.

Shit.

I quickly pulled my phone out and dialed 9-1-1. They answered on the first ring. I shook my head, remembering how 9-1-1 had been busy the night Melanie had called them. Shitheads. I gave the operator the lowdown, hung up, and turned back to Colin.

"It won't be too long now," I told him. "The ambulance will be here soon."

I wasn't sure if I should try to feed him. What had we done for Talon when we found him? I couldn't quite remember. He had gone straight to the hospital as far as I knew. I had only been thirteen. Damn. How was I supposed to help this guy?

He reached up my forearm with his bony hand. "Don't want to talk."

"You won't have to. Not until you're feeling better. Right now you need to be in a hospital."

"Haas..." He closed his eyes.

"Colin, your father has been desperate to find you. I'm going to call him, okay?"

His sunken eyes shot open. "No. Don't."

"Why not? He needs to know that you're alive."

"No!"

"All right, all right. I won't." I put my phone back in my pocket. The hospital would call his father anyway. I would do as he asked for now.

★ ★ ★

I followed the ambulance to the hospital. It was nearly an hour to the next city that had the facilities to care for him, but he was getting care from the paramedics, so he'd be okay.

I screeched to a halt along with the ambulance when we reached the hospital and then followed them in.

"Male, mid-twenties, dehydrated and malnourished. Multiple lacerations and contusions. Physical and sexual abuse." The paramedics handed him off to some ER doctors.

"Let's get an IV started," a doctor said. "Danny, get a rape kit," he said to an orderly.

Two police officers approached the paramedics. After they had answered their questions, the officers turned to me.

"I'm Officer Jones, and this is Officer Goldman," one of them said. "I understand you found this man?"

"Yes, sir," I said. "He was being held captive in a basement at this address." I handed him the piece of paper on which I had written the address that Trevor Mills, one of the private investigators Talon had hired, had uncovered.

"Good. We'll check it out," Jones said. "I'm going to need your name."

"Jonah Steel."

"You're one of *the* Steels?"

"I am."

"So what were you doing at that address?"

I let out a heavy sigh. "I'm afraid that's a really long story."

"Well, we've got time." Jones pointed to a couple of chairs in the waiting area that were secluded. "Let's sit down, and we'll have a long talk."

After I had related my entire story, Jones made a few telephone calls. When he was done, he turned back to me.

"Your story checks out."

"Of course it checks out. What? Did you think I had some hand in torturing this poor guy?"

"Well, he *is* your brother's girlfriend's ex. And your brother was arrested for beating him up."

"For God's sake. My brother has also paid his debt for that. And I'm not my brother."

"Mr. Steel, I know you're an upstanding citizen and business owner here in Colorado, but we have to check everything out."

"Sure, sure." I threaded my fingers through my hair. "But I was just held at gunpoint by one of the men—possibly two of the men—who kidnapped and tortured my brother twenty-five years ago, and then I found out they were doing the same thing to this poor guy. So my patience is wearing just a little thin. I'm sure you understand."

Jones cleared his throat. "Sure. Of course."

"Look, Colin didn't want me to contact his father. I'm not sure why. But I do know how to get in touch with him. My brother's girlfriend has the number. His name is Ted Morse."

"No worries. We'll figure out how to get in touch with him,

Mr. Steel."

"Sure. That's your call."

"Can you tell us anything else about the other guy? The one wearing a black ski mask?"

"Only that he had really bizarre blue eyes."

"What do you mean 'bizarre?'"

"They looked... I don't know. Almost fake."

"Can you be more specific?"

"I don't know. I was staring down the barrel of a Glock, for God's sake. They were just really blue."

"All right." Jones took a few more notes. "We'll get in touch with you if we need more information, Mr. Steel. You're free to go."

Thank God.

All I wanted to do was go home. To Melanie.

But Melanie was no longer there.

CHAPTER SEVEN

Melanie

Had I just heard Ruby correctly? Gina's parents knew?

I opened my mouth, but no words emerged.

"I see that surprises you."

"Hell, yes, I'm surprised. Right now, the two of them are blaming me for their daughter's suicide. And quite frankly, I'm not exactly sure it was a suicide."

Ruby nodded. "I'm not so sure either."

My heart nearly jumped right out of my chest. Here was someone who maybe agreed with my theory? That Gina hadn't committed suicide but had been murdered?

"Do you think her father and mother had anything to do with it? Her death, I mean."

"It wouldn't surprise me. I didn't know either of them very well, but they were terrible parents. They really neglected Gina. So for the short time that I was in their lives, I tried to take her under my wing, but I was still a kid myself who had just lost her mother. There were limits to what I could do."

"Understandable," I said.

"Her mother—my father's sister—she was a mess. In and out of mental hospitals her whole life."

I shot my eyes open. "What?"

"Oh, yeah. She's been committed several times."

"Gina never told me anything about that."

"She might not have known. She was still pretty young when all this was happening, and I'm sure her father covered it up. Said Mommy was on a vacation or something."

"Then how did *you* know?"

"My father told me. Said his sister was crazy and out of her mind and that her husband was a psycho."

"Well, coming from another psycho, I'm not sure how much value I put into that assessment."

Ruby took a sip of her wine. "Agreed. Gina's dad and my dad had a weird relationship. They had this love-hate thing going. I never quite knew what to make of it."

"Have you had any contact with Gina's parents lately?"

"When I found out about her death, I called to offer my condolences. Neither of them were very interested in talking to me. Probably because I was a police officer. That's my best guess, anyway."

"But how do you know? How do you know that Gina's parents knew your father was abusing their daughter?"

"Gina had this friend. Marie Cooke. Marie came to me when I was a young officer right out of the academy. I'm not sure how she found me. She was one of the only people Gina confided in about what was going on, and even then, she wouldn't go into any detail or name any names. But I knew exactly what she was talking about. Remember, my father tried to rape me. That's why I left.

"Anyway, Marie said that Gina's father had come to her and told her not to come around anymore. That she'd better stay away and not breathe a word of anything to anyone, or the same thing would happen to her."

My mouth dropped open. "I suppose he could've been

talking about something else entirely."

"What else could he have been talking about? What else was going on? Gina was your patient for a while. Was there anything else going on that he might have been talking about?"

No, there wasn't. And although I really couldn't discuss what went on in my sessions with Gina with Ruby, it certainly didn't hurt to say one thing. "No. She never gave me any indication of any other traumatic event in her life."

"They're terrible, terrible people. I wish I didn't have their DNA."

"Your DNA doesn't define you, Ruby. Your choices and your actions do. You joined the police force. You're one of the good guys."

"I try to be. But let me tell you, confidentially. There are times when I want to whip out my gun and shoot some of those people."

"Believe me, I know exactly how you feel. My parents were horrible and neglectful people, very verbally and emotionally abusive. But compared to Gina, I was lucky. I was at least never physically or sexually abused by anyone. I've always wondered if I had it in me to be a parent. My own parents were terrible, and I possess their DNA. But you know what? I think I would be a good mother. I think I would like to have a child someday." I chuckled nervously, taking a sip of my wine. That was the first time I had ever thought it consciously—that I might like to be a mother. "Of course, my biological clock is ticking away."

"No, not really. Lots of women in their forties are having children now."

"True. But as a physician, I know the risks of a pregnancy in later years."

"Sure, there are more risks, but the odds are still in your

favor."

I couldn't help a smile. There was something about Ruby Lee that I liked. She had a cautious optimism that was unusual, given her circumstances. "Was Lee your mother's last name?"

She shook her head. "The name on my birth certificate is Ruby Lee Thornbush. That was her maiden name. Her first name was Diamond, no lie. I guess that's where I got my gem of a name." She chuckled. "After she died and I went to live with my father, he had it legally changed to Mathias. Once I turned eighteen, I decided I needed a new start, free of both of them. So I took my middle name as my last name."

"I don't blame you," I said.

"I almost changed my first name as well. I never wanted to be named after a stone. I mean, look at me. I'm sort of a tomboy. With the name Ruby." She let out a raucous laugh.

"Actually, I think Ruby suits you. You have beautiful features."

"Now, don't you start trying to make me over too."

"Oh, God, no. I would never do anything Brooke Bailey would." Ruby had no way of knowing that I was intimately acquainted with Brooke Bailey and that she had come on to Jonah. I had no great love for the woman, but I did feel sorry for her. Her boyfriend was a complete psycho, and although they couldn't prove it, Talon and Jonah both believed that Nico Kostas had tried to have Brooke killed for insurance money. She was still living in Talon's home, recuperating from her severe accident.

"I suppose, as a cop, it's easier to be taken seriously if you don't dress like a froufrou woman."

Ruby looked down and stared at her wine glass. "Yeah. That's it."

She was hiding something. Her mannerisms were feminine, even though she dressed like a tomboy. Something was off. It didn't take my experiences as a psychotherapist to know that. There was more to Ruby Lee than met the eye, and I had a feeling that before this mystery was solved, I would know her quite well.

CHAPTER EIGHT

Jonah

Melanie was no longer at home—at least not at *my* home. I'd told her to leave, to go to Talon's. So that's where I was going. I didn't deserve to see her, but I needed to.

The drive took an hour, and it was near midnight when I rolled toward Talon's ranch house. I didn't expect anyone to be up, but luckily, I could see through the front picture window that the light in the kitchen at the back of the house was on.

I knocked quietly.

Talon's dog, Roger, appeared in the window, his goofy canine smile on his face. Talon followed and opened the door.

"Joe? What are you doing here this late?"

"It's a long story, bro. But I need to see Melanie."

"Melanie's not here."

My skin chilled. "What? What do you mean she's not here? I told her to go to your place."

"I know. When she didn't show, Jade and I figured you had gotten some sense in your head and kept her at your home, where she belongs."

I walked past Talon into his house. "If she's not here, where the hell is she?"

"I don't know. Did you come from your place?"

"No." I helped myself to a cup of coffee and sat down at the kitchen table, where Talon had papers spread out. "I couldn't bear to be there when she left, so I left first."

"Then how do you know she's not at your place?"

"She isn't. The way she looked at me when I told her the truth, that I had ignored her phone call that night she got taken... There's no way she was going to stick around."

"I don't think you're giving her enough credit. She's an amazing woman."

I rubbed at my forehead. "You don't have to tell me."

"Listen, Joe, I don't want to pry, but I have to tell you something. Jade told me that her mother told her that you and Melanie are in love."

"She did?"

"Yes. Did you tell Brooke?"

I shook my head. "No, I didn't. It must've been Melanie, that day she was over here hanging out with Brooke while you and I were talking to Felicia."

"Well...is it true?"

I sighed. "It is on my end. Probably not on hers any longer."

"I doubt that."

"What would you know about it?"

Talon guffawed. "Are you kidding me? What *wouldn't* I know? I fell head over heels in love with Jade, and I tried every trick in the book to stay away from her. It didn't work. That love had a grip on me. It kept me by the shoulders and wouldn't let me go. If Melanie is feeling for you anything close to what I'm feeling for Jade, she won't be able to walk away, no matter what you think you did to her."

"Tal, you know what I did to her. I intentionally didn't take her phone call that night while we were driving to Denver to see Wendy Madigan. I was pissed off because she had sneaked out of my house when you and Jade showed up. I was being petty. I deserted her in her time of greatest need, just like I deserted you."

"Are we really going to get back on that hobbyhorse?" Talon sat down next to me, a cup of coffee in his hand. "You did not desert me that day. You said you couldn't go with me. I chose to go by myself."

"Ryan didn't desert you. Your little brother was there when you needed him, but not your big brother." I fisted my hands in each side of my hair. "Some big brother."

"Oh, for fuck's sake. How long are we going to go through this? Are you going to try to get me to sock you again? That didn't work out so well the first time. You know damned well I can't ease your guilt. No one can, except you. You have to let it go, Joe. And please, if you can't let it go for yourself, let it go for me. I'm happy now. I have the most wonderful woman in the world by my side, I own a quarter of this ranch, and I thought, for a few seconds, that I was going to see my big brother get the same kind of happiness with a wonderful woman."

"Are you saying you're healed?"

"Yes and no. I'm functioning, and I'm happy. Does my past still haunt me sometimes? Of course it does. And I imagine your guilt will always haunt you on some level. But you have to let it go. You have to pick up the pieces of your life and live. Suck out the good in life while you can. Someday none of us will be here."

So here I was, feeling like an idiot again. My brother, who had been through so much at such a young age, was trying to pick *me* up. What a selfish bastard I was.

"Man, I'm sorry."

"Would you stop apologizing to me? I forgave you a long

time ago."

I smiled. "No, I didn't mean for that. I meant for having this stupid pity party for myself right now. It was completely self-indulgent, and I'm sorry."

He returned my smile. I marveled at the fact that I had seen my brother smile more in the last several months than I had in the last twenty-five years. Every smile was triumphant. And he deserved each one.

"No worries, bro. I still get self-indulgent myself sometimes. But Jade is always here to snap me out of it."

"You're a lucky man."

Talon took a sip of coffee. "I am. That's no lie. But you can be just as lucky. The doc is a wonderful woman. Take some advice from someone who knows. Don't let her go, man."

"I don't know, Tal. I don't know if I can get her back." I rubbed the back of my neck. Man, I was tense.

"Joe, you don't even know if she's gone yet. Have you tried calling her?"

"Actually, no. I've been a little busy."

"Yeah? Something going down in the pastures?"

"No, man. You're not going to fucking believe where I've been."

"Try me."

Where to start? I hadn't even told Talon my suspicions—which were no longer suspicions and hadn't been for a while—about Tom Simpson yet. Besides Marjorie, the only person I had told was Melanie.

Now I risked my brother's wrath for not letting him in on it. And also...for letting Tom Simpson get away.

This was going to be a long night.

CHAPTER NINE

Melanie

The talk with Ruby had renewed my vigor. What a strong woman. I had met a lot of strong women in my practice, but never one who'd been on her own since the age of fifteen. On top of that, I'd found a new friend who I had a feeling would turn out to be very helpful to both me and the Steels. I was beginning to look at my own strength in a new way.

I had left Jonah's home to take myself back. But the truth of the matter was I needed to be with him to do that very thing. I would show him the strength I possessed. I would fight for us.

It was nearing midnight when Ruby finally left, and I decided I would not be going to a hotel. I packed up what little I wanted from my loft and got back into my car. I was going back to Jonah's.

I was going home.

★ ★ ★

Jonah's ranch house was dark, but that didn't concern me. It was the early hours of the morning, and he was no doubt in bed. I let myself in, and Lucy bounded to me.

"What are you doing up, girl?" I let her out to do her business and then refilled her water bowl, which was bone-dry. It wasn't like Jonah to neglect Lucy.

I quietly stole down the hallway to his master suite. I knocked lightly on the door. "Jonah?"

No answer.

I opened the door slowly and walked in. I didn't want to turn on the light and wake him. My eyes adjusted to the darkness, and I went through the sitting room and into the bedroom.

The bed was made, and Jonah was nowhere to be found.

Where was he?

Oh, God. Images of his BDSM club floated through my mind. He wouldn't go there, would he? He said he hadn't been there in years and had no desire to go back.

But that darkness still lived within him, a darkness I had only seen glimpses of.

And he had been in a bad way when he left.

Worry clenched at me. I sucked in a breath and left the bedroom. I went back outside to my car and brought in my things. It took me two trips, but I got it all, including the box that I had put all of Gina's files in. Then I let Lucy back in and gave her some loving pets on her soft head. "I guess it's just you and me tonight, girl."

She followed at my heels as I took my things to the guest room where I had been staying before. My file cabinet still sat there, undisturbed. Well, of course. I hadn't yet been gone twelve hours.

Where was Jonah? Why hadn't he come home?

I thought about calling him. Would he answer? I wasn't sure. After all, he didn't know where I was. He thought I had left.

Boy, did I have a lot to tell him. And to tell Talon.

"Oh, for God's sake, Melanie," I said aloud. "Just call him.

You'll drive yourself crazy if you don't."

My cell phone was nearly dead, so I hooked it up to the charger and hit Jonah's number.

"Hey," he said softly when he answered.

"Hey. Where are you?" I asked.

"I could ask you the same thing. You're supposed to be at Talon's."

"How do you know I'm not?"

"Because *I'm* at Talon's."

Relief swept through me. Jonah was all right. He hadn't gone running off to the BDSM club or into the arms of some other woman. I hadn't realized how tightly I was strung until my muscles relaxed.

"Thank God."

"Why do you say that?"

"Because I've been worried about you, Jonah."

He paused a moment. Then, "Where are *you,* Melanie?"

"I'm home."

"Your loft? I thought that was still a crime scene. And I thought you said you couldn't stay there any longer."

I cleared my throat gently. "I got a call from the insurance guy earlier today. The police have wrapped up their work, so I can come and go as I please."

"Are you sure you're safe there?"

"I'm perfectly safe where I am." And I was amazed that I actually believed what I was saying. I was safe at Jonah's place, even if he wasn't there. I had done what I had set out to do. I had taken myself back. I was no longer going to let the fear of being abducted again rule me.

"I want you to leave there, Melanie. Come here to Talon's. I need to know you're safe."

"Like I said, I'm perfectly safe where I am."

"Fine. Don't move. I'm coming to get you."

"You don't have to. I told you. I'm home." I smiled, knowing full well he couldn't see me. "*Our* home."

Silence again.

"Jonah?"

"You... You didn't leave?"

I chuckled. "Oh, yes, I left. But I came back. I'm not going to let you run away from this, Jonah. I happen to think we're worth fighting for."

CHAPTER TEN

Jonah

I couldn't speak. Couldn't breathe. Had I heard her right? She wasn't leaving me?

"Jonah?" Her voice was soft and questioning.

"I'm here. I just can't... I can't believe it, Melanie. I let you down."

"You did, but you were perfectly within your rights to be angry with me that evening. And what were the chances of someone coming to my place and kidnapping me?"

"Considering my family's history, I should've known they were pretty damned good."

"I'm not going to let you torture yourself, Jonah. Not anymore. Not over what happened to Talon, and not over what happened to me. You're a good man. A strong and protective man who would do anything for those you love. I know that, and it's time for you to know that too."

Words failed me.

"So would you please come home? Please? Come home to me?"

I hadn't yet had the chance to tell Talon what had happened tonight. He deserved to know. Again I was stuck with a choice. Stay and help Talon, or go home and make things right with Melanie.

"I will. I'll come home. But there are some things I have to talk to Talon about. I won't be long, so don't worry."

"Okay," she said. "I understand."

"I'll explain it all to you when I get home, baby. I love you. I love you so much."

"I love you too, Jonah. Always."

I ended the call and went back into the kitchen.

"So?" Talon raised his eyebrows.

"She's at home. My home."

A broad grin split Talon's face. "What are you waiting for then? Get on home to her."

I shook my head. "I need to tell you what I was up to today. I have some news—news that concerns all of us."

"Joe, you're my big brother. I want to solve this whole thing as much as you do. But right now, go home to your woman. It took me a long time to figure out what's really important in life. Don't make the mistake of letting her go."

"Tal, you don't understand. This is some big shit."

"Then come back tomorrow. Bring Doc with you. We can all have dinner here."

Dinner? This couldn't wait that long. Jade would get the news in the morning from Ted Morse. I had to tell Talon before then.

"How about breakfast?"

"Breakfast? Don't you eat burritos out in the pastures?"

I nodded. "Usually, but not tomorrow. We'll have breakfast here. What time does Jade go to the office?"

"She leaves around eight thirty to get in by nine."

"Great. Melanie and I will be here at seven. Make sure Marj wakes up too. And keep Brooke in her room."

"Wow. This is *that* big?"

“I’m perfectly willing to stay and talk to you now.”

“No. I’m not going to let you screw this up with Melanie. Now that I know what love is, I want you to have it too.”

“But how...”

He silenced me with a gesture. “I’m dying to know what you have to say to me. Don’t get me wrong. I know how devoted you are to me. I know how responsible you feel. But I’m telling you this. The doc needs you right now. And Joe, you need her.”

★ ★ ★

Melanie was waiting for me, sitting in the kitchen sipping some water. I was tired, but awake. I was glad I’d had that cup of coffee with Talon. I had so much to tell Melanie.

She smiled at me serenely, gliding her fingers through Lucy’s soft fur. Melanie was beautiful, clad in soft cotton pajamas, her face devoid of makeup, her long hair pulled back in a sloppy ponytail.

How could I have even *thought* of letting her go? She had said we were worth fighting for. Of course we were worth fighting for. Why hadn’t I trusted her to know that? To feel that?

And it dawned on me then. That even though I loved her more than anything, to the sun and stars and back, I had never quite believed that she loved me the same. I had never felt worthy.

I had to make this work. Not just for me, and not just for Melanie, but for Talon as well. My brother knew how important this was because it was what he had with Jade. He was willing to forgo hearing my news if it meant I could work things out with the amazing woman sitting in front of me.

"Hey, sweetheart," I said.

"Hey, yourself."

I had never in my life pictured myself doing what I did next. I knelt before her, took her hand in mine, and laid a gentle kiss upon it. "Can you ever forgive me?" I looked into her emerald-green eyes.

"I already have."

I laid my head in her lap, and she gently stroked my hair.

And I finally understood true love.

She stood, pulling me up with her. Saying nothing, she led me to my bedroom, undressed me slowly, and pushed me gently onto the bed. Then she unclothed herself.

So beautiful. Her breasts were rosy, her nipples red-brown and hard. My cock was thick and ready for her when she lay down next to me.

I held her naked body against me, savoring every inch of her as I stroked her, caressed her. I kissed her—not with the fervor and passion that was normal between us, but with love. Only love. Pure emotion. Our lips slid against each other's, our tongues tangling. And when I entered her, with no foreplay other than kissing her, she was wet for me.

She clasped me so sweetly, almost reverently, as I slid in and out of her heat. Her soft sighs whispered against my cheeks, and she clamped her legs around me, drawing me farther into her.

We were one being, bonded by our love.

As I released into her, claiming her, she shattered around me, and we climaxed together.

As one.

★ ★ ★

My alarm clock went off at its usual five a.m. I'd only gotten three hours of sleep, but I had certainly functioned on less in the past. I nudged at Melanie, who was softly breathing beside me.

"Mmm," she murmured.

"Baby." I nudged her again. "I need you to wake up. We need to talk, and then we need to meet for breakfast at Talon's at seven."

She opened her eyes. "What?"

I smiled. She was so beautiful in the morning, her blond hair in messy tangles on the pillow.

"I'm sorry. But we need to talk."

She shot up. "Is everything okay?"

I took her into my arms. "Yes. I have some new information and a lot to tell you."

"I have a lot to tell you too."

"You do?"

"Yes. You won't believe what I found out."

"And baby, you won't believe what I found out. Let's take a quick shower, and we can talk before we go over to Talon's."

She smiled seductively. "All right. Except for one thing."

"What's that?"

"I don't really relish a *quick* shower."

CHAPTER ELEVEN

Melanie

Jonah sprinkled a few drops of lavender oil in the shower and turned on the water. Within a few seconds, a fragrant, steamy paradise surrounded us.

We hadn't slept much, but that was okay. I was home, where I wanted—*needed*—to be. Jonah was here, stepping into the shower behind me and then pulling me into his arms for a passionate kiss.

I opened for him, as I always did, and welcomed his tongue into my mouth. Unlike last night, the kiss was full of the desire and passion that was the norm for kisses between Jonah and me. We ravished each other's mouths, both giving and taking, surrendering to the love and passion between us. When I broke the kiss to take a much-needed breath, his dark eyes were full of fire, full of lust, full of desire. His skin was red from the heat of the shower, and his larger-than-life cock stood out proudly.

Without hesitation, he lifted me and sank me down upon his hardness.

I moaned. The sweet stretching, the purposeful joining—it was all so perfect.

This was where I belonged. This was where I would take myself back. With this man at my side.

I cupped his cheeks, staring into those dark eyes full of love. "I love you," I said. "I love you so much, Jonah."

He groaned. "God, baby, I love you too. How did I ever think I could exist without you?"

"You don't have to." And then I unraveled around him, my orgasm spiraling me upward, until every cell in my body was tingling. I breathed in, the lavender infusing through me as my body pulsated around the man I love.

Jonah's hips pistoned frantically as he plunged in and out of me. "That's it, sweetheart. Come for me. Come all over me."

Then he thrust into me so hard, I almost believed he touched my heart and my soul.

As he shuddered, my climax soared again, and we flew together over the tops of the Rocky Mountains, releasing, flying.

When his trembling finally ceased, I slid off of him, against his hard body, my head tucked into his wet shoulder. We stayed there for a few timeless moments, the hot water pelting us, and I listened to his heart thudding against his chest. My own beat in synchrony with his.

And that's when I knew the truth.

Jonah Steel and I could get through anything, as long as we were together.

★ ★ ★

Once we were dressed, I made a pot of coffee in the kitchen while Jonah took care of Lucy. Then he sat at the table, and I brought over two mugs of the fresh brew.

"Who should go first?" I asked.

He shook his head. "Hell if I know, baby. All I can tell you is that what I have to say is big."

"Me too."

"Well"—he took a sip of coffee—"I always say ladies first."

"All right." I smiled but then got serious as I told him what I had learned from Ruby Lee the previous night.

"I can't believe it," he finally said, after a few moments of silence when I stopped talking.

"I can't either. Seems we now have proof that Nico Kostas, alias Theodore Mathias, is Talon's third abductor."

"I just don't get it though."

"What?"

"Who the hell is this guy with blue eyes? The one who kidnapped you?"

"Most likely he was a hired gun. He pretty much told me that himself."

"But the guy who went to Felicia, who threatened her and forced her to leave that rose for Jade, he had blue eyes, and also..."

"What?"

"I came in contact with another guy yesterday. A guy with really bizarre blue eyes."

"You did?"

"Yeah. It's a long story." He looked at his watch. "And we need to get to Talon's. I'll tell you everything in the car."

"No," I said. "I'll wait until we get to Talon's. Whatever you have to say, he deserves to hear it first."

★ ★ ★

When we walked into Talon's, Marjorie was busy at the stove, making bacon and eggs. I inhaled the appetizing aroma.

"Morning, Marj," Jonah said.

His sister turned around. "You better have a good reason for getting us all up at the butt crack of dawn, Joe."

Talon walked quickly into the kitchen, followed by Jade. "Well, Sis, we're all used to getting up at the butt crack of dawn."

Marjorie laughed and scooped eggs onto a platter. The table had already been set, and glasses of orange juice sat at each place. Jade brought the coffeepot over and filled the mugs.

"Everybody, sit down," Talon said. "Joe says he has something important to talk to us all about."

"You don't have to worry about my mom being here," Jade said. "She stayed in the city overnight for therapy with her nurse."

A little bit of tension released from Jonah. And from me as well, to tell the truth. I still couldn't wrap my head around the fact that Brooke Bailey had tried to seduce him.

I took a seat next to Jonah. Marjorie sat on my other side and began passing around a platter of eggs, bacon, and toast. Once we were all served, Talon spoke.

"So, Joe, it was your idea to get us all together for this breakfast. Let's hear it."

I was antsy. I had no idea what Jonah was about to tell us, and my nerves were doing a little jig underneath my skin. After he was done with his news, and if there was any time left, I'd let them all know that I had almost positively identified the third abductor. I wondered if that was bigger news than what Jonah was about to say.

I didn't wonder for long.

"Colin has been found," Jonah said.

A chorus of gasps came out of all of our mouths.

"How did you find him?" Jade asked.

"It's a long story," Jonah said. "I went after one of your abductors yesterday, Tal."

"Say what?"

"You heard me. I know who another one of them is."

I kept my eye on Marjorie. She was chewing on her bottom lip. She knew as well, but no one had told Talon yet.

"Who the hell is it?" Talon said through clenched teeth.

"It's pretty unbelievable, Tal. I didn't believe it myself at first, but we have proof. It's Tom Simpson. The mayor. My best friend's father."

Talon stood, clenching his fists. "The fucking bastard."

"It's true, Talon," Marjorie said. "I've seen his birthmark. It's exactly how you described it."

"And nobody told me any of this?"

I itched to say something. Raising voices would do no good, and I, as a psychotherapist, could be the voice of reason. But I wasn't a member of this family, at least not yet, so I kept my mouth shut.

"We didn't have any solid proof, other than the birthmark." Joe rubbed at his chin.

"Who the hell else would have a birthmark just like the one I remember?"

"That's fair enough," Jonah said. "But I have proof now. I found the motherfucker."

"Jesus Christ!" Talon grabbed a fistful of his hair. "Where the hell is he?"

"Well, that's the bad news. He got away."

"Oh, for fuck's sake." Talon sat down hard.

"Talon," Jade said soothingly. "Let's hear him out."

Jonah inhaled and let out a slow breath. "Mills and Johnson found the address where Simpson was holed up. He disappeared about a week ago. Bryce told me. Anyway, I went there to confront him. He had a bad dye job on his hair, but it was him. He finally admitted who he was. And Tal? Where he was holed up? I'm pretty sure it's the same place you were held."

Talon's forearms tensed. "The same place?"

"I'm pretty sure. It's just how you described it."

"How did he get away?" Talon asked through clenched teeth.

"I'm sorry about that. I didn't have a choice. When I first got there, Tom wasn't there. So I searched the house. When I went down to the basement, I found that they were keeping yet another prisoner. This was a grown man. His head had been shaved, and he had been beaten and abused."

Jade clasped her hand to her mouth.

Jonah nodded at her. "Yes. It was Colin."

Talon shook his head. "I certainly can't say I like the guy, but I wouldn't wish that on my worst enemy."

"Anyway, I was in the process of untying him and I got him unbound, but then I heard something upstairs. I told Colin to stay still and, if I didn't come back in half an hour, to get the hell out of there if he could. He looked so weak though, I wasn't sure if he'd be able to move.

"So I went upstairs, and lo and behold, who should be coming in with a bag of groceries, but Tom. He had dyed his hair dark brown, but I recognized his blue eyes. They're just like Bryce's. He denied it at first, tried to get away, but I tackled him to the ground, got him tied up with his own duct tape, and then I threatened him with...bodily harm."

Jonah visibly tensed. What had he threatened Simpson with? I would ask him about that later. Or maybe not. He would come to me if he needed to.

"Anyway, I was getting ready to call the cops on him, when a guy all in black wearing a ski mask barged in, holding a gun." He gripped the edge of the table. "I've never stared down the barrel of a gun before."

I reached over and rubbed Jonah's thigh. I hoped I was offering some comfort. I certainly wasn't feeling comfortable myself. My nerves were on edge. The man I loved had been held at gunpoint. I kept quiet...for now.

"I decided to bluff. I told them I had already called the cops, that I'd let the guy in the basement go and told him everything. I told them they could kill me if they wanted to, but they wouldn't get far." He raked his fingers through his hair. "I'm not sure I've ever been so fucking scared in my entire life."

I squeezed his thigh. I was scared myself right now.

"What happened then?" Marjorie asked, her eyes wide.

"He took Simpson and got away. But now we know for sure, Talon. Tom Simpson was one of your abductors."

"What about Colin?" Jade asked.

"He managed to get up the stairs, and I took as good care of him as I could until the ambulance got there. He's at a hospital in Murphy. He'll be all right. He's dehydrated and malnourished, has probably been raped, but he will survive."

Jade's eyes glistened. "I've been nothing but angry with him for the last several months, with good reason, but I would never wish this on him."

"None of us would, blue eyes." Talon sighed. "So now we know who two of them are for sure. I never thought I'd see the day."

Jonah turned to me and nodded.

For the first time, I opened my mouth. "Actually, Talon,

we know for sure who all three of them are."

He stood again. "Doc?"

I quickly related the story about Ruby Lee and her father.

"So Gina's uncle is one of the same men who abused Talon?" Marjorie said.

"Yes."

Talon sat still, staring at the cup of coffee in front of him.

"Tal?" Jonah said.

"I can't believe it," Talon said, still not moving.

Jade stroked his forearm. "This is good news, Talon. We now know who they are. Both of them. Now we can find them."

"I can go see Larry Wade again," Jonah said. "Now that I know who they are, there's no reason for him not to tell me any information he knows."

"The guy who came to the house," Talon said. "The one who held the gun on you. Were his eyes brown?"

Jonah sighed. "I wish I could say they were. But they weren't. They were very stark blue. Almost an unreal color of blue."

"The man who kidnapped me had weird blue eyes too," I added. "He told me he was a hired hitman. And I believe the man who threatened Felicia also had blue eyes, right?"

"So it wasn't Nico Kostas or whatever the hell his name is." Talon sighed.

And then a light bulb went on over my head.

CHAPTER TWELVE

Jonah

Melanie was thinking. She was gnawing on her lower lip as if her life depended on it.

"What is it, sweetheart?" I asked.

"You said his eyes looked unreal. Maybe they were."

"What do you mean?"

"He was wearing colored contact lenses. The kind that can make dark-brown eyes blue."

I smiled. "Why the hell didn't the rest of us think of that?"

"I don't know," Jade said. "Now that you mention it, Melanie, that makes perfect sense. I'm not sure why I didn't think of it. Remember those funky cat-eye contacts you had in college, Marj?"

Marj chuckled. "Oh, yeah. They were yellow."

"They were creepy," Jade said.

"I suppose there's no way to know for sure," I said. "But all three of us seem to think that the eyes were bizarre looking. Unreal looking. Granted, the guy who took Melanie said he was a hired gun, but it's not so far-fetched for him to have been lying."

"It makes sense that Gina's uncle is the one who abducted you, Doc," Talon said. "First of all, you knew what he had done to Gina. Second, he probably also knew you were my therapist and assumed I had told you everything."

Footsteps thumped in the foyer. In a few seconds, Ryan popped his head in the kitchen. "I'm sorry I'm late. An issue in the vineyards early this morning."

"You missed quite a revelation," Marj said. "Sit down. I'll make you some eggs."

"Don't bother. I had a couple doughnuts this morning. What's going on?"

★ ★ ★

After Ryan had been filled in, Jade had to leave for work, and Marjorie left with Ryan to help him in the vineyards. Talon refilled our coffee cups.

"You okay, Tal?" I asked.

He was a little pale, but he nodded. "Yeah. I'm not the one who was held at gunpoint yesterday. I should be asking if you're okay."

"I'm good, bro. I'm just sorry I let him get away."

Melanie caressed my forearm. "You didn't have a choice. None of us want you dead."

"That's for sure," Talon agreed.

My phone beeped. "Excuse me." I took a look. "Damn."

"What is it?" Melanie asked.

"I got another text from my stalker. Have we ruled out Brooke for sure?"

Talon nodded. "Jade searched her room. She only has the one phone, and she couldn't have hidden it anywhere else, since she can hardly move. Someone is usually here with her. Either Marj or Felicia, since she came back to work."

"I guess I'll just put up with it for now."

"Why don't you have Mills and Johnson find out who the number belongs to?" Talon said.

"I don't want to take them off your case. It's way more important that we track down Tom Simpson and Nico Kostas. Or rather, Theodore Mathias."

Talon shook his head. "Tom fucking Simpson. I can hardly believe it."

"Believe it," I said. "He's way worse than Larry Wade. He's an iceman, Tal. Nothing fazes him. He's been hiding his true nature all these years. From his wife. From his son. It was freaking me out every time I thought of little Henry in that house with his pedophile grandfather."

"You don't think he would hurt an innocent baby, do you?"

"He hurt an innocent ten-year-old boy," I said and then winced. "Sorry."

"Don't be. It's old news now." Talon shook his head. "Everyone knows. I've had to make my peace with that. It's embarrassing. Humiliating. But it happened."

"There's no reason for either of those emotions," Melanie said. "What happened wasn't your fault."

"I know that. It's just..."

Melanie smiled. "I understand. But believe me, no one thinks any less of you. We all admire your strength."

"She speaks the truth, Tal," I said. "And no, I don't think Tom hurt the baby. Evelyn was always home, and Bryce was usually there as well. So I figured that Henry was okay."

"Oh my God," Talon said. "Does Bryce know any of this?"

I nodded. "I told him my suspicions before I knew for sure. He wasn't happy with me."

"He wasn't happy with you? What the hell would he have against *you*?"

"It's his father, Tal. As far as he's concerned, Tom was a good father. And I was very happy to hear that, because now I know he never touched Bryce and probably not Henry either."

"True. But he had no reason to get pissed off at you."

I took a drink of coffee. "He'll come around. I have faith in our friendship. Especially now that we have proof. We just need to find the bastards."

My phone buzzed again, this time with a call. I frowned. "I don't recognize the number. Do you mind?"

"Of course not," Talon said.

Melanie shook her head.

"Jonah Steel," I said into the phone.

"Mr. Steel, this is Officer Jones in Murphy. We need you to come back in for questioning and a blood test."

"A blood test? What the hell for?"

"To check your DNA."

"And again, what the hell for?"

"Well..." Jones cleared his throat. "The man you brought in, Colin Morse? He...uh...he says you're the one who raped him."

I dropped the phone.

That asshole.

"What is it?" Melanie asked, stroking my arm.

I pulled away from her. My mind raged in an angry red haze. I had saved that shithead's life, and this was how he repaid me?

I picked up the phone and power walked into the foyer. "What? That's a fucking lie," I yelled into the phone.

"We have to explore all evidence, Mr. Steel. We're just doing our jobs."

I clenched the phone in my hand. "I can't believe this. You

can all go to hell."

"Mr. Steel, if you don't cooperate, we'll get a warrant and force you to take the test. Do you want that?"

"You want my blood, motherfucker? You come and get it." I ended the call and threw the phone onto the floor.

Melanie rushed toward me, her green eyes wide. "Jonah?"

"Leave me alone." I nudged away from her.

"Hey, Joe," Talon said. "That's not like you. What the hell is wrong?"

"Nothing." How could I say this to the brother and woman that I loved?

My phone beeped again. I picked it up. It was still working, thanks to the case I used. Jesus Christ. Another text from the stalker.

If I can't have you, no one will.

CHAPTER THIRTEEN

Melanie

Jonah was walled off all of a sudden. I couldn't get near him. Physically, I was standing two feet away from him, but emotionally, he was miles away.

"Did you get another text?" I asked.

He didn't answer. He shoved his phone into his back pocket and then raked his fingers through his disheveled hair.

"Joe, man, what's going on?" Talon approached him.

"Back off, Talon." Jonah's eyes were dark and angry.

"Please." I edged toward him. "Who was that? What did you mean by telling him to take your blood?"

"I have to get out of here." He turned to Talon. "Can you see that she gets home safely?"

"Of course, but Joe, you have to tell us what's going on."

"I've got nothing else to say." He stomped out, his cowboy boots thudding out of the kitchen, across the marble-tiled foyer, and out the door of Talon's ranch house.

My heart thumped wildly. Something wasn't right. Who had made that phone call?

"You all right, Doc?" Talon asked.

And then I realized I was shaking. I forced myself to calm down. "Yes. I think so. I'm just...worried about him. What made him act like that?"

"I don't know. But Joe gets that way sometimes. He gets stuck in his own head and won't let anyone in. We used to call it his 'dark mood' when we were kids."

Dark?

I knew he had a darkness locked within him, but I always thought it had more to do with his sexual preferences. This wasn't sexual at all. This was him retreating inside himself. And why? That's what I needed to find out.

"Tell me more about his 'dark mood' when you were younger," I said to Talon.

"I don't know if I should. I mean, he never swore me to confidence or anything, but it's not something Ry and I ever talk about. Then, after I got taken, I was the one who was always in a blackish mood, so I didn't notice Joe's as much, but Ry always said it was still there."

"Look," I said. "I love your brother. More than I've ever loved anyone. I want to help him. So please. Tell me."

Talon sighed. "I hope my brother knows how lucky he is to have you."

Normally a comment like that would have made me smile, but right now I was too worried about Jonah. "I don't know what he's thinking. That's why I need you to tell me what you know."

Talon cleared his throat. "It was actually our mother who coined the term 'dark mood.' There were times when Joe would go off by himself. We never knew why, and he would eventually return. And while I'm speaking somewhat metaphorically, he also physically left. Sometimes he would camp out in the pastures for a few days, only coming in for meals. He still did his duty. He was responsible to a T. But he wouldn't talk."

"It almost sounds like he was suffering from depression,

although the fact that he still did his duty around the ranch wouldn't seem to indicate that."

"Oh?"

I nodded. "Depression can be very debilitating. In its severe form, a person can hardly get out of bed in the morning. They find no joy in anything, even things they normally enjoy."

"That sounds kind of like Joe. But yeah, he never shirked his duties. And as an adult, he's never avoided them either."

"Tell me what you remember."

"Well, I don't really remember. But Ryan told me that he got really bad after I got taken. According to Ryan, Joe didn't talk for over a week and a half at one point. It was summer, so there was no school. He did all his work around the ranch, but he had completely isolated himself."

The guilt. The guilt was eating him up, but had he had these "dark moods" before Talon had been taken?

"You think Ryan would talk to me about that time?"

"You'd have to ask him, but I don't see why not. He loves his brother, just like I do, and if you can help him, I'm sure he'd be up for it."

"What about before you were taken?"

"Yeah. It would happen every now and then, for no reason."

"Did your mother explain anything else about these moods?"

Talon shook his head. "We were kids, Doc. We just accepted what she told us."

"I understand. So what happened in the days before you were taken?"

"Like I said, he would just go inside himself for a day or two. Usually no longer than that. He wouldn't talk. He spent his time alone in his room, doing God knows what. My mother told us not to bother him."

"Yet he never shirked his duties."

"Nope. Never. Joe was about as responsible as they came."

"Tell me, did your mother ever have these same kind of moods?"

"Not that I remember, but Wendy Madigan did tell Joe and me that our mother was mentally ill. I look back, and I realize that must have been the case. Mentally fit people don't normally commit suicide."

"Do you think your mother had mental problems before your abduction?"

"The three of us always thought she killed herself because she couldn't deal with what had happened to me and almost losing Marj as a result. But Wendy Madigan insists that she had been having mental issues long before then, and she's a respected newswoman. Though I know Joe has his doubts about that."

My ears perked up. "What do you mean he has doubts?"

"When we went to see Wendy Madigan a few weeks ago, she told us some stuff that was in direct conflict with what Larry Wade had said. Now personally, I think a newswoman's word trumps a criminal psychopath's word. But Joe's not buying it."

"I know Jonah wants to look into the Wendy Madigan situation further," I said. "But the point I was getting at is that depression is often hereditary. If your mother suffered, that could explain why Jonah suffers from depression."

"So you think it is depression?"

"He would need a full psychological work-up for me to make that assessment. The good news is, even if it is depression, I don't think it's severe. Otherwise he wouldn't be able to keep working."

"Please, Doc. Can you help him? I don't want him suffering. I'm so tired of everyone suffering because of me."

"Talon, if Jonah is suffering from depression, it's not your fault. It's no one's fault. It's his body chemistry, nothing more. He probably inherited it from your mother. Be thankful you and Ryan didn't."

"I'm not so sure I didn't. Remember, there was a time when I wanted to get my ass shot off."

"Your depression was situational, due to what happened to you. I'm assuming you didn't have a history of dark moods before that?"

He shook his head. "No. I was a pretty happy kid."

"Exactly. Now that you're working through what happened to you and the consequences of it, you no longer feel that way."

"No, I sure don't."

I succumbed to a small smile. Knowing Talon was healing made me so happy, but knowing Jonah was suffering nearly negated all of it.

"Talon," I said, my voice serious, "you don't think he would harm himself, do you?"

"No. He never has. And whatever that phone call was about, you know I will always have his back."

Whatever was going on with Jonah, the phone call had been the catalyst. Something about his blood. I ached to call him, to help him, but I wasn't sure if that was the direction to go. Still, he needed to know I was here for him.

"I'm going to call him. He may not answer, but I want him to know we're worried about him. Then, would you drive me home?"

"Sure."

I retrieved my phone and made the call. As I suspected, I got his voice mail.

"Jonah, it's me. I don't know what's going on, but Talon and I are worried about you. Please call me. I love you."

CHAPTER FOURTEEN

Jonah

I skidded into a parking spot at the hospital where that shithead Colin Morse was. I should have fucking left him in that basement to rot. This was my thanks for being a good Samaritan?

No more.

From now on, I'd let the darkness that I kept at bay take center stage. I was tired of this shit. At times, I held on by only a single thread. A line so thin that it was imperceptible. But I held on. I didn't let the darkness take me.

Until now.

I swiped my hand over the Glock I had hidden in my ankle holster. I possessed a concealed carry permit, but I hardly ever used it. I hadn't even stopped to arm myself before I went after Tom Simpson yesterday. No, I'd been too focused on my ultimate goal.

Right now, though, I was ready to snap.

How much was I supposed to take?

My phone buzzed.

Goddamnit! Probably another text from my psycho stalker. I threw the phone on the passenger seat. Screw it.

I opened the door but then looked at the phone again. What if something was wrong?

A voice mail. I keyed in my code and listened.

"Jonah, it's me. I don't know what's going on, but Talon and I are worried about you. Please call me. I love you."

Melanie.

Melanie loved me.

I sighed as I unclasped my ankle holster and locked the gun in the glove compartment. What had I been thinking? I'd gone dark. I'd told her to leave me alone. The most wonderful woman in the world loved me, and I'd told her to leave me alone.

This wasn't me. I couldn't let it be me.

Had I really thought I was going to walk into a hospital and shoot a patient? Thank God for Melanie. What if she hadn't called me?

I'd been ready to kill before, and something always happened to talk me out of it.

Or maybe I was talking myself out of it.

Who the fuck knew?

I took a deep breath and counted to ten. Then I got out of the car and walked into the hospital. Officer Jones had told me to meet him in the ICU waiting area.

Jones approached me. "Mr. Steel."

"Here I am." I patted my arm. "And here's a good vein. I assure you that you won't find any trace of me anywhere near Colin. At least not where you're looking for it."

Another man approached, wearing a suit and tie. "Mr. Steel," he said.

"Yeah? Who are you?"

"I'm Ted Morse. Colin's father. Might I have a word?"

"I have nothing to say to you." I turned back to Officer Jones.

"Please. I think you'll be interested in what I have to say."

I rolled my eyes. "Fine. Please excuse me," I said to Jones.

I followed him out of the waiting area and into a hallway. "What is it?"

"I have a proposition for you. One I think you'll find intriguing."

"I doubt it."

"My son is willing to drop his allegations against you."

"Great. I didn't do a damned thing except save his life, so let's get moving, then."

"He says otherwise. However, I think he could be persuaded to change his story for a price."

"Of course. A price. I'm innocent here. You and he both know that."

"I know nothing of the sort. I wasn't there."

"He was. And I know the guys who tortured him. Their names are Tom Simpson and Theodore Mathias. That's who you should be after."

"Nonetheless, he swears it was you."

"He's lying."

"Perhaps. It doesn't really matter. What matters is that he is the victim here, and he swears you are the perpetrator. But I guarantee you he'll recant for five million dollars."

"Are you out of your fucking mind?"

"That's chump change to you."

"So what? I didn't do anything to him. I saved him!"

"Consider it a payment for his suffering. He says both you and your brothers threatened him the day before he was taken. In fact, your brother Talon beat him bloody."

"Talon went to court for that. He's paid his debt."

"My son wanted to be in court that day, to tell his side of

the story. But he wasn't. And who would have the most to gain by him not being there? Your brother. And you."

Oh my God. Was this truly happening?

"Look, we had nothing to do with that."

"As I understand it, only Talon has an alibi. Jade. And that's sketchy, given her history with Colin. But you and your brother Ryan have no alibi for your whereabouts after you left Colin that night. For the five mil, this all goes away."

"This is all ridiculous. All I need to do is have the stupid DNA test and you'll find out I'm innocent."

"Are you sure about that?" His eyes glinted with slime.

What the fuck? Was he trying to frame me? There was no way any trace of my DNA could be found anywhere near Colin's private parts.

Would it be easier to just pay him off? I could afford it.

Then—

"Wait a goddamned minute. I want to talk to your son."

"I'm afraid that's not possible. Only family can see him."

"This isn't his idea at all, is it? He never told anyone that I raped him. You made that up to extort money from me. He knows I saved him."

"Mr. Steel—"

"You are a goddamned piece of work, Morse. I'll tell you the same thing I told Jones when he called me. You want my blood? Come here and take it." I glared at him.

He backed away slowly.

"You know what my brother did to your son, and that was only because Talon saw Colin kissing his woman. Let me tell you something. I'm way meaner than my brother could ever hope to be. What do you think I could do to a guy who's trying to frame me for kidnapping and rape?"

"You had better think before you threaten me, Mr. Steel."

"This isn't a threat. It's just the way things are. You and I both know I never touched your son. In fact, I think I'll go get Officer Jones, and I'll tell him exactly what you said to me during this conversation."

Morse pursed his lips. "You still haven't seen the last of us."

"Look, I'm really sorry about what happened to your son. Those degenerates did the same thing to my brother when he was only ten years old. I wouldn't wish it on anyone. But I will not take the blame when all I did was find him and save him."

He looked at me sternly, his eyes betraying nothing.

"I don't think I'll be having a blood test today after all," I said. "Unless you let me talk to Colin first."

"That won't be necessary." Morse turned and walked away.

The fucking asshole. Trying to extort money from me by accusing me of such a despicable act. Nausea rose in my throat. Part of me wished I had kept my Glock in my ankle holster, but I knew that wasn't the answer.

I had Melanie back now. I wasn't going to screw up my life.

I checked in with Officer Jones before I left. "I think you'll find that my blood test is no longer necessary when you talk to Mr. Morse. In fact, the asshat just tried to extort money from me. You should arrest his sorry ass."

I walked out of the hospital.

CHAPTER FIFTEEN

Melanie

Talon dropped me off at Jonah's, and I had been home only a few minutes when the doorbell rang.

When I opened the door, I had to stop myself from dropping my jaw to the floor. Outside stood one of the most beautiful women I had ever seen. She had auburn hair and blue-gray eyes. She was slightly shorter than I was and was dressed in hip-hugging jeans and a T-shirt that showed a sliver of belly along with her ample breasts. She had full and pouty pink lips, and her eyelashes were long. I didn't see any indication of mascara.

"Yes, can I help you?"

"I'm looking for Jonah Steel," she said in a high-pitched voice, reminiscent of Minnie Mouse.

At least something about her wasn't perfect. She sounded like a little kid.

"He's not here right now."

"Oh." She turned her lips into a frown. "I'm only in town for the evening, and I really want to hook up with him."

Hook up? I didn't like the sound of that.

"Like I said, he's not here, and I'm afraid I don't know when he'll return." Unfortunately, that was the truth. He hadn't called me back, and I had no idea whether he'd gotten my voice mail. "You want to leave a message for him or something?"

"Actually, do you mind if I come in? He still has some stuff of mine that I want."

My hackles rose. "Who are you?"

"I'm Kerry. Kerry Ross. Joe and I used to...date, I guess."

Kerry.

Jonah had told me about Kerry. They had dated for a while, had frequented the BDSM club together. She had wanted him to be her Master, not just in the bedroom but in all of life. I looked her over. She didn't look like a slave, but what did I know? I had never met a slave before, at least not that I knew of.

She was so beautiful, so perfectly formed. Except for that voice of hers, she had no flaws at all. Jealousy surged through me.

"I don't know. Like I said, he's not here, and I have no idea where your things might be."

"Oh, don't worry about that. I know exactly where they are." She walked past me and into the foyer.

I couldn't believe it. She barged into what I now considered my own home.

"Excuse me? I'm not sure I should be letting you in here."

She gave me a dazzling smile. Even her teeth were perfect. "Oh, I know he won't mind. I've been meaning to stop by for a while now and pick up all the stuff."

"Why don't you tell me where it would be, and I'll get it for you?"

"Honestly, it's no bother. It's just downstairs." She walked into the kitchen and to the other wing of the house, one I'd hardly ever been in. She opened a door, which led down to the basement.

I walked down the stairs behind her. I knew Jonah had a basement, but I'd never been in it. I'd had no reason to go down there. It was finished into a beautiful rec room, complete with a pool table, a big-screen TV, and a full bar. "Wow, this would've been a great party room when I was younger," I said.

"Oh, I know. Joe and I used to have the best parties down here."

The envy lanced through me again. He had parties with her down in the gorgeous room that I didn't even know existed?

She walked toward a door near the end of the room. She turned the doorknob. "Shoot, it's locked. No worries, I think I still have the key."

She had a key to a room at Jonah's house?

She pulled a key chain out of her purse and unlocked the door. She walked in as if it were perfectly normal to do so and flipped the light switch.

And I gasped.

"What is this place?"

"Oh, I'm sorry. This is Joe's dungeon."

Joe's dungeon? Acid bubbled up in my throat. He'd talked about doing scenes at the BDSM club. He hadn't said anything about his own private dungeon.

The walls were painted dark blue, and part of the room looked completely normal. Against one wall was a large bed covered in a blue silk comforter with black brocade pillows. At the foot of the bed sat a settee of the same black brocade. On the opposite end were a sofa and a lounge chair, a slightly lighter blue, again with black pillows.

But on the adjacent wall...

On hooks hung handcuffs, rope, scarves, blindfolds, riding crops...and a lot of stuff I couldn't name. What looked like some kind of stockade stood nearby. A strange-looking table jutted out from the wall as well. And it looked like—no lie—the table I lay on when I went to the gynecologist's office.

My skin prickled around me.

Several crates sat beneath where the implements hung, and while Kerry walked to them and began sorting through them, my gaze was drawn to the chair in the corner.

It resembled a standard wingback chair, but it was much larger than normal. Its fabric was black leather, the wood black lacquer. It was oddly beautiful yet terrifying. And though I'd never seen anything like it before, I knew what it was.

It was a Master's chair.

Jonah was the Master in this room.

I shivered.

Did I really not know the man I loved at all? Was this the true extent of the darkness?

Kerry pulled out and held up a pair of red fur-covered handcuffs. "Found them," she said. "I've never been able to find a better pair of cuffs. I can't believe I left these here so long."

I closed my eyes for a moment, and the image of Kerry, her beautiful naked body spread out on the table, her hands bound with the red handcuffs, Jonah whipping her with a riding crop...

I opened my eyes.

Now she was holding up a riding crop, also red.

I cleared my throat, determined to stay polite and nonchalant. "Is that all you need, then?"

"Yes. I suppose I should've called before barging in. I hope I didn't bother you. It's just that I'm only in town today, and I really wanted to get these."

She walked out of the room, and I followed along like an

obedient puppy.

She walked up the stairs, through the kitchen and foyer, to the door before she turned to me.

“Please tell Joe I’m so sorry that I missed him.” She whipped the riding crop through the air, and it gave a hiss. “I’ve sure missed this thing.” She smiled. “Thanks so much for allowing me to get these. It was so nice to meet you... Oh, I guess I never got your name.”

“Melanie,” I said, biting my lip.

“Melanie, great. Please tell Joe I stopped by and that I hope he’s doing well.” She walked out the door and shut it behind her.

I stood in the foyer for a few moments, attempting to swallow the lump that had lodged in my throat.

This was crazy. Totally crazy. When Jonah had told me about his time at the BDSM club, I had been freaked out a little, but I was determined to accept every part of him, even the darker side of his desires.

Why hadn’t he told me that he had a dungeon in this house? In this house he’d invited me to live in?

Surely he would have thought I might go exploring while he wasn’t here. Now that I knew he had a beautiful rec room in the basement—

Wait! The door to the dungeon had been locked.

I wouldn’t have been able to get in, except that Kerry had a key.

She still had a key to Jonah’s dungeon.

My heart sank.

Would I ever be able to please him? He was still keeping things from me, still not revealing the true extent of his dark yearning.

My curiosity getting the best of me, I walked back down the stairs to the room that was still unlocked.

It was such a strange combination of beauty and grandeur mixed with darkness and kink.

Did Jonah fantasize about taking me in this room?

He had never said anything about it. In fact, he had been loath to even discuss his darker desires with me. I had taken the lead and asked him to show me some of what I might be missing.

He'd said he hadn't been to the club in years. Was it possible he hadn't been down in this room for years either?

There was only one way to find out. I would have to ask him about it.

I walked over to the Master's chair and ran my fingers over the supple leather. I pictured Jonah sitting in the chair. It wasn't a stretch. He exuded dominance. It was an easy image to form in my mind—him sitting in this chair, a submissive on her knees in front of him.

What was difficult was imagining that the submissive was me.

Was that what he wanted from me?

And if it was, would I be able to give it to him?

I knelt in front of the chair, imagining Jonah sitting there, me serving him.

I gazed around the room, focusing on the thing that looked like a stockade and then the strange table. But if I looked just to the right, I saw a beautiful bed that almost looked like it belonged to a decadent bedroom, along with the settee, couch, and marble-topped coffee table.

I stayed, kneeling in front of the chair, for a long time.

CHAPTER SIXTEEN

Jonah

When I got home, I made sure Lucy had fresh water, and when I didn't find Melanie in the family room or the kitchen, I figured she might be resting in the bedroom. I sighed. I had a lot of explaining to do to her. It hadn't been fair of me to walk out on her and Talon without telling them where I was going or why, and I really shouldn't have told her to leave me alone. I had just been so angry. And then to be blackmailed on top of everything else. Colin Morse and his father would not get one penny from me. Well, his father wouldn't. I had no problem helping Colin, if he needed it and as long as he wasn't perpetuating lies about my family or me.

Whoever and whatever he was, he didn't deserve the treatment he had received at the hands of Tom Simpson and Theodore Mathias.

I walked to my bedroom to find Melanie. She wasn't there, so I checked the guest room she had been using. Not there either.

I grabbed my phone and called her. Oddly, a phone began ringing, and I found it on top of the dresser in the guest room.

She would never go anywhere without her phone, so she must be around here somewhere.

Instantly I began to panic. What if she had been taken

again? Those two sickos were still out there.

I ran out of the bedroom down the hallway. “Melanie? Melanie? Where are you?”

Then I noticed the door to my basement was cracked. I usually kept it shut. Perhaps she had gone down there.

I walked down the stairs slowly. “Melanie?”

And then my heart raced. The door—*that* door—was *open.*

Oh my God.

I ran into the room.

There she was, kneeling in front of my chair, her cheek on the black leather cushion.

I stood, silent, for a moment. Kneeling at my chair, she was beautiful. I had always imagined her in that position. So lovely. But—

How had she gotten into this room? I kept it locked for a reason. I hadn’t used it in years, not since Kerry. I had always meant to have it redecorated and converted into another spare bedroom. Damn. Why hadn’t I? Or why hadn’t I just told her about it? What must she have thought when she stumbled down here on her own?

But I was sure it had been locked, and I had the only key.

“Baby?” I said tentatively.

She lifted her head and twisted her neck to face me.

“What are you doing in here, sweetheart?”

“I...didn’t mean to be nosy or anything. But...Kerry stopped by.”

Kerry? “What was she doing here? She moved to California a couple years ago.”

“She said she was just in town for the evening and you still had a few things of hers. She just walked on down here, knew her way around and everything, had a key to open the door...”

Melanie closed her eyes.

What had I done?

"Baby, I can explain all this."

But could I? I hadn't told her about this room. In truth, I just hadn't thought of it. I'd never dreamed she'd see it without me being there to explain.

"You...don't have to explain anything."

I went to her, took her hand, pulled her to her feet, and then led her over to the bed and sat down. "I'm sorry you had to find out this way, that you had to see this room this way. I didn't realize Kerry still had a key. I'll change the lock immediately."

"I've been worried about you." She cupped my cheek. "Where were you? Are you okay?"

I closed my eyes and inhaled. This room had been a complete surprise, and who knew what had gone through her mind? But her first concern was me.

Just one more reason I didn't deserve this wonderful woman.

"I'm fine. It's a long story and I'll explain it later, but everything is all right. Right now, I need to know. Are *you* all right?"

She chewed on her lower lip. God, she was always so beautiful.

"Kerry was...very nice. Very pretty."

"Yes, she is." I wasn't sure what I should say.

"She didn't look like a submissive."

"Most people in the lifestyle don't go around town wearing their leathers." I attempted a smile.

"Yes, I know that. She said you had parties here."

"Yes. A few times, we had parties here. With others in the lifestyle."

She nodded.

"Baby, are you sure you're okay?"

"Why didn't you tell me about this? You told me about the club, and I understood. You said you had no desire to ever go back there, yet I find your own personal club in your home."

"I'm sorry. I've actually been meaning to have this room redone for a while. There's always so much going on around here, and I just haven't had the chance to hire someone to get it done. I'm so sorry you had to find out about it this way. I would've shown you eventually."

"Why didn't you show me when we talked about this?"

"I don't know. I wasn't thinking. I knew it was all so much for you to...digest."

She nodded. "That's an understatement."

"Look, baby. Most of this is in my past. I don't expect you to..." Didn't expect her to what? Would I love to see her bound for my pleasure, ready to take my hard cock?

Yes, I would.

But I could never ask her to do that. Especially not after she had been kidnapped and bound and nearly killed.

"I'll tell you what," I said. "Why don't you take over the redecorating and make this room into whatever you want? An office, maybe. You'll need a home office after all. It won't be long until you're practicing again."

"I couldn't."

"Of course you can. This is your home now, Melanie. I want you to have your own space here."

"I understand that, Jonah. I just can't have...*this* space. Knowing that you were down here with other women..." She let out a small laugh. "I suppose that doesn't make any sense. I'm sure you had other women in your bedroom from time to time."

"Yes, from time to time."

But this did bother her. I could see it in her eyes. She was trying to understand, but this was disturbing her. How much, I wasn't sure.

"All right. We'll make this into another guest room. You can use one of the upstairs rooms for your office."

"No," she said. "I don't think this should be a new guest room. I mean, you have plenty of guest rooms."

I caressed her silky hair. "Then what would you like to do with this room, my love?"

She looked at me, still biting her lip, her emerald eyes shining. "I want you to show me what you do in this room. I want you to show me now."

CHAPTER SEVENTEEN

Melanie

I trembled inside. Was I actually ready for this? I wasn't sure. All I knew was I loved this man with all my heart and soul, and I wanted to understand him more than anything. If surrendering to him in this dark dungeon would please him, that is exactly what I would do.

"Baby, this isn't necessary."

"No, Jonah, it *is* necessary. I just met a woman who you were intimate with in this room, a room I didn't even know existed, despite the fact that I've been living here. I made myself a promise yesterday when I left here. I promised to take my life back, to take my*self* back. I've been looking at myself in a different way since my kidnapping. It made me look at Gina's death in an entirely different way, a way that may turn out to be correct. Maybe finding this room is part of the journey I need to take. If you and I are going to be together, I need to understand you. In every way. I know there's a part of you that still craves this." I drew in a deep breath and let it out. "Tell me, honestly. Is there part of you that wants to see me tied down on this bed or that table?"

He tensed up, his brow furrowed. "Melanie, I love our relationship exactly the way it is."

"That's not what I asked you. I believe you. I believe

you love me and you love our relationship as it is. But tell me honestly. Is there something inside you that would love to see me naked, bound, ready for your pain and pleasure?"

He swallowed audibly, and my eyes were drawn to his Adam's apple as he did so. Still, he did not respond.

I knew the answer. If it were no, he would have no problem saying so.

But Jonah could not lie to me, any more than I could lie to him. Our love bound us, not just physically but emotionally.

Now I knew the truth.

The only question up in the air was whether I could give in to his deepest desires.

I wanted to try.

I surveyed the wall where the straps and paddles hung. He had given me a slight slap with his hand, and though it had made me uncomfortable, I hadn't hated it.

"Tell me how it makes you feel, Jonah," I said. "How did it make you feel when you slapped my behind?"

He sighed. "Melanie, do you really want to go there?"

I drew him toward me, cupped his cheeks, and pressed a soft kiss on his lips. "I love you. That will not change. Now I want to *know* you. Deeply. Please tell me. What do you feel when you slap me on the ass?"

He closed his eyes for a moment. After a few timeless seconds, he opened them. "No one has ever asked me that before."

"Really?"

"That surprises you?"

"Yes, very much. I love you, and I want to know everything about you. Everything you feel."

His lips fell into a beautiful smile. "That must be the

difference, then. None of my other partners ever loved me."

I shouldn't have been so surprised. He had told me as much when we first discussed his enjoyment of BDSM activities. He hadn't told any of them that he loved them, and apparently they hadn't loved him either.

"Does that mean you don't have an answer?" I asked.

"It's not something I've ever put into words, Melanie."

"Could you try? For me?"

He rubbed his temple, sighing. "For you, I will try. I would do anything for you, Melanie. Anything at all. And although I've always known that, I don't think it hit me with full force until right now. For you, I will try to put this into words."

He took my hand, rubbing my palm with his thumb. "I see you looking at those instruments on the wall. Yes, I've used them, but no, I don't always use them. Sometimes I only use my hand, as I did on you. But whether I use an implement or my hand doesn't seem to matter. When I use a prop, it's for the submissive's pleasure, not my own. I get the same pleasure no matter what I use. It's like the riding crop, or the paddle, or whatever I use becomes an extension of me. As it comes down on the submissive's flesh, I feel it as if it is my own flesh touching hers."

I closed my other hand over his. "That's fascinating. I never would've known."

"I'm not sure I knew it consciously myself. Not until I just put it into words."

"What else do you feel?"

"Although I am the one inflicting the pain, I feel it. I feel it in my hand. The sting, the tingle. It travels through my fingers, up my arm, and into my entire body. It soaks into my groin, and my cock grows hard."

I nodded.

"And then the redness of the submissive's flesh... I feel that warmth in my own body, and sometimes, when I looked down at my chest, I become red as well, even though no one has slapped me."

His words had a dark beauty to them, and although I still didn't quite understand his full motivation for the play he enjoyed, I was beginning to see a little more clearly.

"In a way," he continued, "it's not all that different from normal vanilla sex. When we're close, Melanie, and you become wet for me, I can feel your arousal, even before I touch you between your legs."

"I understand. I feel your arousal too."

"When I'm taking control over a submissive, my arousal becomes almost..." He shook his head. "It's primal, but in a different way than you're thinking. I can feel my adrenaline rushing through me. It's not that I want to physically hurt my partner, at least not in a bad way. But those endorphins that my partner emits as the pain turns into pleasure somehow transfer to me. When she begs for more, my arousal intensifies and comes to a boiling point."

"From a medical standpoint, that makes sense," I said. "A person in pain will produce endorphins. They act kind of like... Well, like narcotics. They block the pain receptors and can cause euphoria. But that doesn't explain why you get those feelings as well."

"Not from a physical standpoint, no. What drives me is producing it in the person. The feeling of being in complete control of someone else's pleasure. Something in me opens. I feel every slap of the riding crop, every prick of the needle, every burn of the melted candle wax on the submissive's flesh."

He closed his eyes. "It's arousing to be so in control yet so out of control at the same time."

I squeezed his hand. "I never knew it could be like that."

"For me, it feels good. It feels *right* to me to be in a dominant role, to know that another person trusts me that much. But I've learned something, Melanie. Although I love being in control of someone else's pain and pleasure, and though I feel every bit of it myself as if it is happening to me, I have no more power than the person I'm dominating."

"Why do you say that?"

"Because it's not so much about power. If she doesn't like what I'm doing, she can stop the scene at any time. If I don't like how things are going, I can stop. It really doesn't have anything to do with power. The power is equal between us."

Jonah's words struck a chord within me. Power. That was the problem I was having with this, with surrendering to him. I was afraid of giving up my power.

But if what he said was true, I wouldn't be giving up any power, and neither would he. The power would be equal between us. All I needed to do was trust him—trust that he would never harm me.

And I did. I trusted Jonah Steel with my heart, my life.

Now was the time to take myself back.

CHAPTER EIGHTEEN

Jonah

Melanie stared at me, her green eyes as beautiful as ever, nibbling on that luscious lower lip of hers. That red lip, the lip I had taken between my teeth and bitten on so many occasions, that I had run my tongue over, that I had kissed with wild abandon as well as soft sweetness.

She was beautiful, my Melanie. Beautiful and strong and brilliant.

She had asked me questions in her innocence, and I had answered them to the best of my ability. Had I made a mistake in doing so? I had to believe that I hadn't. If we were meant to be together, we had to know each other unequivocally. There could be no barriers between us.

I understood that now.

And now I had the answer to the question she had asked at the beginning of this conversation. Was there a part of me that wanted to see her naked, bound, at my mercy?

She probably already knew the answer.

I had fought my baser desires, and I knew I could be happy just making love with her for the rest of our lives. After all, making love took many forms. If my intimate time with her was simply vanilla sex, I could handle that. Giving her up was not an option, and it never would be.

But now was the time for me to be honest. She trusted me, and I owed her that much.

I leaned forward and pressed my lips to her peachy cheek.

I pulled back.

"I hope this doesn't scare you," I said, "but the answer to your original question is 'yes.' There is a part of me that longs for your submission. I hunger for it, Melanie. I hunger for those feelings that I have when I'm taking control of another person, but not only because it's so arousing for me. It's more than that. It's because this is part of me, and I want to share with you everything I am."

She smiled. "I can't say I understand every bit of it, but I want so much to make you happy."

She fingered the beautiful diamond choker around her neck—the one I had bought weeks ago, the one I had originally planned to give to her as a formal collar, denoting the Dominant and submissive relationship between us.

I had decided to give it to her anyway, regardless of whether we ever had that kind of relationship. It sparkled around her alabaster skin, and I knew no one else could ever wear it, no matter what kind of relationship she and I ended up with. The piece was made for her. No matter what happened between us, I hoped with all my heart she would never remove it.

"I want to make you happy too, baby. So no pressure. I'm sorry I didn't tell you about this room. I was being honest when I told you I hadn't used it in years and that I had eventually planned to get rid of it."

"I believe you. But if this is a part of who you are, you shouldn't have to get rid of it for me. It wouldn't be fair of me to ask you to do that, and I don't want you to."

"I understand," I said, "but we don't have to use this room. I am perfectly happy making love with you the way we normally do in our bedroom."

She smiled. "You said '*our* bedroom.'"

I returned her smile. "It *is* our bedroom, sweetheart. Everything in this house is yours as well as mine. I can't imagine ever wanting another woman."

She stroked my cheek with her soft fingertips. "And I can't imagine ever wanting another man."

I leaned forward and took her lips with mine, sliding them open with my tongue. She met my kiss with sweet eagerness. The kiss became more passionate, and when I finally broke it to take a breath, her green eyes were alight with fire.

"Show me, Jonah. Show me what you do in this room."

I groaned, and my cock thickened beneath my jeans. At least now she knew what she was asking. "Are you sure, baby?"

"I'm sure. Just be gentle at first. I'll need to go slowly."

"God, of course. I don't ever want to harm you. Please tell me you know that."

She smiled. "I do know that. I believe you with all my heart, and I trust you, Jonah."

I clamped my lips onto hers once more, and this time the kiss was ferocious, fueled by lust and passion. She began unbuttoning my shirt with her slender fingers, and my heart pounded.

We undressed each other slowly, and when she was naked, her beautiful body bare to my view, I felt, for a moment, that I could be content just looking at her. Basking in the beauty of her, the happiness she had brought into my life, the trust she gave me so freely. The love.

I could see the love in her eyes, and I hoped with all my

heart that she could see the same thing staring at her from my own.

My cock was thick and hard, already aching for release. But I would do as she asked. I would show her a little bit of what we could do in this room, of how we could create amazing pleasure for each other.

I wasn't ready to put her on the table. For now, we would use the bed. The headboard was made of brass with posts perfectly situated for binding. I went to the wall and chose two silk scarves. Silk was never my first choice, because it was harder to untie in case of an emergency, but it was soft and feminine, and after what Melanie had been through during her abduction—being bound with rope and duct tape—I thought silk the best thing to start with.

I would only bind her hands to the headboard and leave her feet free.

I took my dominant stance, standing over her. "Lie on the bed, Melanie. Facedown."

Her swift obedience surprised me, and my heart melted even further. Here was a woman who loved me, who didn't understand everything that I was about, but wanted to please me nonetheless.

I swept the soft fabric over her body. "These are silk bindings, Melanie. I'm only going to bind your wrists to the bedpost this time. If you're uncomfortable at any time, you just tell me to stop, and I will. Do you understand?"

"I understand," she replied.

The silk caught on my calloused fingertips, but I swiftly went to the head of the bed, took one of her wrists gently, and bound it to the post, not too tightly but enough that her hand wouldn't slip through. Then I repeated the action with her other hand.

"Does that feel all right?"

She nodded.

"I need you to answer verbally."

"Yes. Yes, it feels fine."

I sat down next to her on the bed and caressed the soft flesh of her ass. "Are you nervous, baby?"

"A little," she admitted.

"Do you want to continue?"

"Yes," she said unequivocally. "I want to continue."

"I'll use my hand this time, unless you want to try something else. Some of the riding crops feel nice."

"No, just your hand. And start slowly."

"I love you," I said. "Thank you for letting me share this side of me."

She smiled, and the curve of her lips was so beautiful that my heart nearly burst. I was still caressing the globes of her beautiful ass, aching to slap her.

So I did.

She jerked just a little but didn't say anything.

I smacked her ass again.

And again. And as I did, I felt the tingle through my own body, from my hand, up my arm, traveling outward. My cock tightened. Her ass shone a gorgeous shade of light pink.

"Okay so far?"

"Yes."

"You're so beautiful, Melanie. Your ass is so rosy." I leaned down and kissed her soft cheek. Then I slapped her again.

And again.

My cock stiffened further.

"How does that feel?" I asked.

She turned her head and bit her lip. "It's...painful...sort of." But she wiggled her ass. "Again, please."

Slap! Slap! Slap!

The light pink turned to deeper rose.

So beautiful.

I inhaled and smelled her arousal—that heady scent of apples, ginger, and female.

I climbed behind her and pushed her knees forward so her ass was in the air. I gave each cheek another slap, and then I leaned down to taste her gorgeous pussy. She sighed as I swiped my tongue from her clit all the way up to her asshole. Then I went back down and smacked her ass one more time.

She jerked under my slap, but let out a moan. A deep moan. A moan I had heard many times before.

Her moan of pleasure.

It was happening.

She was beginning to surrender.

And God, it was driving me crazy.

I sucked at her pussy again, slapping her with one hand and then driving two fingers inside her wet heat with the other. I tongued her tight hole and still slapped her ass.

She whimpered beneath me. "Jonah, God. I need to come. I need to come so badly."

So did I, but I had a lot to show her first.

"You don't come until I tell you to, baby."

A muffled whimper was her response. I continued to fuck her with my two fingers, adding a third because she was so wet, so responsive. As I continued to lick her asshole, I went a little longer between slaps. Her ass was so gorgeous and deep pink now. I felt the heat of her flesh through my own body, the pleasure-pain of the stinging, the tingle of a thousand needles jabbing into me.

I had to have her.

"I want to fuck you now, baby," I said. "I'm going to shove my cock into you, and when I start to come, I want you to come with me."

CHAPTER NINETEEN

Melanie

"God, yes, please," I said breathlessly.

He jammed into me. My ass still stung from the spanking, and now as he thrust in and out of me, my entire body quaked. This was why he enjoyed pain play—the tingling, the point where pain and pleasure were indistinguishable. I had found that point.

I wanted more.

He thrust and he thrust, and I was on the verge of coming, but I held myself in check, determined not to come until he told me to.

He pumped above me, thrusting upward, taking me, making me completely his.

Then he pulled out, waited a few timeless seconds, and said, "I'm going to plunge into you now, Melanie, and I want you to come. Come, baby, with me."

He surged deeply inside my pussy, and I imploded. My entire body prickled as the orgasm floated through me like a hundred shooting stars.

My whole world became my pussy. Everything I felt in my center I felt throughout the rest of my body. The pleasure ran through my body, coursing through my bloodstream and out my fingers, and then came lancing back, pulsing into me with the strength of a tidal wave.

Jonah groaned above me, clasping my hips, so deeply embedded inside me that we were like one.

I was so in tune with him I could feel the tiny contractions of his cock.

When my orgasm finally began to subside, I pulled at my hands, trying to release myself. I wanted to turn over and touch Jonah, wanted to look into his eyes and tell him how much this had meant to me.

But he had other ideas.

In a few minutes, he withdrew, came to me, and unbound me. I turned onto my back and gazed at him, his dark eyes afire.

"That was amazing, Jonah. I never knew."

"Baby, that was only the beginning."

He got up from the bed, rummaged through one of the boxes, and came back with a satin blindfold. He tied it around my eyes.

"Stay on your back, baby. I'm going to bind your wrists to the posts again."

As soft silk whispered over my breasts, my nipples hardened, and my pussy began to throb. I had just had an earth-shattering orgasm, and I was already ready to go again.

I had no idea what to expect. Again, he didn't bind my ankles.

For a while nothing happened, and just as I opened my mouth to speak, something touched my nipple. Coldness burst through me.

It was ice.

The chill hardened my nipples even further, the heat of my body melted the ice, and tiny rivers of water meandered over my body.

"Spread your legs, baby," Jonah said.

It never occurred to me not to obey. In a flash, the cold ice touched my clit, and then his warm mouth glided over the hard nub and erased the coolness.

I was so sensitive from my orgasm, but oh my God, I wanted to come again. I spread my legs farther, threatening to disjoint my hips, wanting so much for my hands to be free so I could push his tongue deeper into me.

But they were not free. I could not touch him, and I longed to.

And that was very erotic.

As he continued to lick me, the combination of coldness from the ice and warmth from his mouth titillated me. I was near the urge again when he forced two fingers into me and commanded, "Come."

I hadn't thought I was close to another orgasm, but at the commanding tone of his voice, I unraveled again.

Shivers raced through me, morphing into heat, morphing into fire, and the flames burst through my veins.

When I finally came down, he withdrew his fingers slowly. And then, before I knew it—

Slap!

Something came down over my breasts, over my still very hard nipples.

Was it one of the riding crops?

I felt the blood rushing to my breasts, and the soft whoosh of the riding crop met my ears with a loving hiss. The pain turned quickly to pleasure, culminating in my pussy once more.

Slap!

The crop came down on my breasts again.

Slap! Slap!

This time on my thighs.

The heat barreled through me like something I'd never imagined. So this was what he was trying to give me. This was why he had a dungeon in the basement. For these kinds of hot, kinky pleasures.

My nipples were straining, wanting to be sucked.

As much as I'd always thought I didn't want any of this pleasure-pain, I had always liked my nipples sucked hard.

Slap! The cropping came down on my breasts once more. *Slap! Slap!*

The tingling flew through my body again, landing in my pussy, and then moved again, all the way down to my toes and back up to my core.

"How does that feel, sweetheart?"

I bit my lip. How did it feel? I wasn't sure how to answer, because these were feelings I'd never felt before. My orgasm was magnified, and the heat in my body was electrifying.

"Wonderful." Yet that word wasn't enough to describe anything like what I was feeling. Yes, it was wonderful, but it was so much more than that.

He pushed my thighs forward and stroked my folds with his tongue.

"I have a surprise for you, sweetheart."

He began licking my puckered asshole, and then something cold dribbled over me.

"Just a little bit of lube, baby."

And then, the stretching. The slight pain until the rim of muscle relaxed.

"Easy," he said softly. "It's just an anal plug."

Something bulbous forced its way into my anus, but then

the pain subsided as the muscles wrapped around it.

"You keep this in for a little while, okay?"

Not that I had a choice, my hands being bound.

The feeling was different from when he breached it with his finger. That feeling had been wonderful, but I had been ready for it. This was...different. I had just come down from an orgasm, and he hadn't gotten my ass ready.

But the feeling was, oddly, not bad. Only unusual. I was being stretched for a reason I didn't know.

Would it be okay to ask? "Jonah?" I said tentatively.

"Yes?"

"What is that thing for?"

He chuckled softly. "We're going to do a little bit of training."

"What do you mean?"

"I'm going to train your ass, baby. Train it to take my cock."

The thought both terrified me and turned me on. Jonah had a large cock. Larger than any man I'd ever been with, larger than anything I'd ever imagined. Would I ever accommodate it...there?

Warmth enveloped me. The thought was...arousing.

"You keep this in for a little while. I'm going to give you another orgasm while it's in your ass. And I want you to tell me what it feels like."

I shuddered. Already I was ripe for a new orgasm. This entire scene had taken me by surprise. I should've known there was more to this than met the eye. There was a reason Jonah enjoyed this. I was seeing those reasons now.

"All right, Jonah."

"How do you want your orgasm, baby?"

"My nipples. I need you to suck them."

"You got it." His soft lips clamped around one, and he squeezed the other between his thumb and forefinger.

I nearly spiraled out of control right there. My nipples had been neglected during this bout of play, and they were ready for some attention.

He sucked them hard, twisted them, and they grew harder. My pussy grew wet. I inhaled the musk in the air. It hung around us like an early morning fog.

As he continued to suck and play with my nipples, he trailed his fingers over my abdomen, threading them through my blond curls and finding my clit. He inserted two fingers into my wet heat, moistening them, and then he began rubbing my clit.

God, so good.

This wouldn't take long.

"Yes, Jonah. Please suck my nipples. Feels so good."

And as he was pleasuring me, his fingers hit just the right spot, and I soared once more.

"Yes, yes, yes! Oh, Jonah, I'm coming for you."

"That's right, baby," he said against the soft flesh of my breasts. "You come for me. No one but me."

And as I spiraled outward, to the sun, moon, and stars, I knew, without a doubt, that my surrender had begun.

CHAPTER TWENTY

Jonah

Melanie and I sat on the deck that evening, the fire pit burning, sipping martinis.

We didn't talk about what had happened in my dungeon, other than my asking her afterward how the plug had felt. She had bitten her lip and smiled shyly, saying only "good." I had only begun to show her the pleasures I could give her down there. We'd be revisiting that room soon. But now, I had to tell her what happened today, that Colin Morse's father had tried to frame me for his kidnapping and rape.

"I'm so sorry," she said after I'd spilled the story. "Talon and I were wondering why you took off so quickly."

"I'm the one who's sorry," I said. "I shouldn't have left you that way. But when the officer said I had to take a blood test, I didn't know what to do."

"Unreal that Ted Morse would try to frame you like that, and after what you did for his son."

"He doesn't really see it that way. He blames all of this on our family. After all, Colin wouldn't have been in that situation if Talon hadn't punched his daylights out in the first place."

"I'm not condoning what Talon did, but you and your brothers are not responsible for these sick men."

"If only I had gone with Talon that day..."

"We've had this discussion." Melanie touched my hand. "Stop playing the 'what if' game. We don't know, and we never *will* know, what might have happened if you'd gone with him. You might've both been taken. Perhaps neither of you would've been taken. Perhaps you would've gone a different way. We just don't know."

My head told me that she was right. My heart still wasn't sure. At any rate, I had to let it go.

"So has Colin dropped his accusations against you?" she asked.

"Like I said, I don't think the accusation even came from Colin. He was in no condition to form a story like that. I think his father made the whole thing up. Since I haven't heard from him again, I assume the case is closed."

"That's good. I suppose at some point I need to contact my malpractice insurance company and deal with the lawsuit the Cateses filed against me. The answer is due in a few weeks, and I certainly don't want to default."

"Baby, I will get you the best lawyer out there."

"You don't have to. I have insurance. They will pay."

"I can find you a better lawyer."

"It probably won't come to that. I doubt the case will go far. But let me use the insurance I've been paying for the past fifteen years. I might as well get something for my money."

I couldn't help a smile. She had been through so much, but she was moving forward. The least I could do was move forward as well.

Time to really let go of the guilt now. To stop saying it and really do it.

I hoped I could.

"Another thing happened. I got another text from my

stalker."

She dropped her mouth open. "We've got to find out who's doing this. If it's not Brooke, someone is after you, and I don't like it."

"I think it's probably harmless," I said, and I truly believed that. But it was still starting to creep me out.

"I think you should have Mills and Johnson look into it." Melanie sighed. "I know you don't want to take the time away from Talon's and my cases, but look how much we've found out already. We know who the other two abductors are."

"But we don't know *where* they are."

"Honestly, how much time is looking into a phone number going to take away from finding Tom Simpson and Theodore Mathias?"

She had a point, and I was sick and tired of the stupid texts.

"All right. I'll call them and have them look into it."

"Good."

"As long as you promise to call your insurance company and get this lawsuit taken care of."

She let out a breath. "All right."

"Have you heard anything from the medical board?"

She shook her head. "Not yet. I'll have to talk to Miles Bennett at the hospital, see what they've found out. I'm hoping my leave of absence will end soon. I need to get back to work. I need to focus on something other than all this stuff."

"I hear that one." I took a sip of my martini. "It has pretty much taken over our lives."

"So what's the next step?" she asked.

"For me? I'm going to go to the city again and see Larry Wade."

"I figured as much. Do you think Talon will go with you

this time?"

"I don't know. That's a lot to ask of him, Melanie."

"I agree. Although it may benefit him to look Larry in the eye at some point."

"I'm not sure it will tomorrow."

She nodded. "It's still too soon. Do you want me to go with you?"

Now that was an idea. "I honestly hadn't given that a thought, Melanie, but it makes perfect sense. If there are two of us, we'll have to use the visitation room, and there will be no barrier between us. Plus, your input as a psychotherapist will be invaluable. I never would've asked you to do this, but would you like to go?"

"I will go. Do I want to go? Not really. I mean, to come face-to-face with him isn't high on my list. But I've been thinking for a while now that maybe I should go. Not just to support you, but to try to help Talon in any way I can. I still consider myself his therapist."

"We all do." I took her hand and rubbed my thumb into her palm.

She sipped her martini with her other hand. "When do you want to go tomorrow? I'm sure you have things to do around the ranch."

I nodded. "I do. Let's say we leave here around two in the afternoon. That will get us to the city by three. We can visit with Larry and then maybe catch dinner before we drive home."

She smiled. "That sounds good to me."

★ ★ ★

Melanie was visibly tense as we sat at the table in the visitor's room at the prison, waiting for the guard to escort Larry to us.

"I don't mean to be so jittery," she said.

"I understand completely. I was jittery the first time I met him as well. I'm still jittery to a certain extent. This man—my uncle, for God's sake—did terrible things to my brother. That thought never leaves me as I talk to him. Yet I have to keep my cool, keep my head, because I'm trying to trip him up. I'm trying to get him to give me information."

"Do you think he'll be a little more forthcoming today?"

"I'm banking on it. I don't know for sure, but now that we know who the two other culprits are, there's no reason for him to keep anything from me. They already know that we know."

"True," she said. "But don't underestimate him. He may have his own reasons for keeping silent that have nothing to do with his fear of Simpson and Mathias."

I widened my eyes. That thought hadn't occurred to me. "What other reason could he have?"

"We may never know. The man is a psychopath. He doesn't understand empathy or remorse. What is inherently wrong to a sane individual doesn't seem wrong to a psychopath, and even though he knows he's hurting someone, he feels no remorse or sorrow for his offenses."

"So are you saying you think he might've been pulling my chain all along?"

"I'm saying it's a possibility."

I looked up. A guard was escorting Larry to our table.

"Steel," Larry said, plunking into a chair. He had two black eyes that were sunken, and lacerations and bruising covered his arms. "What the hell do you want now?" He looked to Melanie. "And who the hell is this?"

"This is Dr. Melanie Carmichael. She's a psychotherapist."

"Oh, you want her to shrink my head? Believe me, I've been through more psych evaluations since I've been in here than I know what to do with."

"She's not here for that. She's here because she's my friend. She's here to support me."

"Hello, Mr. Wade," she said.

"Aren't you courteous? Please call me Larry."

She didn't bat an eye. "All right, if you prefer, Larry. You may call me Dr. Carmichael."

I had to bite my lip to keep from smiling. Melanie never ceased to amaze me. Professional even in the most dire circumstances.

"You're probably wondering why we're here, Uncle," I said.

"Nah. I know why you're here. You want information. Information I've already told you I can't give you."

Melanie's gaze was focused on Larry. She was reading him, or trying to. I couldn't wait to hear what she had to say when we were done with this visit.

"I'm definitely here for information. I've identified Talon's other two abductors."

Larry narrowed his eyes, but his expression was not one of surprise. "You have?"

"You already knew I was on the right track. You already knew whom I suspected. And you all but told me I was right the last time I was here."

Larry shook his head. "I did no such thing."

"Tell me, Uncle. How was your night that night? The night after I last visited?"

Larry looked down into his lap, presumably staring at his handcuffed hands. His neck and cheeks turned ruddy.

Apparently, my generous tip to the guards last time had paid off.

"Don't think things can't get worse. We still have a lot to go over, as you already know."

He looked up at me, his eyes gray and sunken. "What the hell is it that you want?"

"I need to find Simpson and Theodore Mathias."

CHAPTER TWENTY-ONE

Melanie

Jonah's voice never cracked, his intonation never wavered. But the muscles in his forearms were tense as he looked his uncle straight in the eye.

"I don't know anything about those two," Larry said.

"Stop the innocent act," Jonah said. "We've already identified them as the other two abductors. Right now, they're on the run. I need your help to locate them."

Larry shook his head. "They never shared a lot of their information with me."

I regarded Larry's countenance. He was looking Jonah straight in the eye. He wasn't fidgeting. His body language indicated he was telling the truth, but there was no way for me to let Jonah know that.

"Sure, Uncle Larry. And I have a couple acres of swampland in Florida I'd like to sell you."

"Think what you want. I don't know where they are. I've never known where they hid. They weren't there for me when I needed them, and the cops found me in New Mexico about ready to cross the border. You think I would've been caught if I'd had their help? The two of them are pros. They never get caught."

"They're going to get caught this time. We're going to see

justice for Talon and Luke Walker, and for Gina Cates."

"You know about that?"

"Yes, thanks to a source I'm not going to reveal to you."

Jonah was clearly talking about Detective Ruby Lee. I was glad he didn't say her name. I didn't want her in any more danger. She was at risk already, being the daughter of one of them.

Jonah's friend Bryce and his baby son, Henry, crossed my mind. They were the son and grandson, respectively, of the other. Were they in danger too? Had that occurred to Jonah? I trembled, clenching my fists together to cover it up.

Larry looked at me, scrutinizing. "Shit. You're her therapist, aren't you?"

"You only talk to her if I tell you to." Jonah cleared his throat. "So you see, Uncle, we found out without your help. Finding them and bringing them to justice would be a lot easier if you cooperated." Jonah eyed the guard standing about five feet away from Larry. "And I think you know what I can make happen if you don't cooperate."

This side of Jonah didn't surprise me. Inside, I knew he was wound tight as a drum, but he didn't let anything faze him. I had seen him take on Gina's father, threatening him without batting an eye. Jonah believed in what was right, and he would do anything to protect and avenge those he loved, even break the law himself.

It was a side of him I hadn't come fully to grips with yet.

"Look," Larry said. "Those two are still at large, and they probably think I ratted them out. Believe me, my time behind bars is limited. Meaning, they're not going to let me live. And the more I tell you, the shorter my time on this earth will be."

"Not necessarily. My offer to pay for the best lawyer in

Colorado still stands. If you help me find these two."

Larry rolled his eyes. "I don't know where they hole up. They never told me. You think I'm lying to you? What would I have to gain at this point?"

Jonah let out a laugh. "Hell, yes, I think you're lying to me. You've been lying to me this whole time. I looked you straight in the eye and asked you if Tom Simpson was one of Talon's abductors. You told me no."

"I never said no. At least not that I recall. I said I wasn't rolling over on them, whoever they were."

"You knew I was on the right path, yet you said nothing. I've found them now. I know who they both are, although one of them does go by a dozen different names."

"Look, all I can tell you is this. Don't underestimate those two. They're way beyond psychopaths, especially Mathias. That man is dangerous."

"Uncle, are you concerned about me?"

"Stop with your bullshit. I'm trying to be straight with you here. I don't fucking know where they are. I have never known where they are, but I know *what* they are. They're both criminally insane."

Jonah scoffed. "That's an interesting assessment, coming from someone who's criminally insane."

"Look, I'm far from perfect. Okay? I have certain urges that most people don't have. I'm not proud of it, and I'm serving my time, but I'm telling you again. Don't underestimate the two of them. They make me look like a fucking angel."

Again, as far as I could tell, he wasn't lying. Of course, pathological liars were often very good at it and left no evidence that they were lying. But what if Larry was telling the truth? What if he was, as he'd put it, an angel compared to the other two? He probably wasn't as good at lying as they were.

I decided to chime in. "Larry, there has to be something you can tell us about those two." I kept my voice as soft and feminine as I could. Perhaps Larry would respond to that. Perhaps not. But it was worth a try.

"Sorry, *Dr.* Carmichael."

Jonah stood. "This is a fucking waste of our time."

I touched his forearm. God, he was so tense. "Let's not leave yet," I said. "Let me ask a few questions."

Jonah sat back down. "Melanie, I think you're walking toward a dead end, but go for it if you want to."

I bit my lip and looked straight at Larry Wade. "What high school did you go to?"

"That's probably a matter of public record," he said.

"Maybe it is, but I don't have access to those records right now. Why don't *you* tell me where you went?"

"Tejon Prep School in Grand Junction."

"Good. Tom Simpson told us that you and he went to the same high school. Or rather, he told Jonah."

Larry stiffened.

"Did anyone else we know go to that high school? Theodore Mathias, perhaps?"

Larry stiffened further, but he did not answer.

"All right, let's attack this from another angle," I said. "You want to live through tonight?"

Jonah looked at me, his eyes unreadable. Perhaps he hadn't thought that I could play hardball.

"Lady," Larry said, "I've had a contract out on my life since I got here. Do I want to live through tonight? Sure. But you can't give me any guarantee that I will."

"Don't ever refer to her as 'lady' again. She's Dr.

Carmichael," Jonah said.

I squeezed his thigh, hopefully showing him that it was okay, as long as Larry was talking.

"What can you tell us about Wendy Madigan?" I asked.

Jonah darted his gaze at me again. Was he confused? I wasn't sure, but I had a reason for asking this question.

"She's a newswoman. Retired."

"We already know that. I'm looking for something deeper. I want to know how she was involved in the attack on Talon."

"You'll have to ask her."

"As you know, Jonah and Talon *have* asked her about it. Her story doesn't jibe with yours. You say Talon was never meant to be taken. She says Talon was taken on purpose, and the plan might have been to take all three of the boys."

"Doesn't surprise me."

"What doesn't surprise you? That all the boys were meant to be taken?"

"No. It doesn't surprise me that she's lying to you."

Jonah was rigid next to me. He'd had a bad feeling after his meeting with Wendy, thought there was more to her than met the eye. Clearly he was correct.

"Why doesn't that surprise you?"

"Because she was obsessed. Obsessed with Bradford Steel."

"You mean my father and she were not lovers?" Jonah said.

"They were a long time ago. She was a great-looking woman in her younger days. And Brad was no saint."

"Do you know for sure whether they were lovers?" Jonah asked.

"I can't say for sure. I mean, I never saw them in bed

together, but it was pretty much known when they were younger. They went out during high school." He shook his head. "She may play the part of the competent newswoman, but don't be fooled. She has a dark side. And that dark side was obsessed with your father."

"You claim you didn't get the five million dollars that mysteriously disappeared from one of my father's accounts twenty-five years ago," Jonah said.

"Correct. I didn't get any."

"Then where did it go?"

"How the hell should I know? It would've been a nice gesture for them to give me some money. They chased me out of town after I helped your brother escape."

"Gee, I don't know why my parents would chase you out of town," Jonah said. "After you fucking abused their son."

"Let me get straight to the point here," Larry said. "I *did* help him escape. He was never supposed to be taken. None of us wanted to incur the wrath of the Steel family. That would just be stupid. You can think what you want about all three of us, but we were never stupid."

"Seems you were stupid to get involved with the other two," Jonah said through clenched teeth. "Seems you have their backs, but they never had yours."

I squeezed Jonah's thigh again, hoping he would calm down a bit. "What else can you tell me about your high school experience?" I asked. "Were you and Tom good friends?"

"We were both members of the future lawyers club. That's how we met."

"And was anyone else a member of the club?"

"Lady— Excuse me. *Dr.* Carmichael, I'm not saying another word about Simpson or the other one. But you can find the information you seek very easily."

CHAPTER TWENTY-TWO

Jonah

Melanie squeezed my thigh again. "Jonah, I think we can go now."

"Fine." I signaled the guard. "We're done here."

The guard led Larry away, and I grabbed Melanie's hand. "I need to talk to the guard on duty."

"Why?"

"I'm giving him a few hundreds to have Larry roughed up tonight."

She touched my upper arm. "Don't do that."

"Why the hell not?"

"Because he just gave us a clue."

"Are you kidding me? What clue did you get out of that?"

"His high school. The future lawyers club."

"How in the world is that going to help us?"

"The last thing he said was that we could find the information we needed easily. Since the only information he gave us was where he went to high school and the club he and Tom Simpson were in, that means we start there."

"We go to his high school?"

"That's right. We go to his high school right now, and we ask to see their old yearbooks."

"How would that help?"

"I've dealt with my share of unstable and psychopathic people. They each follow a certain type of logic, which in their minds makes sense, even though it doesn't make sense to the rest of us. Did you ever see *Silence of the Lambs*?"

"Yes."

"Remember when Clarice first goes to see Hannibal Lecter? He tells her to 'look inside yourself.' He wasn't referring to Clarice finding herself. He was referring to a Your Self storage company. What Larry said isn't that different. He told us we would find what we need at his high school and the future lawyers club."

He smiled. "You're fucking brilliant."

She laughed. "I don't know that I'm brilliant. I could be completely wrong. It's possible he's sending us on a wild goose chase. But the way he looked at me when he said we already knew where to find the information we sought... Honestly, I think it's worth checking out."

"I trust your judgment, Melanie. That's why I brought you along. Let's visit the good people at Tejon Prep School. Hell, we're already here in the city."

★ ★ ★

A half an hour later, we arrived at the school. Classes were over for the day, and after-school activities were in full swing. Melanie and I walked into the school to find the office.

A redheaded receptionist sat behind a desk.

"Excuse me," I said.

"May I help you?" she asked.

"Yes. I'm Jonah Steel." I handed her my business card. "Of Steel Acres ranch. We'd like to look at some of your old yearbooks."

"Nice to meet you, Mr. Steel." She smiled broadly. "Which yearbook are you looking for?"

I looked at Melanie.

"We're not sure," she said. "Probably at least thirty years ago. We'll have to look to find the ones we need."

"We keep copies of all of our yearbooks in the school library and the school archives. Are you two alumni?"

"No," Jonah said. "But my uncle is. We're trying to find some information for him."

"We don't normally give access to our library and archives to anyone other than current students. I can have you fill out a form to request access, but that probably won't be necessary." She smiled.

She was flirting with me. Melanie tensed a little beside me. I figured she would understand if I used this to my advantage.

"Oh? Would you be willing to bend the rules a little for us"—I glanced at the name on her desk—"Jordan?" I gave her my best smile.

"I'm afraid I can't do that." She batted her eyes coyly. "But all of our yearbooks are on our website. All your uncle needs to do is open an account."

I sighed. "My uncle is...incapacitated at this time. Are you sure you can't grant us access to the library?"

"I wish I could. It's just not possible right now." She nodded toward an office door marked "Principal."

Melanie grabbed my hand. "That's quite all right. You've been very helpful. Let's go." She pulled me out of there.

When we got outside, I said, "Are you crazy? I could've gotten access for us."

"Why bother? We can open an account in Larry's name

and get the information ourselves from the website."

"It's not that easy, Melanie. We'll probably need his year of graduation to get in. Or his Social Security number."

"You're so funny, Jonah. Jade can get all of that information for us. From the lawyers registration file in Colorado."

"Still... I could've gotten in."

"Pardon me if I don't want to see you flirting with some bubble-headed receptionist just to get something you want. This is an easier way. We can research it at home, and no one will be looking over our shoulders."

I squeezed her hand. "All right. You know, you're cute when you're jealous."

She smiled at me. "Admit it. Part of you liked that you had her in your clutches. You wanted to see how far you could get her to go with the principal in the next office."

"All right, I can't fault your perception. But you're right. Doing it in the privacy of our own home will be much easier."

"And if it doesn't work?" Melanie said. "I will personally accompany you back here tomorrow, and the two of us will reduce that receptionist to jelly, okay?"

I laughed.

★ ★ ★

Though we had originally been planning to eat dinner in the city, both Melanie and I were eager to get home and explore this new avenue. On the way home, Melanie called Jade at her office and got the information we needed—Larry's date of birth and year of graduation from Tejon Prep School. When we got home, I let Lucy out while Melanie filled her food and water. Then I threw two of my home-chef-prepared frozen meals in the microwave, opened a bottle of wine, and fired up my laptop.

Melanie sat next to me, positioned so she could see the screen as well, as I typed in the correct website. I typed in Larry Wade, his birthday, and graduation year.

And jolted when it came up "nothing found."

"Damn."

"Maybe his real name is Lawrence," Melanie said.

"Good point." I tried again.

No dice.

"Shit," I said. "We're going to have to see the hard copies of the yearbooks."

"Wow, I feel bad," Melanie said. "This was my idea."

"Not your fault, sweetheart. You were right. This would have been easier. This isn't the first time these guys have hacked in and changed databases. It wouldn't surprise me if Larry Wade was erased from this one."

"If they were able to accomplish that, they were probably able to get into that school's library and destroy the pertinent yearbooks."

"Yes, probably." Would we ever be able to get this information? Seemed like they were always one step ahead of us.

My phone buzzed. Damn, not another text from my stalker.

But no, it was a phone call, from a Grand Junction number I didn't recognize.

CHAPTER TWENTY-THREE

Melanie

Jonah put the phone to his ear. "Jonah Steel."

He was silent for what seemed like forever but was only several seconds.

"I see. And how can you do that?"

I had no idea what he was talking about or to whom he was speaking. Probably work related.

"Won't that get you into trouble?"

More silence.

"I'm near Snow Creek. How soon can you get here?"

Now I was curious.

He rattled off the editions of the yearbooks we needed from Tejon Prep School, and my curiosity piqued again.

"Thank you. You're a lifesaver. I'll make sure you're well compensated." He clicked off his phone.

"What was all that about?" I asked.

"You won't believe this. That was my admirer, Jordan Hayes, the receptionist at Tejon. She's going to sneak into the school archives and get the books we need. We'll meet her at Murphy's in an hour."

"What?" I let the words sink into my head. "You must have made more of an impression on her than you realized."

He smiled. "I guess it's not just you women who can use

your looks to get what you want."

I gave him a loving smack. "I don't do that."

"No, I'm betting you don't." He smiled. "You're too classy for that."

"How did she get your number?"

"I handed her a business card while we were there. Maybe you didn't see me."

Then I remembered. He had handed her the card when he introduced himself. He hadn't introduced me. Perhaps he'd had the idea in his head the whole time to flirt his way into what he wanted. That was neither here nor there. If we could get the information that had been deleted from the website and possibly from the library, this was a good thing.

"I suppose you're going to want to go alone to meet her at the bar. If I tag along, you won't be able to work her as well."

"No, Melanie. I want you to go. You have a way of reading people that I don't. She'll just have to get used to the fact that she's not getting anywhere near this body."

I smiled. "You did say you would compensate her handsomely."

"Well, my body won't be her compensation. Money will have to do."

"How can she sneak into the archives?"

"The archives are off-site, at a storage place."

"That doesn't mean that Simpson and Mathias haven't figured it out and destroyed everything that was in the archives."

"Yes, I thought of that. I assume she'll call me back if she can't find what we need. But for now, let's be hopeful. If we don't get a call within a half hour, we head to Murphy's in town."

★ ★ ★

Jordan hadn't called, and now I sat next to Jonah in a booth at Murphy's, waiting for the spunky receptionist to walk through the door. It was nearing eight o'clock, and she had to drive all the way from Grand Junction. I had no doubt that she would show, though. The way she had looked at Jonah when we had been at the school earlier confirmed my beliefs.

A-ha. The bell on the door chimed, and in she strolled, her red head bobbing. She couldn't be more than twenty-five, but she wouldn't be the first younger woman to be attracted to Jonah Steel. How could a woman not be attracted to his dark handsomeness?

Jonah stood and motioned her over. She smiled and trotted toward us, but then her face fell when she noticed me sitting on the inside of the booth.

"Have a seat." Jonah gestured to the bench across from us. "Can I get you something to drink?"

"Sure. What are you drinking?"

"We're just having a glass of wine."

"Perfect. I'll have the same."

"Hello?" I nudged Jonah.

"I'm so sorry. This is Dr. Melanie Carmichael."

I held my hand across the table. "Maybe you remember me from this afternoon? When we came to the school?"

"Of course. So nice to meet you." She arranged a large tote bag on the seat next to her.

"Since I didn't get a call from you and you're here now, I assume you have some good news for us," Jonah said.

"I sure do." She licked her lips. "I hope you know I could get fired for this."

"I know that, and I really appreciate this," Jonah said. "We'll just get the information we need, make copies, and then we'll get these back to you as soon as we can. I will personally bring them back to your school."

"Oh, no. Don't bring them to school. You'll have to bring them to my home, and then I can sneak them back to the archives."

Jonah smiled. "Sure."

I smacked his thigh under the table.

Jordan pulled out four yearbooks from the tote bag and set them on the table. "Here you go."

Jonah grabbed one and opened it.

I nudged him again. "Shouldn't we take these home? And look at them privately?"

"We will. But Jordan hasn't had a drink yet." He motioned to a waitress and ordered a glass of wine for her.

I couldn't argue. The woman certainly did deserve a drink for her efforts. After all, she could lose her job if anyone found out she had sneaked into the archives.

"Jordan," I said, "why do you keep your archives off-site?"

She pursed her lips. "No reason."

Yeah, she was lying. "Really? Seems like there would be a reason. I'm sure you have plenty of storage space at school."

"Oh, that's where you're wrong. We are so overcrowded. If the alumni don't come through with more gifts, we may have to close down."

Good answer. But I still didn't believe that was the only reason.

I would leave it for now. If I could get Jonah alone, I could tell him my suspicions, and I could get him to turn on the sweetness and soften her up. Of course, I wasn't in any mood for the two of them to be alone.

I opened the yearbook in front of me, the one from Larry Wade's junior year. I leafed through the pages. Juniors... Juniors... There they were. I flipped to the end and looked under W. There he was, Lawrence Wade. But for the fact that he was balding and graying, he looked about the same. Pretty forgettable. I backtracked to S, looking for Simpson. He wasn't there. Well, that didn't mean anything. Tom Simpson could have been in a different class. I turned to the seniors. Sure enough, there he was, Thomas Simpson. Blond, light-eyed, and very good-looking.

"Bingo," I said. I shoved the yearbook in front of Jonah.

He gawked at it. "Oh my God. That's exactly what Bryce looked like in high school, except with a different hairstyle."

Jonah hadn't opened the book in front of him. He had been making small talk with Jordan. The waitress brought her wine, and she took a sip.

I continued looking through the book. Lo and behold, there was Theodore Mathias, also a senior in this book. The photo was in black and white, but he appeared dark-haired and dark-eyed with an olive complexion. So Simpson and Mathias were both a year older than Larry, or at least a year ahead of him in school. Next thing on my list was to see if there was any mention of a future lawyers club anywhere in the yearbook. As I began to flip to the index, something caught my eye back in the Juniors section.

"Oh my God," I whispered.

CHAPTER TWENTY-FOUR

Jonah

Something in Melanie's whisper gave me pause. I turned to her, and she had become pale. "Sweetheart, what is it?"

She shoved the yearbook in front of me, pointing. "Check out who else was in Larry Wade's class."

The pictures were in black and white, so I couldn't tell if the hair and eyes were right, but the name I recognized.

Rodney Cates.

My heart thumped. This was all getting just a little too eerie.

My phone buzzed on the table in front of me, and I glanced down. Another text.

Our time is coming, my love. Soon we will be together for eternity.

Shit.

"What is it?" Melanie asked.

"Nothing. Work related." I hated lying to Melanie, but I would tell her later. I didn't want to say anything in front of Jordan. The less she knew about this whole situation, the better. We were putting her in danger just by having her get these books.

"I hope I'm not prying," Jordan said, "but what do you need these books for? You said you needed to find some information for your uncle."

"Yes," I said. "My uncle is...dying from cancer."

She clasped her hand to her mouth. "Oh! I'm so sorry."

"It's okay. He's lived a good life." Lying really didn't come easy for me. "He was hoping to get in touch with a few of his classmates."

"How would the yearbook help that? It would be easier to find them online. They're probably all on Facebook."

Of course. This was why lying didn't come easy to me. I sucked at it.

"Oh, it's not information so much he was looking for," Melanie said, stroking my arm. "It's photos. You see, all of his photos were destroyed in a fire a few years ago."

And again, the hand on the mouth. "Goodness, what terrible luck."

Melanie nodded. "I know. He's been through so much. Now, as he is nearing the end of his life, he not only wants to talk to these people that he hasn't seen in decades, but he also wants to remember them with these photos."

"I completely understand. I'm so glad that I could be of help to you." Jordan took a sip of her wine.

I tried not to stare at Melanie in awe. She had just lied her way out of this situation. I had never known her to be anything except completely honest, and I knew she would be when it mattered. But here, the way she was able to save the situation impressed me. To her mind, she was in a session right now, trying to extract information. Brilliant.

I took a sip of my wine. Now we knew that three abductors had been at the same high school, two of them in the same class, one a class below. Rodney Cates was there too... What else did they have in common?

"We truly do want to compensate you for your time," Melanie was saying.

"Goodness, the drink is more than enough. I'm glad I could do something to make your uncle's last days better."

I nearly choked on my wine. I took my wallet out of my pocket and pulled out a hundred-dollar bill. "Please, take this."

"I can't take so much."

I shoved the bill across the table. "I insist. You've helped us more than you'll ever know."

"Are the two of you...involved?" she asked.

Before I could open my mouth to speak, Melanie said, "We're just good friends."

I couldn't read the look on her face. She had body language down to a T. Anyone looking at her would think she was telling the truth. It unnerved me a bit.

The alpha in me urged me to take her by the hand, pull her toward me, and kiss the life out of her. But Melanie never did anything without a reason. If she thought it would be better for Jordan not to think we were involved, I would go with that.

Did she want me to ask Jordan out or something? Beyond the yearbook, there wasn't really any information Jordan had that I needed. I'd talk to Melanie about it later.

"I have to use the ladies room," Melanie said. "If you'll excuse me for a few minutes?"

"Of course." I stood and let her out of the booth. I couldn't help watching her as she walked toward the restroom. She moved with such beauty and confidence.

She was giving me permission to do something. I just wasn't sure what it was. What more help could Jordan be to us?

Unless Melanie thought knowing why the archives were

in a storage facility was important.

“Let me ask,” I said. “How long has your school kept the archives off-site?”

“I’m not sure. I’ve only been at this particular school for two years, and archives have been off-site the whole time. But I’ve heard rumors.”

“What kind of rumors?”

“Evidently, the school was broken into about five years ago. Some yearbooks were stolen from the library. You know what’s funny? They’re the exact same yearbooks that you requested from me.”

This woman clearly wasn’t the brightest. I lifted my eyebrow. “Really? That’s strange.”

“It is strange, isn’t it? Once I realized that, I called you with the offer to go to the archives. I figured if they weren’t in the library, they probably hadn’t made it online either.”

Okay. Not so dumb after all.

“Anyway, I wanted to help. I mean, you and your friend hardly look like the type who would try to put something over on me. You’re just so...” Rosiness crept into her cheeks.

This was my cue to ask her out. But that wasn’t going to happen. “I’m just a nephew who loves his uncle and will do anything for him.” I stopped, waiting for lightning to strike. I really did hate lying, and that was a big one.

“That’s so very nice of you,” she said.

“Yeah, well, I’m a nice guy. Can I get you another drink?”

“No, thank you. I have to be driving home.”

“I understand.” I stared down at the yearbook Melanie had been looking at. I flipped through a few pages, landing on clubs. French club, German club, Fellowship of Christian Athletes, National Honor Society... Where were the future lawyers?

And then they appeared in front of my eyes. Not the future lawyers, but the future lawmakers. There was Larry, there was Tom, there was Theodore Mathias, and—

My heart nearly stopped. The club had three additional members.

“Are you okay?” Jordan asked.

“Fine.” My voice was tight. Thank God, Melanie was returning from the restroom.

She touched my arm. “Jonah, do you mind if we leave? I'm not feeling very well.”

I went into protective mode. “Of course.” I looked to Jordan. “Do you mind? We'll need to cut this short.”

“Not at all.” She stood. “Thank you so much for the drink.”

I stood and gave her a hug. “Thank you. You've made my uncle very happy.”

“Just call me when you're done with the yearbooks, and I'll arrange to meet you somewhere to get them.”

“Will do.”

She turned and walked out the door.

“What's wrong, baby?” I asked Melanie.

Melanie sat down next to me. “Nothing. I decided it was time to get rid of her. Did you get any information out of her?” Then she looked at me, touching my cheek. “Jonah, what's wrong?”

I pointed to the future lawmakers club.

“This.”

CHAPTER TWENTY-FIVE

Melanie

The photo showed six students, five male and one female. I quickly perused the faces. Larry, Tom, and then Theodore Mathias.

One of the two other men was none other than Rodney Cates.

The woman?

My heart stopped.

Wendy Madigan.

I looked to Jonah. And then back down at the book. The last male was taller than the other four and virtually identical to the man sitting beside me.

Bradford Steel.

"Oh my God."

"Melanie, I have no idea what to make of this. My father *knew* these men. Was in some lawmaking club with them. What the hell does all this mean?"

I stroked his arm. "I wish I knew. But I can tell you one thing. We *will* find out."

"We need to keep these yearbooks. We can't give them back to Jordan."

"We don't want to get her in trouble, Jonah."

"No, I don't want to do that," he said. "But we need these

original documents. And I need to talk to Wendy Madigan. Goddamnit, someone is going to tell me the truth if I have to beat it out of them."

"Jonah, you're not going to hit a woman."

He raked his fingers through his hair. "Of course not, baby. You know I would never do that."

"You know," I said, "this could mean nothing. So the six of them knew each other in school. That was eons ago. It doesn't mean a thing."

He looked at me, straight in my eyes, his own burning. "You don't believe that."

I sighed. "No, I don't. But we have no reason to believe that your father was involved in anything nefarious. He certainly wouldn't have participated in the kidnapping and rape of his own son."

Jonah shook his head, his pallor lightening. "At this point, Melanie, I just don't know. I keep coming back to what Larry said to Bryce and me. 'The truth is overrated. Once you open the door to that dark room, getting out is damn near impossible.' I'm now seeing the ironic truth of those words."

I took his hand, rubbing my thumb into his palm. "I can't promise you what we'll find, but I promise you this. We will get to the bottom of this. You and I together. And Talon, Jade, Ryan, and Marj. We will find the truth."

★ ★ ★

Jonah didn't speak much on the drive home, and when we entered the house, he didn't even stop to pet Lucy when she trotted up to meet us. He grabbed me, pushed me up against the wall, and crushed his mouth to mine.

The kiss was angry, and while I knew Jonah wasn't angry with me, I understood why his emotions were coiled up the way they were. He had just found out that his father actually knew all of Talon's kidnappers, indeed had been in a club with them in high school. Perhaps his emotion wasn't anger so much as it was helplessness, probably a combination of the two. Whatever it was, I would be here for him. I would see to whatever needs he had.

His tongue tangled with mine, and he groaned against me. When he pulled back a little, he nipped at my lips, sucking the lower one into his mouth and biting it. Then he crushed our lips together again in a demanding, punishing kiss. I knew he wasn't punishing me. This was his way of punishing the world around him, the world that had delivered to him such a feeling of helplessness.

When he finally broke the kiss and sucked in a deep breath, he grabbed me, holding my face in one hand. "I need to take you downstairs, Melanie. I need that more than I can even put into words right now."

"Jonah..."

"No, Melanie. I could go out and swim a hundred laps in my pool, or I could go on a run, or we could go to my bedroom and fuck each other's brains out. But none of those will give me peace, not right now. I need to take you downstairs. And I don't know what I'll do if you say no."

I was not about to deny him. Things tonight might go farther than I was ready for, but I had pledged my love to this man. I had pledged my life to him, and right now he was in pain, big-time emotional pain, and I would do what I could to ease it for him.

I looked at him straight into his dark brooding eyes. "I'm

not going to say no."

He touched his forehead to mine. "Thank God." Then he swooped me up in his arms, walked me through the foyer and to the door that led to his basement. He thumped down the stairs quickly, turning, walking through the rec room and then opening the door to his dungeon.

"I can't be gentle with you," he said. "Not tonight. But I won't hurt you. I'd never hurt you."

Fear sliced into me, but I was determined to give him what he needed. "I know you won't. Take from me what you need, Jonah. I'm here for you."

He set me down and took a seat on the bed. "Undress." His voice was firm, commanding.

I wasn't sure whether he wanted me to undress slowly and give him a striptease or just get naked as quickly as I could. So I decided to compromise and try to be sexy while getting undressed quickly.

I unbuttoned my blouse and slid it over my shoulders. I bent forward and unclasped my bra, so he could see my breasts pointing downward as I removed it. Then I stood straight and put one foot on the bed, unzipping my ankle boot. I removed it and then my sock, and then repeated the motions with my other leg. I stood straight again and unzipped my jeans, sliding them over my hips and thighs and stepping out of them.

He groaned. "Still that damned beige cotton."

I bit my lip. My cotton underwear was angering him tonight?

"Come here," he growled.

I walked toward him slowly, and he grabbed my hips and unceremoniously ripped the panties off me.

"From now on," he said, "you do not enter this room

wearing beige cotton. Is that understood?"

I bit my lip again and nodded.

"Only lace and satin will be allowed in this room," he said. "I'll make sure that you possess adequate garments after tonight."

I nodded again.

"I need to put you on the table tonight, Melanie. I need to bind not only your wrists but also your ankles this time. I need you surrendered to me, laid out for my pleasure. You understand?"

I nodded, but then remembered what he'd said about answering in words. "Yes."

I looked toward the table. It was rectangular, with stirrups attached. There was a black skirt around it, so I couldn't see what, if any, mechanism lay underneath. There were clamps attached where I assumed he would bind me.

He came toward me, lifted me in his arms, carried me to the table, and set me down upon the black leather that covered it.

"Don't be afraid," he said in a husky voice.

That was a little too much to ask. I *was* afraid. Goose bumps had erupted on my skin. I was trembling. But I trusted him, and I wanted to do what he needed.

"Lie down."

I obeyed. He took one of my hands, bound my wrist to one end of the table, and then repeated with my other hand. The bindings were made of leather and were tight but not tight enough to be painful.

I was face up.

He moved to the foot of the table and repeated his actions with each of my ankles. He then removed the stirrups from the table. I secretly sighed in relief. I didn't really want to go there tonight.

Oddly, my legs weren't very far apart, but he soon remedied that situation. He unlatched a mechanism at the bottom of the table, and the two sections moved apart until I was spread-eagled before him. He could now position himself between my legs.

I was still trembling, but my nipples had hardened into berries. My skin was heating. I didn't know what was going to happen, and that alone was starting to turn me on. This surprised me. I could tell my pussy was getting wet. I had that telltale tickle between my legs.

Jonah inhaled. "God, you're ripe. So fucking ripe."

"What are you going to do to me?" I asked.

"You'll see. And from now on, don't talk until I tell you to."

The sternness in his voice unnerved me for a moment, but I was determined to get through this, to show him I could be what he needed. I loved this man so much, with my entire heart and soul. I wanted nothing more than to bring him some semblance of peace tonight. If this is what it would take, I would gladly participate.

He came back to the head of the table and placed a silk blindfold over my eyes. Just as well. I wasn't sure I wanted to see what he'd be doing anyway.

"I'm going to use nipple clamps tonight, Melanie. I think you'll enjoy it."

I shuddered. I opened my mouth to say something, I wasn't sure what, but then closed it. He'd told me not to speak unless told to.

"Your nipples are already hard. They're so beautiful. They're going to get very red when I clamp them. You'll feel it in your pussy, baby. You'll feel it through your whole body, and I'll feel it too, as I watch you."

Again I said nothing, but tensed up a bit, waiting for the clamps.

"First, I'm going to slap your breasts, baby. Slap those pretty titties."

Swat!

Something came down on me. I was blindfolded, so I had no idea what he was using. The sound as much as the sting made my nipples tighten further.

I cried out, not from pain so much as pleasure.

"You like that, baby? You like when I punish your breasts?"

Did that mean I had permission to talk? "Yes," I said.

"Good. Ready for the clamps?"

"Yes." I bit my lip.

I was expecting cool metal, but what touched me felt more like vinyl. I gasped as the clamp tightened around my nipple. Soon the other was in a clamp as well, and as he tightened both of them, I cried out.

"Too much?" he asked.

"God, no." I gritted my teeth. It was painful, yes, but oh, so amazing at the same time. My nipples were being twisted in the most wonderful way, and I felt it all the way down to my pussy, just like Jonah had said I would.

"I'm going to chain the clamps together now, Melanie, and tug on them."

I groaned.

Soon my nipples were being pulled. God, so good.

"Jonah," I gasped. "I need you. I need you now. Your cock inside me."

Slap!

Something came down upon my abdomen.

"I told you not to speak without permission."

I started to open my mouth to say I was sorry but bit my lip instead.

I was at his mercy. He could do with me whatever he wanted right now. If he hurt me, I could tell him to stop, and I trusted that he would. So far, he wasn't hurting me. The clamps were...surreal. As much as I loved having my nipples sucked hard, the clamps were something completely different. Yes, they were influencing the same nerve endings, but it was a different sensation, different than a suck, different even than a bite. Perhaps it was because it was prolonged. I didn't know, and I didn't rightly care. All I knew was my body was hot, so hot.

This was more physical for me than it had ever been before. Right now I wanted to be fucked.

But Jonah obviously had other ideas.

"I'm going to put some clamps on your thighs. Let me know if it's too much," he said.

I sucked in a breath at the first pinch on the top of my thigh.

Too much? Hell no.

I breathed out. A few seconds later, he pinched my other side in the same spot, about a couple of inches below my groin.

"Okay?" he asked.

"Yes." I wasn't sure if I was allowed to say any more.

He applied two more to each thigh, one in the middle and one right above the knee.

I tensed, letting the pain course through me, letting it grow into something that wasn't quite pleasure but was amazing at the same time.

"This is why I like this kind of play, Melanie," Jonah said. "I know what it does to you. It's doing exactly the same thing to me. Everything I produce in your body I feel in my own. I don't know why, but I do. I have such a hard-on right now for you, Melanie." His erection pressed against my hand that was bound. "Feel me. Feel what you do to me. Feel how much I want you."

Then fuck me! I longed to shout. But I would not disobey him again. I kept my hand on his bulge until he moved away.

Slap! Tiny smacks that didn't hurt—in fact, felt amazing—came down on my abdomen and then on my clamped thighs.

Slap!

This time on the blond curls between my legs, and then again, between them, against my slick folds of my pussy.

I bit my lip to keep from crying out, so hard that I actually drew blood. The tangy metal taste made its way to my tongue. If only he would fuck me, fuck me hard.

As if he were reading my mind, two fingers suddenly forced their way into my pussy.

I let out a gasp. "Oh!"

Something slapped against my clit.

"I told you not to speak."

He tugged on the chain joining the clamps again, and oh my God, without any clitoral stimulation, I began to orgasm.

How was this possible?

I couldn't help myself. I tried to stop it because he hadn't given me permission to come. But it was too late. The convulsions started in my pussy and spread outward until I tingled all over, and sparks of electricity surged through my entire body, culminating in those places where I was bound, where I was clamped.

"Good, baby. Enjoy it."

I flew and I flew, and when my pussy finally stopped pulsating and the tingling in my body subsided a bit, I said, "I'm sorry."

This time he didn't discipline me for speaking out of turn. "Why are you sorry?"

"Because you didn't tell me I could come."

He let out a little laugh. "No, I didn't. But I didn't tell you that you couldn't, either."

I smiled.

He touched my lips. "You need to stop biting your lip so much, Melanie. You're bleeding."

"May I speak freely?"

"Yes."

"I was biting my lip to keep from begging you to fuck me."

Another chuckle. "I may never again put any restraint on your talking."

I let out a soft laugh myself at that.

"I will fuck you, Melanie. But all in good time."

CHAPTER TWENTY-SIX

Jonah

She was so beautiful. Laid out before me naked, each of her limbs bound, her legs spread, her nipples and thighs clamped. She did this for me because she knew I needed it.

She hadn't completely surrendered to me yet. That wouldn't happen until she knelt at my feet while I sat in my chair. But this was enough for now. I could not push her any further tonight.

I grabbed a feather boa from one of the boxes near the wall and delicately drifted it over her.

I was done inflicting pain for tonight. Now I would give her only pleasure. She sighed against the touch, and after she was sufficiently relaxed, I removed the clamps from her thighs, relishing the pink marks they left. Although I would show no pink marks on my own skin, I felt every place those implements touched her. I closed my eyes, sighing, my cock hard as granite.

I would keep the clamps on her nipples for now. She responded well to them, and when she came again, this time with me embedded deep inside her, she would be glad of the clamps.

I slowly removed my shirt and then my boots, socks, jeans, and boxers. My cock was the biggest it had ever been, harder than normal even. I was ready to put it inside her, to complete the scene and make her mine. I knelt between her legs for a moment and licked her folds. She was so juicy and glistening. She sighed.

"I'm going to ram into you, Melanie. Fuck you hard and fast. It won't be gentle."

I climbed onto the table and slid my knees into the notches that had been built to my own specifications. I was primed at the right angle, and I entered her with one swift thrust. She let out a gasp as I embedded myself into her balls-deep.

She began biting her lip again.

"You can speak now, Melanie. Speak at your will."

"God, thank you. You feel so good inside me, Jonah. I've been longing for this all night."

I groaned. "Me too." I pulled out all the way so the tip of my cock was only barely touching her slick folds. I waited for a moment, even though my instinct was to plunge back in.

I wanted to tease her a little.

But only a little.

I thrust back into her, all the way, pulled out again, and thrust back in.

She screamed my name.

And I thrust again.

My entire body was tense and rigid, in need of release.

So I pulled back out again, tickling her folds with the head of my cock, and then thrust into her violently, letting my orgasm release into her.

As I emptied into her, the tension and stress left my body.

And I knew, with this woman by my side, I could get through anything.

Anything at all.

★ ★ ★

After we showered, we sat together in the bedroom, Melanie with her laptop.

"What are you working on?" I asked.

"Just some basic searching. Trying to find out what the future lawmakers club is. Maybe it's some national thing, like National Honor Society. So far I haven't found anything though."

"None of this makes sense. I always thought my father went to Snow Creek High School. That's where he always said he went."

"Your family has a lot of money, Jonah. It also makes sense that he'd go to a private preparatory school like Tejon."

"Wendy Madigan told us so many lies."

"I know. But remember, you're the one who had a feeling she wasn't trustworthy when you met with her. Turns out you were right."

"Great. I was right. So why do I feel so awful?"

"You know the answer to that as well as I do. Because this is an awful situation. And now you need to find out what your father's role was."

I shook my head. "I've always wondered why my father swept Talon's abduction under the rug and never let any of us deal with it. I always wanted to know why, for my own sake as well as Talon's. Now that I know about a link to the three abductors..." I raked my fingers through my hair. "Melanie, I'm afraid."

"Afraid of what?"

"Afraid of finding out who my father truly was."

She put her laptop away, came to me, and then, taking a

seat on my lap, curled her arms around my neck. "Our parents are never really who we want them to be. I know mine aren't."

Her words made me feel selfish and self-indulgent. I had been focusing so much on my own familial turmoil, and here she was, the woman I loved, and I knew next to nothing about her own family. "Tell me about your parents, sweetheart."

"There's not much to tell, really. It's not something I like talking about."

"I want to know you, Melanie. I already know that I love you more than anything, but I need to know *you*, everything about you. Beginning with your childhood."

She heaved a sigh and then gave me a kiss on the cheek. "It's not a happy story, but it's not horrible either. My parents gave me everything I wanted or needed...except their love and affection."

I looked at her beautiful face. She must've been a gorgeous child. How could her parents not have loved her? "I'm sorry, baby."

"I've long since gotten past it. At least I like to think I have. It has come back to me a little since Gina's death. I think part of the reason I wanted to help Gina so much was because my own parents were a lot like hers. She sought love and affection from someone else because her parents weren't giving it to her. That someone else turned out to be her uncle, and you know where that led."

"Did you seek love and affection from anyone else?"

She shook her head. "No. I threw myself into school. I was a basic nerd, always had my nose in a book, always made straight As. I ended up getting scholarships for most of my college and medical school, and for what didn't get paid for, I took out student loans. My parents could've helped me, but I didn't want to take their money. That was all I ever had from them, and I vowed, at that time, that I was done taking it. That I would make it on my own. So far I have. I've never asked them for a penny since I left for college."

"I've said this before, Melanie. You're the strongest woman I've ever known."

She bit her lip. "I'm stronger now than I was mere weeks ago. It's funny how things get put into perspective. Even with all my successes, I always thought of myself as average. If I'd been anything great, my parents would've loved me, so I must not have been anything great. The truth is that no matter how old a child gets, somewhere in the back of his mind—it can be fully subconscious—he always longs for his parents' approval and affection."

I opened my mouth to speak, but she placed two fingers over my lips.

"You're going to tell me how wonderful I am." She smiled. "I can see it in your eyes. Every time you look at me, Jonah, I can tell how much you love me, and that means more to me than you'll ever know."

"Are your parents still around?"

She nodded. "But we don't talk much. There's no reason to."

"I'd like to meet them," he said.

"There's no reason for you to meet them."

"Melanie, if you and I are going to have a future together, which I hope we will, I *do* need to meet your parents."

She let out a sigh. "All right. We'll drive to Denver to meet them sometime. But not anytime soon, okay?"

"Okay."

"I never thought I'd have kids. I didn't want to make the

same mistakes my parents did."

"I never thought I'd have kids either, Melanie. But now that I've met you, I think I might want to try."

She smiled, shaking her head. "I may be too old for that."

"I doubt it. Lots of women are having kids in their forties."

She laughed. "Someone just told me that same thing."

"Oh? Who?"

"Ruby Lee. She and I had quite a talk the other day."

"She's another one we probably need to talk to further," I said. "After all, her father was one of Talon's abusers. A member of that 'future lawmakers club,' whatever that could mean."

"I think Ruby will be cooperative," Melanie said. "She wants to see her father behind bars. She told me so."

"Damn it, so do I. I want to see my brother avenged."

She touched my cheek. "We will, my love. I know we will."

CHAPTER TWENTY-SEVEN

Melanie

I woke up at about nine a.m. and stretched. Jonah had taken the yearbooks to his office early that morning to have Dolores make the copies we needed. Then we had to return them to Jordan before anyone noticed they were missing. He was going to get back to the house as quickly as he could, because he and I were taking a trip to Denver to see Wendy Madigan.

I wasn't sure what her story was. She had obviously been a respected newswoman, so on the surface, at least, she was intelligent and hardworking. But who knew what went on in her mind?

She was a sophomore in the yearbook where she was shown as one of the members of the future lawmakers club. Tom Simpson and Theodore Mathias were seniors, and Brad, Rodney Cates, and Larry were juniors that year. Wendy had told Jade that her family had moved from the western slope to Denver when she was sixteen and Brad was seventeen. She didn't appear in any yearbooks after that year, so perhaps she had been telling the truth.

What was that club truly about? Larry had called the club the "future lawyers." Had he made that mistake on purpose, trying to throw us off track? Or had he simply misspoken? After all, he and Tom were the only ones who actually became lawyers. I shook my head to myself. No, he had given us the wrong name on purpose. I was sure of it.

I would find out later. Right now, I had to get Lucy fed, take a shower, and get ready for Jonah to come home so we could drive to Denver this afternoon.

When I stood, a vibrating buzz met my ears. My phone was still hooked up to the charger in the bedroom, but I looked around.

Jonah's phone sat on the kitchen counter. Very odd. He never went anywhere without his phone, but there was a first time for everything. I grabbed the phone. It was a text.

Now you are mine.

I dropped the phone back on the counter with a clatter. Icy chills crept up the back of my neck. He was still getting those texts. Had Mills and Johnson traced that number yet? Had Jonah even called them? I had no idea. Well, I had the number right in front of me now. I would call and get to the bottom of this. Taking Jonah's phone with me, I walked swiftly to the bedroom where my own phone was. Quickly I dialed Trevor Mills's number.

"Mills."

"Hi there, this is Melanie Carmichael, Jonah Steel's... girlfriend."

"Of course. What can I do for you, Doctor?"

"I need you to trace a phone number for me." I rattled off the number. "Jonah's been getting some unusual texts from this number, and all we could find is that the area code is in Iowa."

"I'll get on it. Anything else?"

"No. Just give me a call when you have any information."

"Will do. Have a good day."

I stared at Jonah's phone for a moment, again questioning why he'd left it here. Probably just an oversight. I walked into the bathroom and started the shower.

★ ★ ★

Jonah was late getting back from the pastures. I couldn't call him because I had his phone. So I decided to call Dolores at his office.

"Steel Acres."

"Hi, Dolores. This is Melanie Carmichael. Is Jonah still in the office?"

"Jonah hasn't been in this morning," the secretary said. "I just assumed he went straight out to the pastures."

My heart nearly stopped. "You mean he didn't go in this morning and ask you to make some copies of some old yearbooks?"

"No, Melanie. Sorry."

My skin prickled, and my pulse raced. What was going on?

"So you haven't seen him at all today?"

"No, I haven't. Is anything wrong?"

I didn't want to worry her. "Everything's fine. Thank you." I ended the call.

Now what? I bit my lip, drawing blood. Where was he? I paced around the house, Lucy following my heels.

Maybe he hadn't gone into the office after all and had just been delayed out in the pastures. That would make sense. What didn't make sense, though, was how he had forgotten his phone. That was so unlike him.

I looked around, finding nothing more in the kitchen and

bedroom. I walked into the other wing of the house, to Jonah's study. I gasped.

On his desk sat the four yearbooks.

There was no way he would've forgotten both the phone and the yearbooks.

Something was wrong.

Very wrong.

My adrenaline surging, I flipped on his printer and copier and quickly went through each yearbook, making the copies we needed.

Then I let the fear take me. My heart pounded and my nerves bristled. Nausea crept up my throat. Someone had Jonah. He wouldn't leave without a trace unless someone had taken him.

Blood rushed to my head, and I was caught in a haze of white noise.

No!

I had to do something. The police. I'd call the police.

I quickly made a call to 9-1-1 and alerted the authorities that Jonah was missing. What next?

I let out a breath and rubbed my shivering arms.

I would have to call Talon. I just didn't relish telling this man who had been through so much already that his big brother was missing.

My phone rang in my pocket. I picked it up and recognized Mills's number.

"Hello?"

"Hey, Doctor, this didn't take long at all. We got a name for your number. Definitely an Iowa area code, as you know, but as far as we can tell, the person with the number never lived in Iowa."

Right. The number of the person who'd been stalking Jonah. Of course. I willed myself to stay in control. "Okay."

"The number is registered to a female in the name of Selena Winters."

"Jonah has never mentioned anyone by that name. Why would she be stalking him by phone?"

"With a little more research, we found out that Selena Winters is an alias. The person who uses this number is a retired newswoman living in Denver. Her name is Wendy Madigan."

The phone flipped from my hands. I quickly picked it up, my pulse racing. "I'm sorry. Wendy Madigan?"

"That's right. She's had this phone number for nearly ten years. But it doesn't get used very often."

"Can you get her phone records?"

"Yes, ma'am. Working on it."

"Great. Call me when you have something." I hung up quickly.

Oh God oh God oh God.

The text I'd read forced its way into my mind.

Now you are mine.

She had him. Wendy Madigan had my Jonah.

I quickly called Mills back.

"Yeah?"

"Melanie Carmichael again. I need you to drop everything. Jonah is missing, and it's most likely that he's with this Wendy Madigan. I've called the police, but I want you on this. All I know is that she lives in Denver with her mother, but we need to find her. Scratch that. I don't give a damn about her. I just need to find Jonah."

"We'll get on it, Doctor."

"I don't care what it costs. Please. Find him." I ended the call.

Now I definitely had to call Talon.

But I wasn't looking forward to it.

CHAPTER TWENTY-EIGHT

Jonah

I opened my eyes to pastel blurs.

Where the hell was I?

I had gotten up at five a.m., showered quickly, and was filling my travel cup full of coffee when...

My mind was blank after that.

I was in a bed. A king-size bed crammed into a small bedroom. I wasn't tied down, so I sat up.

Whoa. Really woozy.

I moved my knees over the side of the bed and stood, but my knees wouldn't hold me. I toppled over on the floor.

Someone came rushing in. "Goodness, my love, you shouldn't be up yet."

I strained my eyes, but the woman in front of me was a blur. She had short hair, maybe blue eyes.

"Lie back down, Brad. You'll be feeling better soon."

Brad? I opened my mouth to argue with her but only garbled noises emerged.

What the hell was going on?

"I'll be bringing in your lunch soon," the woman said. "Once you're feeling better, we can talk. I've missed you so much, Brad." She left the room, closing the door behind her.

Brad. That was my father's name. My father whom I

didn't know anymore.

My mind seemed to be working fine. It was my body that was having trouble catching up. What happened? Was I dreaming? Did I have a stroke? Why wasn't my body working?

Drugs.

Someone must've drugged me. I had been in my kitchen, getting ready to pour coffee...

I squeezed my eyes shut, desperately trying to remember anything beyond that moment.

Nothing came.

I patted the back pocket of my jeans for my phone.

It wasn't there.

Damn. I never went anywhere without my phone. I had set it on the kitchen counter because I was in the middle of reading an e-mail when I went to fill my coffee cup...

It must still be there.

What time was it?

I was supposed to meet Melanie back at the house so we could drive to Denver...

I tried standing again, to no avail. I would have to wait until whatever I had been drugged with left my system.

Think, Joe, think. What could be going on? Who would be calling you Brad?

The door opened again, and the woman, still a blur, came in with a tray.

I said nothing. Just sat, squinting, trying to make out who it was.

And then I knew.

Brooke Bailey had never been stalking me.

The person stalking me, who was now talking to me as though I were my father, was none other than Wendy Madigan.

She couldn't have gotten me here by herself. Someone was helping her.

Was I in Denver? How much time had passed?

Wendy set the tray down on a TV tray and brought it to me. "I hope you're hungry. I made my famous beef stew. I remember how much you used to love it."

Should I play along? Not like I had much choice until I could work my body. Right now I was tingling all over. From nerves? Probably. But maybe also from whatever drug she'd given me wearing off. Hopefully.

She hadn't bound me, thank God, but she was probably locking the door behind her while I was in here. But the room was sunny and had a window. I could easily get out of here.

What to do until then? Appease her? That would probably be the safest thing, but it wasn't in me to do that without trying to get out first.

"You made a mistake," I said. "I'm not Brad. I'm his son, Jonah. Brad was my father."

"Always the same thing, Brad," she said. "Always trying to deny what has always been between us. That's why I brought you here. That's why I've been texting you. It's time that you finally surrendered to our love."

She was crazy. My skin compressed against my muscles, and I remembered the last time I had seen Wendy Madigan. She had said more than once how much I looked like my father, more so than Talon and Ryan did. That much was true, and I recalled the way she'd stared at me, to a point where I'd become uncomfortable.

Now she had clearly flipped her wig.

I tried not to worry about my fate. Melanie would notice I was gone, and she would go to Talon and Ryan. They would put Mills and Johnson on the case, and I would be found soon. Still, I needed to try to escape.

"I'm ovulating, Brad. I think we may finally get that baby we've been wishing for."

Nausea crept up my throat. Ovulating? Wendy was in her sixties. Not only crazy but delusional as well. No way was this happening.

"Enjoy your stew. I'll be back to check on you later."

"Look, Wendy, you know I'm married. Daphne and I have four children."

"Silly, you only have three. Three boys. You say you love Daphne, but I was always your first and only love. You told me so yourself."

All right. No wonder she thought she was ovulating. She was stuck in the past, obviously before Marjorie had been born. I could work with that. "That was a long time ago. We were just kids."

"Not that long ago. You know as well as I do that we were always meant for each other. I forgave you when you impregnated that slut Daphne."

I chilled. The need to defend my mother rose up within me, but would that be the right attack?

"I'd appreciate it if you wouldn't talk about Daphne that way," I said. "She is, after all, the mother of my children."

Wendy stiffened, picked up the bowl of stew on the tray, and hurled it against the wall. "*I* was always supposed to be the mother of your children. You know that as well as I do. You took that chance away from me." She pointed to the mess she had made. "Now clean that shit up." She walked out the door, slamming it, the lock turning.

I had no intention of cleaning up her mess. I wasn't hungry

anyway.

I walked to the door to examine the lock. It was a deadbolt, so picking it was out of the question, especially since I didn't have any tools. I could turn this room upside down looking for something, but I'd check the window first. I walked toward it and looked out. I was on the second story of what appeared to be a house in a decent neighborhood. Was this the same house Talon and I had visited in Denver? I had no idea.

The window wasn't locked, so I unlatched it and slid it open. However, instead of a screen, another pane of glass had been installed. Not a huge problem. I could break glass, and I could probably jump to safety, even though I was on the second story.

When I heard the lock being tinkered with on the door, I hurried back to the bed and sat down.

Wendy walked back in, locking the door behind her. She looked toward the mess she had made with the stew earlier, looked at me, and then back at the floor. "Brad, please forgive me. You know how I get sometimes."

How many personalities did this woman have? I tried standing again, and my knees wobbled a little less this time. I managed to stay standing for a second until she walked toward me and pushed me back down on the bed.

"You shouldn't be up. You need to rest. Just lie down while I clean up this mess. Again, I'm so sorry." She walked out the door for a moment and then came back with some rags and a shop vac. She worked quickly, as if possessed by a manic streak, and within ten minutes, the mess was gone.

Now, instead of beef and carrots, the room smelled like beef, carrots, and carpet shampoo. Great.

She slid the shop vac outside the door and then returned.

"I'm so sorry, Brad. Please forgive me."

I was at a loss. How should I approach this? Obviously, I should approach it as my father would have, but it had become increasingly clear to me that I didn't know my father at all. How would he have acted?

Like the domineering man he had been. He had been a kind father, but he had been strict, teaching us responsibility and the value of hard work. He had been a sexist, to Marj's chagrin, believing a woman's place was in the home and not out on the ranch. I smiled. Marj had set him straight on that. Once she'd stood up to him, he had spoiled her rotten.

How would he have treated Wendy?

I had no fucking idea.

I knew one thing, though. He wouldn't have put up with her little tantrum and throwing food.

I looked at her with all the anger I could muster...and I had a lot of it pouring through me at the moment. "If you ever pull a stunt like that again, Wendy, I will walk out of here and never come back."

She fell at my knees, sobbing into them. "Brad, please don't leave me. You know we were meant to be together. You can't deny it. You don't love Daphne the way you love me. You know you don't."

Would I get further with her if I pacified her, told her I loved her? Or would I get further if I defended my mother? If only I knew what my father had done.

According to what Wendy had told Jade, Wendy and my father had been in love and had engaged in an affair while he was alive. Was that true? Or was it part of Wendy's delusion?

She had been instrumental in covering up what had happened to Talon, and I still didn't understand why my father had swept it all under the rug.

Maybe I could find out...

"I'm sorry, Wendy," I said, "but I can never forgive you for your part in what happened to my son."

CHAPTER TWENTY-NINE

Melanie

I sat in Jonah's kitchen with his brothers.

"Joe tried to tell me," Talon said. "He thought something was off about Wendy Madigan, but I kind of brushed it off. She had been a huge help to Jade, and Jade spoke highly of her." He shook his head. "I should have listened to my big brother."

"Don't beat yourself up, Tal," Ryan said.

"Yes, don't," I agreed. "Right now we have to find Jonah." I sank my head into my hands.

Talon touched my shoulder. "Doc, it's going to be okay."

I let out a sigh. If only... I was in a position right now that I was never supposed to be in. Not only was the man I loved missing, probably taken by a woman who was clearly mad, but someone had to tell Talon what Jonah and I had learned from the yearbooks. That was never supposed to be me, but right now, I didn't have a choice.

"We'll get through this, Tal," Ryan said gently.

He shook his head. "I still can't get over it. One of those motherfuckers was here the whole time, and I didn't know it. The fucking mayor. He congratulated me on my heroics overseas, officiated at that stupid-ass ceremony they did for me in town. And all that time..."

"I'd like to tear his fucking head off," Ryan said, tensing.

"I think we all would, Ryan," I said.

"And the other one... I was right. Jade's mother's boyfriend." He shook his head again. "I was actually right."

"You were," I said.

"Funny," he said. "It doesn't feel good to be right."

"Of course it doesn't. It doesn't change what happened to you. I always told you that your healing didn't depend on finding those three." I rubbed at my forehead. Now wasn't the time for a therapy session. "But there is a silver lining to this cloud. We know who we're looking for now. And they can't hide forever."

Talon stood, his eyelids heavy. "I don't even care anymore, Doc. I just want my big brother back."

So did I. Tears emerged at the corners of my eyes. I sniffled. "I'm worried and scared, just like you two. But we need to take solace in the fact that if Wendy has him, she probably won't hurt him. After all, she was in love with your father."

As I said the word "father," my heart sank. The next step was to show Talon and Ryan the yearbooks—and the connection between Rodney Cates, Wendy, the three abductors...and Bradford Steel.

I doubted they'd take it any better than Jonah had.

I inhaled a deep breath.

This wasn't going to be easy.

★ ★ ★

After half an hour of telling the story and looking at Talon's and Ryan's mouths wide open, we were all ready for a drink. Ryan played bartender at Jonah's bar, mixing up a bourbon for Talon, a martini for me, and then, in a surprise twist, a bourbon for himself.

"I thought you were a wine guy," I said.

"Today screams for something stronger," he replied, taking a sip of his bourbon and then clenching his jaw. "We need to get out of here. We should be out looking for Joe. He'd be doing that for us."

"True," Talon said, standing.

I hadn't been able to shake the nausea I'd been experiencing since I realized Jonah was gone. I'd thought a drink might be a good idea, but I couldn't choke any of it down. "The police are on it. So are Mills and Johnson. There's nothing more we can do."

"The hell there's not," Ryan said, downing his bourbon like a shot. "Let's go, Tal."

"If you two are going, I'm going with you," I said.

Talon turned to me, handing me the yearbooks. "You stay here, Doc. Joe would never forgive us if we put you in harm's way." He checked his watch. "Jade should be home from work soon. I'm going to text her and tell her to come stay with you. I don't want you to be alone."

"You're crazy." My blood was rushing through my veins. I could almost hear the whoosh. "I'm not staying here."

"Please," Ryan said. "Stay here. We need to know you're safe. For Joe."

For Joe.

They knew the words that would get to me. I would do anything for their brother. Finally, I relented. I would stay, but I elicited a promise that they would text me every half hour. I didn't need to be worrying about them, as well.

"Why hasn't Mills called? Or the police?" I pulled at my hair.

"Jonah's strong, Doc," Ryan said. "He'll be all right."

"I can't lose him now. I just can't. I don't know how I'll go on."

"If Wendy loved our dad the way she said she did, she won't hurt one of his kids," Ryan said.

Talon jolted on his bar stool. "Oh my God..."

"What is it, Tal?"

"Oh, God," he said again. "Melanie..."

Talon had never called me Melanie before. Always Dr. Carmichael or Doc. His use of my first name couldn't signify anything good. I inhaled, gathering what courage I had left. "What is it?"

"If Wendy was in the group, this future lawmakers club, with my father and my three abductors... What if she was somehow involved in my kidnapping?"

I heard the words Talon didn't say. If what he proposed was true, and if Wendy had been involved in his abduction, she certainly wasn't above hurting one of Brad's children.

I rubbed my shoulders as cold fear pressed through me. My breath came in rapid pants. Couldn't breathe. Couldn't see...

I fell into Talon's arms.

CHAPTER THIRTY

Jonah

Wendy stared at me, but I couldn't read the look on her face. My vision was still too blurry. She advanced toward me.

"Brad, you know as well as I do that what happened to your son was your own fault."

What? Fiery rage pulsed in my veins. How dare she blame my father for what happened to Talon? I opened my mouth to say as much but then closed it quickly.

Had Wendy orchestrated Talon's kidnapping to punish my father?

Had she been telling the truth? That my father had an enemy? And that *she* was the enemy?

Then again, that would contradict what Larry had said—that Talon was never meant to be taken. Larry's story made more sense, as Talon and Ryan had gone searching for Luke Walker that day, and there was no way that Tom and the other one, whichever name he was using at the time, could've known where they had gone. Wendy couldn't have known either. She lived in Denver, not Snow Creek, at that time.

What could I say to get the most information out of Wendy?

"It was *not* my fault, Wendy," I said. "You and I both know the truth." I had no idea what truth I was speaking of, but maybe she would start talking.

"The only truth I know, Brad, is that we are meant for each other. We have always been meant to be together. And I will use whatever means I must to make you see that ultimate certainty."

While I was thinking about how to respond, she stalked toward me, pushing me down supine on the bed. She began unbuttoning my shirt. "It's time, Brad. It's time for you to impregnate me. I'm ovulating, ripe as a tomato ready to fall off the vine. I'm ready to take your seed, to start making your true heir."

My vision was finally coming back. She looked at me with a mixture of love and madness, her blue eyes filled with emotion unreadable. There was no way we were having sex.

I exerted my strength, sat up, and pushed her away. "No. Not after what you did to my son. Maybe we had a future at one time, Wendy. But when you harmed my son, you ended whatever was between us."

"And I told you, what happened to your son was your own fault, not mine. You were the one who refused to surrender to our love. You needed to be punished."

"So to punish me, you harmed an innocent little boy. You're a monster, Wendy. A monster, and I cannot love a monster."

Tears emerged in Wendy's eyes. "Everything I've done, I've done out of love for you. How do you not see that?"

And then an idea popped into my mind. "Wendy, I'll make a deal with you. You tell me exactly how the attack on Talon was orchestrated. Be totally honest so I can punish the people involved. If you do that for me, I will give you the child you so desperately want."

The thought of actually sleeping with Wendy Madigan made my skin crawl, but I had no intention of doing so. It was clear that my father had been able to manipulate her, as I was doing now. It was also clear that she was unstable and this so-called love for my father had blinded her to everything else. Had blinded her into orchestrating the kidnapping of an innocent ten-year-old boy, if what I suspected was true.

"No, Brad. You give me the child first. Then I will tell you everything."

Time to act the domineering male again, an act I was no stranger to. I stood, pulling her up next to me. I looked her straight in her blue eyes, which were now no longer blurry, thank God. "You seem to be forgetting who makes the rules around here. In case you need an answer, I do. Not you."

She fell against me, weeping. "Brad, of course you make the rules. I would do anything for you. You know that."

I pushed her away from me, again meeting her gaze. "Then you will tell me right now. Tell me exactly how Talon was taken and who orchestrated it."

"You know already. You knew what kind of men the future lawmakers were. You joined their club anyway, like I did."

"Refresh my memory. Tell me what that club was about. Tell me why you joined, Wendy."

"You know why I joined. To be near you."

"What about Rodney Cates? Why did he join?"

"He had the hots for Theo's sister. You know that."

Of course. Gina's mother, Theodore Mathias's sister. Things were starting to fall into place.

Sort of.

Why would my father have joined the club? He wasn't a future lawyer or future lawmaker. He was heir to the most profitable ranch in Colorado. What was that club truly about?

"Wendy, I'm losing patience quickly. You will tell me right now what the future lawmakers club was about and how and why the attack on my son was orchestrated. Am I making myself clear?" I gripped her upper arm harshly.

"Yes, Brad. I love it when you get rough with me. Squeeze my arm harder."

Okay, not where I wanted to go with this. "I will not get rough with you. I will not do anything you want until you tell me what I need to know."

"Why? Have you somehow lost your memory? You know how that happened. You were a big part of it. Remember?"

She was lying. No way had my father been involved in any way with Talon's abduction. I gripped her other upper arm and shook her. "Goddamnit," I said through clenched teeth. "You *will* tell me the truth. Now." I threw her down on the bed.

"Yes, Brad, take me." She began unbuttoning her blouse. "I'm yours. Only yours. Take me now."

I needed to get hold of myself. Getting rough with her was not getting through to her, clearly. Plus, even as angry as I was, I wasn't comfortable roughing up a woman, even one who deserved it as much as Wendy Madigan did.

No. That was not who I was. I could never get violent with a woman. Especially not now. I would never be able to look my sweet Melanie in the eye.

And then another thought occurred to me. If she liked me roughing her up, I would do the opposite.

"No." I looked straight into her eyes. "I will not take you. I don't want you, Wendy. I love Daphne."

"Need I remind you, Brad, that talk like that is what got your son taken in the first place? You have two other sons, you know. Aren't you concerned about their safety? Especially the young one?"

"Why you little bit—" I stopped myself from finishing the sentence. Although the rage and ire were consuming me, I had to keep my head. I had to figure out how to get her to talk.

She finished unbuttoning her blouse and pushed the pieces of fabric to each side, showing her bra. "You always loved my breasts, Brad. Don't you remember?"

"We were just kids, Wendy."

I fervently wished she would leave her clothes on. "Button yourself back up. I don't even want to look at you anymore." I turned and walked toward the door.

To my surprise, it opened. I rushed down the hallway and down a flight of stairs to the first floor of the house.

I raced through what appeared to be a living room to the front door and turned the knob. Locked. From the fucking outside. She had locked me in.

Wendy came running down the stairs, the two sides of her blouse flapping. "Just where do you think you're going?"

I turned to her. "I'm getting the hell out of this house. I'm going home to my wife and children."

"No!" She launched herself into me, nearly making me lose my footing. "I'll never let you go, Brad. Never."

I pushed her off me, gripping her upper arms. "You don't have a choice."

I shoved her to the side and walked through the house, looking for a back door. When I found it, I turned the knob, and to my delight, it opened.

I gasped.

I stood facing a man in a black mask, a man with unreal blue eyes. Eyes I had seen before.

He was pointing a gun at my heart.

CHAPTER THIRTY-ONE

Melanie

I woke up on Jonah's bed, a woman removing a damp cloth from my forehead. I squinted. It was Jade.

"Melanie," she said. "Can you hear me?"

I nodded. "What happened?"

"You fainted. Talon carried you in here."

"Did they tell you..."

"Yes." She replaced the cloth on my head. "It's all so unbelievable."

Yes, it was. "Did you look at the yearbooks?"

She nodded. "Talon texted me about them, and yes, I looked at them. He's a mess, Melanie. I'm worried about all three of them right now."

"Talon is strong. He'll get through it. He's gotten through much worse. Is there any word from..."

She shook her head. "I'm so sorry. But we have the cops and Mills and Johnson on it. Plus Talon and Ryan. We'll find him, Melanie. I promise we will."

Jade was an attorney. She knew better than to make such a promise, just as I did as a physician. But I wouldn't bring that to her attention. She was simply trying to make me feel better. I couldn't fault her for that. I would be doing the same thing if our positions were reversed.

I was still a little woozy, but I sat up in bed. "I've made copies of all the relevant pages in the yearbooks. We have to get them back to Jordan Hayes, the receptionist at Tejon Prep School. In fact, I should call her." I moved to stand.

"You should probably stay in bed."

"Nonsense. I'm a doctor. This was a simple neurally mediated syncope."

"Huh?"

"Just a silly fainting spell caused by anxiety. Perfectly normal."

"Have you eaten anything today?"

Had I? "I'm not sure."

"Why don't you let me bring you some dinner in here?" Jade said.

I opened my mouth to protest, but she was right. I needed sustenance. I was feeling a bit nauseated, but that was common after fainting. My body needed the food for strength, even though I couldn't wrap my mind around putting anything in my stomach.

"All right."

"I'll be back in a few minutes."

"Thanks."

I closed my eyes. I had to return the yearbooks, or at least call Jordan and let her know there would be a delay. I would call her later from Jonah's phone. He had the number.

I fell back onto my pillow, a black cloud hovering above me.

Come home to me, Jonah. Please, come home.

★ ★ ★

I woke up the next morning, Lucy at the foot of Jonah's bed. I'd invited her up. Sleeping in Jonah's bed without Jonah seemed so many kinds of wrong.

After I had eaten my dinner the previous night, I had been able to go back out to the kitchen, where Jade and Marjorie were. After we had received several texts from Talon and Ryan, assuring us they were fine, I promised Jade and Marj that I would be fine and told them they should go home.

In truth, I needed to be alone.

They hadn't wanted to leave me alone here, especially considering we didn't know exactly how Jonah had disappeared. Because his phone was still in the house, it was likely someone had been here and had taken him. Either that or he'd left willingly, which none of us thought was the case.

They finally relented after they talked to the Snow Creek police and the county sheriff about keeping an eye on Jonah's house overnight.

Once they had left, I had gone straight to bed, huddled in the fetal position shivering, until Lucy's presence calmed me. A bit.

Last night I hadn't been able to think about the possibility that Jonah wouldn't return. This morning, though, I had to face the reality of that prospect.

Wendy Madigan had somehow taken Jonah from his home. She was an older woman, probably in her sixties, so she would've had help. I had a sinking feeling that help had come in the form of Tom Simpson and Theodore Mathias.

Those two men had been in this house.

From what I knew, I didn't think Wendy Madigan would

harm Jonah. Tom Simpson and Theodore Mathias, on the other hand? They would have no qualms about it.

And that was what frightened me to no end.

But Jonah was alive. I felt it. Knew it in the marrow of my bones. We were connected. I would feel it if he were gone.

I would.

I *would.*

I got up finally, only because I knew Lucy needed to go out. I let her out, filled up her food and water, and was on my way back to bed when I spied Jonah's phone. I had left it in the kitchen last night.

The yearbooks sat on the kitchen table. I didn't have the strength to return them to Jordan today, but I at least owed her the courtesy of a phone call to let her know we would be returning them soon.

I flipped through Jonah's phone to find the number for Jordan Hayes. Once I found it, I was ready to hit dial, but then I stopped.

I just couldn't call her. Not yet. I needed to at least have a cup of tea or something first.

I let Lucy back in so she could have her breakfast and then found the container of tea I had bought when I replenished Jonah's groceries. I put the tea kettle on the stove and then sat down at the table, my head in my hands.

I had come so far. I had gotten through my own private hell, had come out kicking, had fallen in love with the most wonderful man in the world, had begun to surrender to his darkest desires and had found myself in the process.

And for what? To have it taken away from me?

Tears slid from my eyes, and I sniffled. Lucy looked up from her kibble and came to me, wagging her tail. I couldn't muster a smile for the sweet dog, but I did give her a pet on the head.

The tea kettle whistled, and I poured water over my tea bag. As it steeped, I stared at the threads of darkness feathering through the clear water.

Threads of darkness.

I had unraveled Jonah's darkness, and we had become closer than ever.

I wasn't going to give him up without a fight.

I returned to the counter and picked up his phone. I would start by calling Jordan Hayes and arranging to get those yearbooks back to her. The sooner they were back in place, the sooner the poor woman would be out of any danger.

I dialed the number.

"Hello?" It was a male voice.

"Yes, good morning." I cleared my throat. "I'm trying to reach Jordan Hayes."

A gasp met my ears. "I'm sorry. This is Jordan's father." A pause. "Jordan was murdered last night."

CHAPTER THIRTY-TWO

Jonah

My life still didn't flash before my eyes.

But this time, my bowels clenched. Now I had something to live for. I had Melanie—sweet Melanie who had forgiven my transgressions, who had surrendered to me in so many ways, who loved me beyond measure.

I inhaled, gathering every ounce of courage I possessed. "Theodore Mathias," I said. "A.k.a. Nico Kostas, Milo Sanchez, and a host of other names."

"I don't know what you're talking about," the masked man said.

"Where's Simpson?"

"Again, don't have a clue what you're talking about." He walked toward me.

I stepped backward, retreating into the house.

Wendy ran toward me, pushing at the masked man. "Please, don't hurt him."

"Why shouldn't I? He's a fucking thorn in my side."

"He's the love of my life."

"You're crazy as a fucking loon, Wendy," he said. "I'll do what I want with this asshole. One less Steel in the world will be no loss to anyone."

"Please, no." Wendy tried to grab the gun from the masked

man.

The man crashed it down onto her shoulder, and Wendy crumpled to the ground, wailing.

As much as I hated Wendy Madigan, I didn't like seeing any woman mistreated. But I didn't say anything. This was between Mathias and me.

"What do you want?" I asked.

"I want what's been due to me for years."

"And what's that?"

"Your fucking money, Steel. I want it all."

I stopped myself from laughing out loud. I didn't want to give him any reason to shoot me.

"You can kill me," I said, bluffing. "But if you do, the entire Steel fortune goes up in flames."

"That's a goddamned lie and you know it. We've seen your father's will."

"Maybe you have and maybe you haven't. In Colorado, wills aren't a matter of public record. But even if you have seen my father's will, you haven't seen mine. Maybe it escaped your notice, but my father is dead. Everything belongs to me now, and my brothers and sister and I decided long ago what to do with it should any harm come to any one of us. We have things in place with our attorneys. Contracts that override any stipulations that we might be forced to sign at gunpoint. Ironically, we made that decision because of you and what you did to our brother."

"You're bluffing."

"Maybe I am, and maybe I'm not. Do you really want to take that chance? Kill me if you want, but you won't see one penny from the Steels."

"I have had enough Steels to last a fucking lifetime. You

people ruined my life."

"You ruined your own life. You abducted and raped my brother, raped your own niece, tried to kill your girlfriend for insurance money."

His eyes got a little rounder. Only slightly, but I had rattled him.

"Oh, yeah. I know all about you, Mathias. You're legendary around here."

"I don't know who the hell you think I am, but you've got the wrong name."

I rolled my eyes. "You're not that good of a liar."

He moved toward me and nudged the barrel of the gun against my heart. I tried hard not to piss myself.

"Not a good liar? Do you think I'm lying now? I'm going to kill you, Steel. I'm going to put a bullet into your heart."

Wendy surged forward then and plowed into the masked man, making him drop his gun. The weapon slid across the tile floor.

"You will not hurt him! I love that man!"

Before I could think about what was happening, I lunged toward the gun. My hands were clammy, but I got hold of the slick weapon.

I stood over the two of them. "Don't either of you fucking move."

The masked man got to his feet and grabbed Wendy, putting her in a headlock. "You drop that gun, motherfucker, or I'll twist her head right off."

"You think I care?"

"Brad, please!" Wendy cried. "Don't let him hurt me. I'm carrying your child!"

Jesus Christ, this woman was deranged. I looked around

the house. There had to be a landline here somewhere, but I hadn't been able to find one. I had no cell phone.

"Either one of you have a phone?" I asked.

"You think I'm giving my phone to you?" the man said.

"I think you're giving your phone to me," I said. "Otherwise I'm going to put a bullet in your brain." I touched the barrel of the gun to his forehead.

The man was cold as ice. No reaction at all.

Until I heard the cock of a pistol behind me.

"Drop the gun, Joe."

That voice I recognized. Tom Simpson. I had wondered how Mathias had known which door I would try to use to exit this house from hell. Now I knew. He hadn't. Simpson had been waiting at the other door.

"Nice to see you again," I said, although I hadn't turned and I couldn't see him. I didn't dare budge with a gun pointed at me.

"Let her go," Tom said to Mathias, "and move out the door slowly."

The masked man pushed Wendy to the ground and walked backward toward the door.

Tom moved into my vision. He was wearing a mask this time as well, but I recognized his eyes.

"What the hell are you doing?" I asked. "What am I supposed to tell Bryce? What about Evelyn?"

"You were never supposed to know about any of this, Joe," he said. "But you Steel boys wouldn't quit pushing. Our beef was never with you. It was with your father."

"You have no beef with us? You torture my little brother, and you think we're not going to come after you? You don't know any of us very well, and you sure as hell didn't know our father."

"You're the one who never knew who your father really was, Joe."

I froze, chills skittering through my veins.

Tom was right. I just didn't know to what degree he was right.

I would damned well find out.

"Everything was going along fine," Tom continued, "until your brother decided to go into therapy, decided to dredge up all the shit that had been long buried." He held the gun against the side of my head. "You think I won't kill you, don't you, Joe? You think because you're Bryce's best friend, I won't do it."

I scoffed. "Are you kidding me? You killed your nephew, Tom. I know you have *every* intention of killing me. You won't lose a wink of sleep over it. I don't question you at all. I know you wouldn't think twice about pulling that trigger and putting a bullet in my head."

"How do you think it feels to die, Joe? How do you think it feels to have a bullet rip through your body?"

My bowels churned once again, but no way was I going to shit myself in front of Tom Simpson. He was sure as hell not worth that. I would go down fighting.

"Go ahead and kill me if you have to." I willed my voice not to crack. "But I already told your friend here that we made arrangements with our attorneys for our fortune should anything happen to any one of us. You won't get your hands on a cent of it."

"We've seen your father's will, Joe."

"Good for you. I've seen my father's will, also. You seem to be forgetting that my father is dead, so his will is moot. I have my own will. And trust me, it's ironclad."

"We'll see about that," Tom said. "We know what's in his will, and nothing you can do can change what we know to be true. We made sure there were no loopholes."

What the hell was he talking about? My father's will had been read to us by his attorneys after his death. No one had contested it, and his death was common knowledge. His obituary appeared in all the local papers. As informed as these jokers claimed to be, surely they knew that.

This was all a ruse. They were trying to play with my mind. To manipulate me. Well, I was far from a ten-year-old boy or eight-year-old girl. "I'm done with this conversation. Either kill me or get the fuck out of here." I looked to Wendy. "And take her with you."

"We don't want her. She was your father's problem, not ours."

"Come on!" Mathias yelled from the doorway. "Leave him be. We'd never hear the end of it from her if we blasted his brains all over this place."

"We could kill both of them," Tom said. "I'm sick of the sight of them."

"No more than I am, but you know the consequences. Let's get the fuck out of here."

Tom walked toward the door, still holding the gun on me. "You're getting spared again, Joe. But trust me when I say your luck will run out eventually." He shut the door behind him.

I let out a gasping sigh, ready to release my bladder. Wendy was crumpled on the floor.

And I realized I still held a gun in my hand.

I pointed it straight at her.

CHAPTER THIRTY-THREE

Melanie

I dropped the phone, and it hurtled to the floor.

Murdered?

Oh my God.

I hadn't liked the way she had been making eyes at Jonah, but I certainly never wished her dead.

I quickly picked up the phone and put it back to my ear. "I'm so very sorry," I said. "May I ask what happened?"

"Who is this?"

"This is Dr. Melanie Carmichael. I'm a...friend of Jordan's."

"The name that came up on the caller ID was Jonah Steel."

"Yes. Jonah Steel is my boyfriend. I'm using his phone."

"How does my daughter know the two of you?"

I wasn't sure how to answer that question. The fact that she had been rooting around in Jonah's father's past could very well have been what had gotten her killed.

"Jonah's father and his uncle were alumni at the school where Jordan works. They had been in touch with her about getting some information." That seemed tame enough.

"I see. There's not much to tell you. She was shot in her apartment late last night, apparently. There was no evidence of a forced entry, and the police are investigating now."

I shivered as chills swept through me. "Again, I'm very sorry for your loss." I wasn't sure what else to say.

"Thank you." Jordan's father ended the call.

I sat back down at the table. Lucy rested her head on my knee. I absently ran my fingers across her soft head.

Another life had ended. Maybe not technically on my watch, but because of what Jonah and I had been doing. Granted, I didn't know this for certain, but I had a strong hunch.

My heart broke for Jordan. So young. Oddly, she was probably around the same age as Gina. Most likely killed by the same person.

There was nothing I could do about the yearbooks now. So I would keep them. I would keep them until Jonah came home. And he *would* come home. I couldn't think otherwise. I couldn't allow the words to form in my mind.

He had to come home.

"Oh, Jonah," I said aloud. "Please come home to me. Please. I need you so much."

I wasn't hungry, but I walked to the kitchen to fix myself some scrambled eggs.

When I had finished eating, I went back to the bedroom. Talon had texted again, assuring me he and Ryan were fine. I had also missed a call on my cell phone. From Detective Ruby Lee.

Theodore Mathias's daughter.

This was all too much to deal with.

I didn't want to talk to her right now. I didn't want to talk to anyone. But she might have news that would help me find Jonah.

I pushed the button to dial her number.

"Lee," she said into the phone.

"Ruby, hi. This is Melanie Carmichael returning your call."

"Yeah, Melanie. How are you?"

Surely she hadn't called just to ask how I was. "Do you have any news on my case?" I didn't mean to be rude, but my mind was hammering and my head beginning to ache.

"No. Like I told you before, I'm not technically on your case anymore. But I wanted to call and let you know that my aunt, Erica Cates, has been released from the hospital."

My nerves jumped. "Oh?"

She cleared her throat. "Yeah. I haven't spoken to her or Rodney, but I've been keeping tabs through my connections at the hospital. She was released into her husband's care by a Dr. Miles Bennett."

Miles Bennett. The doctor who had recommended I take a leave of absence from my practice. Some recommendation. He'd all but threatened to suspend my privileges if I didn't heed his advice.

"Are they returning to Denver?"

"No. They're staying in a townhome Rodney rented in the city."

"Yeah. I've been there."

"So, I was wondering..."

"What?"

"I'm thinking of paying my aunt and uncle a visit."

"What does this have to do with me?" I didn't mean to be short with her, but my mind was full of Jonah. I couldn't focus on anything else right now.

"I was wondering if you'd like to come with me."

"I'm not sure that's the best idea. Right now I have a complaint with the medical board pending that was initiated by Rodney Cates, plus he's suing me for malpractice." Jade had given me the name of an attorney in Denver, Sherry Malone, who handled malpractice cases and was considered one of the best. Of course, whether my insurance company would agree to pay her rates was still up in the air.

"Why? Have you been told by counsel not to talk to them?"

"No..." I just didn't really want to talk to them. Especially not now, with Jonah missing.

"I understand. I was just hoping for some company. I don't have anyone else to ask."

Ruby sounded lonely. She'd been on her own for so long. Did she even have any friends?

What the hell? I wasn't any use to Jonah sitting around the house worrying. Maybe I could get some clues from the Cateses about everything else we were dealing with. All these people were interrelated somehow. "Okay, I'll go along, but there are a few things I need to tell you first."

CHAPTER THIRTY-FOUR

Jonah

"No, Brad, please! I love you!" Wendy crawled toward me even as I pointed the gun straight at her.

"Don't come any closer, you crazy-assed bitch. I'm getting out of here."

"You can't leave me. You promised we'd be together. What will I tell our child?"

She was so delusional. I wasn't sure I could get anything close to the truth out of her, but I had to try.

"Tell me about those men, Wendy. Why were they here?"

"You know why, Brad."

"Damn it! I'm not Br—" I stopped myself. It wouldn't matter. She had convinced herself that I was my father, and nothing I could say would change her lunatic mind. So far, posing as my father hadn't gotten me any information that was helpful, but maybe that would change. "No, Wendy, I *don't* know why they were here. And why did one of them keep calling me Joe?"

"I don't know. Maybe because that's your son's name."

"I have a son?"

"You have two."

Two? Had she gone back further in time to when Ryan hadn't yet been born? "What is my other son's name?" I asked.

"You know your son's name, silly." She smiled and batted her eyes.

"Humor me." I stood over her, letting the gun sag a bit in my hand. "Tell me my son's name, damn it."

"Some weird name your slut wife picked out. Talmud or something."

"Talon."

"Yes, that's it."

I stood over her, rage pouring out of me. "If you refer to my wife as a slut again, Wendy, I'll rip your throat right out of your neck."

"I'm sorry. Please. Don't leave me, Brad. I need you. Our child needs you."

"Wendy, you know I'm married. Only Daphne is having my children."

"I am. I am. I swear. I went to the doctor just the other day. He confirmed that I'm pregnant. It's going to be a boy, Brad. A boy just like you. More beautiful than your two sons with Daphne, with a shining smile and eyes that laugh. Our son will be a god."

Her words niggled at me. A boy. A Steel son that was considered the best looking and most jovial of the three.

Ryan.

No. Ryan truly was the most handsome of all of us, so he must have come from our mother. Daphne Steel was more beautiful than Wendy Madigan could ever hope to be.

Oh, God...

"Fast forward, Wendy. Tell me about our son."

"He's beautiful, just like I knew he would be. Dark eyes and hair like yours, Brad. But his eyes have a brightness that your other sons' lack. I wanted to name him. I wanted to name him, but you wouldn't let me."

"Why?"

"You had a name in mind. But you let me give him his middle name. Warren, after my father."

Warren? Ryan's middle name *was* Warren, but it had been our mother's maiden—

No, it hadn't. Our mother's maiden name was Wade. We had always been told it was Warren, and in fact, Warren was listed as her maiden name on her birth certificate and her marriage certificate. But Jade had uncovered her original birth certificate. The one in the database had been altered. Her actual name was Daphne Kay Wade. That was how we had first found out she was the half sister of Larry Wade.

No.

This could *not* be happening.

Ryan was not the spawn of my father and this crazy woman.

He looked like us, for God's sake.

But...we all looked like our father. Marjorie was the only one who looked even slightly like our mother.

No. No. No.

Our mother would never have stood for it. She never would have raised another woman's child as her own.

But our mother did as she was told... Always...

"I told them," Wendy was saying. "I told them not to take my son. Only the other one. That's why they let the little one go."

Acid slowly crept up my throat, leaving trails of flame in its wake. No. Talon had saved Ryan. That's why he hadn't been taken that day. Ryan had told the story over and over again. Talon had saved him. Saved him....

But Talon was never supposed to have been taken. That's what Larry had said.

Had Wendy been telling the truth all along? That Talon was taken by my father's enemies? And those enemies happened to be Tom Simpson and Theodore Mathias?

Larry had been lying?

I closed my eyes and inhaled, trying to get my bearings.

If what I suspected was the case, the truth lay somewhere in between.

"Wendy, are you saying you gave birth to my child?"

She nodded, sniffling. "You took my baby, Brad. You took him, and I let you. I let you because I love you and I'd do anything for you. I let you give my child to another woman to raise. That's how much I love you, Brad. But still, it wasn't enough for you. So I made sure you paid the ultimate price for your betrayal."

CHAPTER THIRTY-FIVE

Melanie

After I'd told her over the phone about Jonah being missing and the future lawmakers club, I met Ruby at her tiny apartment in the city. I'd made a conscious decision to push my worry to the back of my mind. Talon and Ryan hadn't let me go with them to search for Jonah, but maybe I could find out something by going with Ruby to see Rodney Cates. After all, he'd been a member of that strange club too.

"I can afford a decent neighborhood now," Ruby said, "but I keep my life simple. Very few possessions and a small place. I like to be able to pick up and leave quickly if I need to."

Ruby was dressed in her usual khaki pants and white shirt, one button unbuttoned at the collar. No makeup, hair pulled back tightly. No jewelry or adornments of any kind other than a chunky black watch on her left wrist. I looked closely. Nope. Even her ears weren't pierced.

"I understand." And I did. She'd been through a lot. Life hadn't been easy for her, and she didn't take anything for granted. I sighed as I took a long look at her. Compared to her life, mine had been easy. Sure, I'd gotten no love or affection from my parents, but at least I hadn't been physically abused. I'd always had a roof over my head. Plenty of books on my shelves. A chance for a top-notch education.

But Ruby? She'd done all of this herself. Starting at age fifteen.

Unreal.

"I did a little research while you drove over here," she was saying. "There's no news on the murder of Jordan Hayes, and nothing about Jonah either. I don't blame you for putting Mills and Johnson on it. They're the best. They'll find him."

"I hope so." Over twenty-four hours had passed, and no news. I was numb.

"Thank you for coming with me. I know how worried you are."

"I was wondering if we could make a stop before we see your aunt and uncle," I said.

"I suppose so. Where do you need to go?"

I pulled my wallet out of my purse and retracted the wrinkled piece of paper with some names on it. Rodney Cates had written down some information the last time Jonah and I had visited him. On this sheet of paper was the name of a woman, Marie Cooke, who had been a friend of Gina's. She had told Rodney that Gina had been in love.

Gina's suicide note, which I'd told Ruby about, had indicated she was in love with me. I wanted to talk to Marie and find out if that was true. I had a suspicion that it wasn't, and that the letter from Gina was a forgery, with the part about her being in love with me thrown in to push me further off track.

It had worked.

I handed the paper to Ruby. "Can you get an address for this name and number?"

"I can try." She called into the station. Within a few minutes, she had a home and work address.

"I hate to bother her at work," I said.

"Police business," she said. "I'll whip out my badge, and she'll cooperate."

"But she's not in any trouble."

"Of course not, but this way we won't have any trouble getting in to talk to her."

"All right." I needed the information, and there was no reason Marie wouldn't give it to me. Gina was gone.

We drove in separate cars to the real estate office where Marie worked as a receptionist. When we walked in, there she sat right in the front. She was a pleasantly attractive young woman with light-brown hair and hazel eyes.

"May I help you?" she asked us.

Ruby whipped out her badge. "I'm Detective Ruby Lee with the Grand Junction Police, and this is Dr. Melanie Carmichael. Are you Marie Cooke?"

"Yes." She bit her lip timidly.

"You're not in any trouble, ma'am," Ruby said, "but we need to speak to you. Is there a place where we can talk privately?"

"Uh...sure. I guess." She picked up her phone. "Megan? Can you cover for me for a few minutes?"

Another girl came and took over the phones.

Marie came out from behind her desk and led us to a conference room. "Is this okay?"

"Yes, this is fine," Ruby said. "We won't take up much of your time."

Marie was still looking nervous.

I smiled at her. "It's okay. You're not in any trouble, like Detective Lee said."

"All right. It's just...weird when the police come looking for you."

"I know." I patted her arm.

"We're actually here to ask about a friend of yours. Gina Cates," Ruby said.

"Oh. Gina is..."

"We know she's dead, ma'am," Ruby said.

I wanted to intervene. Ruby was just doing her job as professionally as she knew how, but her formality was freaking out Marie. I could see it in her eyes.

I looked to Ruby, and she nodded slightly. I hoped that meant I could take the lead here.

"Marie," I said, "Gina's father told us that you told him that Gina had been in love. Is that true?"

She nodded. "Yes."

"Did she tell you who she was in love with?"

"No. She didn't. It was in the beginning phase, you know? She just said it was someone she'd met recently who made her toes curl. They'd only been out together a couple of times."

A-ha! "You mean she had gone out with this...person?"

"Yes."

"Was this person a man?" I asked.

Marie smiled. "I'm assuming so. Are you asking if Gina was a lesbian? Because she wasn't. She was straight."

"We have reason to believe that Gina might have been in love with a woman. Is this something she would have told you?"

"Maybe. We were friendly, but not that close. We were really close when we were teenagers, but her father threatened me when I was about fifteen."

"Yes," Ruby said. "Gina told me about that."

"We connected again as adults, but we were never as close as we once had been. She probably would have told me if she was in love with a woman. But believe me, that wasn't Gina. Gina liked men."

"Is it possible that she could have fallen in love with a woman?" I asked. "Her therapist, maybe?"

"She was in therapy?"

"That was just hypothetical." Sometimes people didn't even tell their closest friends they were in therapy. Nothing strange about that.

"Oh. I can't say for sure about anything. Like I said, we had kind of lost touch. But Gina was straight, and she did say she had been out with this person a few times."

Good enough proof for me. Gina and I had certainly never "gone out," so Marie was talking about someone else. Whether the person was male or female didn't matter at this point.

"Thank you so much. I don't think we need anything else." I looked to Ruby.

"Yes, thank you, ma'am. We'll be in touch if we need you further." She handed a business card to Marie.

In the elevator going down, I turned to Ruby. "I hope I didn't overstep my bounds. She just seemed so uncomfortable."

"I know I take being 'businesslike' to new heights," Ruby said. "That's why I let you do the talking. It was clear she wasn't responding to me."

"Don't be afraid to be..."

"Be what?"

I laughed. "Well, I was going to say 'human,' but I didn't want you to think I was insulting you."

She joined in my laughter. "When you grow up like I did, you don't really learn the finer points of etiquette."

"I understand."

"I've just never let myself get close to anyone. At first it was a defense mechanism. If anyone got close, I'd get caught when I was underage and shipped back to my father. Later, I just got used to it. I like being alone."

"Don't be afraid of people, though. They can help."

She let out a chuckle. "You have no idea how hard it was for me to call you today and ask you to come along."

"But you did it."

"Only because the thought of facing my aunt and uncle alone scares the shit out of me. I mean, these people let their daughter get abused by my father. I haven't seen them in years."

"Are you armed?" I asked.

She pointed to her ankle. "Always."

"Good. Not that I think they'll be violent, but we don't have the muscle Jonah has. He had to get pretty tough with Rodney the last time."

Jonah. He was never far from my mind, even when I'd been talking to Marie. I'd turned on the therapist to make her comfortable and get the information I needed, but still, Jonah niggled at my mind. I couldn't turn off the worry that consumed me.

I couldn't lose him.

I just couldn't.

I *wouldn't.*

Ruby and I drove to the townhome where the Cateses were staying. A new door hung from the hinges. Jonah had cracked the old one, trying to break it down because Rodney wouldn't come to the door.

I grabbed the yearbook that I had brought with me off the dash.

"Here we are," Ruby said.

I clutched at the book. "Here we are indeed."

CHAPTER THIRTY-SIX

Jonah

My body swayed.

No! Had to stay focused. I drew the gun and aimed it at Wendy once more.

"Now you listen to me, you conniving, crazy bitch. You are going to walk me through what happened to my son. And don't you leave out one single detail, or I will put a bullet in your heart and splatter your blood on this cheap carpeting. Do we understand each other?"

She nodded timidly, and I opened my mouth to speak—

The blare of a siren pierced through the silence.

Someone had found me.

At just the wrong time.

Just as I was about to get the information out of Wendy that I needed.

I turned toward the sounds that were growing louder by the second.

"Joe?"

I turned back to Wendy.

"What are you doing here?"

I lifted my eyebrows. "What did you call me?"

"I called you Joe. Short for Jonah. Your name."

Now her sanity kicks in. Great.

"Wendy, where are we?"

"We're in my home. Of course, I no longer live here. I live with my mother in Denver now. How did I get here?"

"You really want to know? You freaking kidnapped me and brought me here. You were convinced I was my father."

She shook her head, her brow furrowing. "That doesn't make any sense. You do look just like him, though."

"You've been sending me stalking texts from some phone number in Iowa."

She shook her head. "I don't have any phone number in—"

Someone banged on the door. "Police! Open up!"

"Gladly," I said under my breath, still holding the gun. I went to the door and opened it.

Two uniformed officers stood there, their guns drawn.

"Jonah Steel?" one of them said.

"Yes."

"Are you all right?"

"Yes. She didn't harm me, other than injecting me with something. I'm recovered now."

They walked in. "Where is she?"

I laid down the weapon and gestured. "Over there."

Now Wendy was cowering in the corner. "Officers? I don't understand what's going on."

"Are you Wendy Madigan?" one asked.

"Yes. I am."

"Get to your feet, ma'am." The first officer pointed a gun at her.

"I haven't done anything wrong."

"You abducted this man, Jonah Steel. How do you think he got here otherwise?"

Her eyes misted up. "I wish I could tell you. The last

thing I remember is... I think I was in Denver with my mother. Maybe... What day is it today anyway?"

"She's got some kind of personality disorder. Or she's just a great liar," I said. "I don't know how I got here. She drugged me with something. She's been calling me by my father's name. She only just came out of the delusion now."

"Is this true, ma'am?"

She shook her head, closing her eyes. "No. I don't remember..."

"She's crazy," I said.

The first officer nodded. He put his gun in his holster and grabbed a set of handcuffs. "Wendy Madigan, I'm placing you under arrest for the abduction, drugging, and false imprisonment of Jonah Steel. You have the right to remain silent. If you choose not to remain silent, anything you say can and will be used against you. You have a right to an attorney. If you cannot afford an attorney, the court will provide one to represent you. Do you understand these rights?"

She nodded, biting her lip. I wasn't sure she understood the rights at all. Clearly she was incapacitated. Her attorney would probably get her off on some insanity plea.

"Officer," I said. "She has information I need. I was just getting her to talk when you burst in."

"We're taking her in, Mr. Steel. You can talk to her at the station. If it's okay with her attorney."

Shit. Now I might never get what I needed. She would no doubt end up in some psychiatric hospital strapped to a bed, and I might never be able to find out what had truly happened to Talon and why.

And then there was the issue of Ryan.

Part of me wanted to disbelieve Wendy. What she said

couldn't be true. But it made an eerie sort of sense.

How could my father have slept with this woman? I shook my head. He'd probably slept with her when he was in high school. That was when her obsession with him seemed to have started. She said herself that she had joined the future lawmakers club to be near him.

I heaved a sigh.

"You all right?" the second officer asked me.

"Fucking fine," I said. "Just no closer than I've ever been to the truth."

"What truth is that?" the officer asked me.

I shook my head. "Nothing. Nothing at all. How did you find me?"

"We got a tip from some PIs."

"Mills and Johnson?"

"Those are the ones. They're legendary all throughout Colorado. They charge a pretty penny."

I nodded. How well I knew.

"You sure you're okay? Should we call an ambulance for you?"

"Whatever she gave me seems to have worn off. My mind came back before my body. My vision was blurry and my legs and knees didn't work for a while, but I'm fine now, as you can see."

"Let's get you an ambulance. That way they can do a blood test on you and see what you've got in your system."

What the hell? I wasn't going to get any further hanging around here. Besides, I needed a ride.

★ ★ ★

“Chloral hydrate,” the doctor said to me. “It’s an older drug. When used with alcohol, it’s called a Mickey Finn. You’ve heard the phrase ‘slipped him a mickey,’ haven’t you?” He pointed to a tender spot on my neck. “Looks like you were injected here.”

“My vision was blurry when I woke, even though my mind was okay. I had trouble standing.”

“Dizziness is a common side effect. You’ll be okay. It’ll be out of your system soon.”

“Damn.” I shook my head. “I can’t believe somebody got into my house and did all this.”

“Do you have a security system?”

“Yes. But I was up. I had turned it off. Why can’t I remember any of this happening?”

“Retrograde amnesia. It’s pretty common. People sometimes lose the few minutes before an attack.”

I shook my head again.

“The good news is there’s no evidence of any other bodily injury.”

So I hadn’t been beaten or raped. I supposed that *was* good news, given what our family had already been through.

“How long do I need to stay here?”

“I don’t see any reason to keep you. You’re obviously fine. The drug will leave your system on its own.”

“Good. Is there a phone around here? I have some calls I need to make.”

CHAPTER THIRTY-SEVEN

Melanie

Ruby knocked on the door of the townhome. "Rodney Cates? Open up. Police."

No response. Not that I expected one.

She banged on the door again. "Open up, or we'll force our way in."

A few seconds later, the doorknob turned.

Rodney Cates stood there. "You don't look like a police officer to me. Where's your uniform?"

"I guess you don't recognize me"—Ruby pulled out her badge—"Uncle Rodney."

He took the badge from her and stared at it. "Detective Ruby Lee." He looked back at Ruby. "Shit, you're Theo's daughter."

"I am. I think you know Dr. Carmichael?"

Rodney glared at me. "What are you doing here? You have no right to be here. I just brought Erica home."

"Good," Ruby said. "I have a few words for you and for her."

"She's not in any condition—"

Ruby grabbed the badge from Rodney's hand and pushed him out of the way, entering the townhome. I did a double take. She was a completely different person in the line of duty.

I followed her in, clasping the yearbook to my chest.

"We have some questions, Uncle Rodney."

"Look, whatever you think is going on, I assure you that Erica and I are not involved."

"Really? Two people are wanted for murder and a host of other crimes right now—two people you knew very well at one time. One of them is your brother-in-law, my father, the man who raped my cousin, which led directly to her death."

"Gina's suicide is no business of yours."

"Isn't it? My father tried to do the same thing to me, as you know. And at this point, we're questioning whether Gina actually did kill herself."

"What are you saying?"

"We think she might've been murdered."

He rolled his eyes. I scanned his features. An eye roll wasn't what I had expected from a distraught father. I walked closer, still clutching the yearbook to my chest.

He regarded me. "What do you have there?"

I handed the book to Ruby. She turned to the relevant page, the photo of the future lawmakers club.

"I want you to take a look at this." She pointed. "That is Theodore Mathias, my father. That is Tom Simpson, who is also wanted right now on charges of kidnapping, raping, and torturing a ten-year-old boy. That is Larry Wade, currently incarcerated and awaiting trial on those same charges. And that, Uncle Rodney, is you."

"Where the hell did you get this?"

"I'm thinking you might already know. A poor woman is dead because of this yearbook."

"I don't know what you're talking about."

"You don't? Then I think I will be going into the bedroom

there to talk to my aunt. I have a feeling she'll be a little more talkative than you are."

"You know I'm not going to allow that."

"That's fine. I can make her talk to me. I can take you both down to the station for questioning. Then you'll have to talk to me."

"You don't have anything on me. Or Erica."

"I don't have to have anything on you. Your brother-in-law is a wanted man. Taking you to the station for questioning is standard procedure."

"Erica is not in any condition—"

"I don't rightly care. I came here for information, and I aim to get it. Now we can either do it here or at the station."

"Fine." Rodney sighed. "I don't want *her* here." He pointed to me.

"No, you don't get to make the rules. She stays." Ruby walked through the living room and into the kitchen. "Let's all sit at the table."

I followed her, determined to be strong. I didn't know what Rodney's connection was to Talon's abductors, other than being the brother-in-law of one and being in the same club as they were decades ago, but I knew one thing. Whatever the connection was, it wasn't going to be good.

We sat at the table, and Ruby slid the yearbook in front of Rodney. "I need to know about this club. What was the purpose of it?"

"It's pretty simple. The club was exactly what it says it was. For future lawmakers. People who wanted to go into law, whether as an attorney, or legislator, or lobbyist. Politicians."

"Doesn't it seem a little strange that three of these people are criminals? We already have Larry Wade in custody."

"Larry Wade is a creep."

"I can't fault your observation. Why were you in the club?"

"None of your damned business."

"I think it is. You're a linguistics professor. You didn't go into lawmaking of any kind."

"I don't have to tell you anything."

Ruby looked at her chunky black watch. "I suppose you don't. But I'm not leaving here without what I came for, and I don't have anywhere to be. Do you, Melanie?"

"No." I gathered my courage and looked Rodney Cates in his eyes. "I don't have anywhere to be. You made sure of that."

"Look, you let my daughter die. I was well within my rights to file a grievance and a lawsuit against you."

"We're actually not here to talk about that," Ruby said. "We're here to find out the link between Larry Wade, Tom Simpson, and Theodore Mathias. They have obviously known each other for a long time, and they got into some really bad shit. You're going to tell me why."

Rodney started to tremble. "I can't."

"Why the hell not?"

"They'll kill me."

Now we were getting somewhere. It was time for me to bring in my psychological expertise.

"Look, Dr. Cates," I said. "I know what you think of me. You're wrong, but I understand why you think it. Right now Jonah Steel is missing. We're pretty sure that some members of this club are responsible."

"I don't have anything against the Steels, except for the fact that one of them barged in here recently with you in tow, Doctor."

"Jonah had his reasons."

"I'm sure he thought he did. Didn't stop me from having to replace the door."

"He paid for that door and then some. Right now he is missing, and we're worried about him."

"He's getting what he deserves."

"I thought you just said you didn't have anything against the Steels."

"I don't. Except for that one."

"Rodney," Ruby said, pulling her bad cop routine. "I'm about this close"—she gestured with two fingers—"to dragging you down to the station. In fact, I'm thinking I might have you arrested."

"What for?"

"For not cooperating with an investigation. We have a missing person here. This is serious business."

"For God's sake. What do you want to know about that stupid club?"

"What it was. What it truly was," Ruby said, putting her feet on the table. "And I have all fucking day, Uncle."

As I prepared to hear what Rodney Cates would say, my phone buzzed.

CHAPTER THIRTY-EIGHT

Jonah

The hospital no longer had a pay phone, but since I didn't have my wallet, I wouldn't have been able to pay for a call anyway. The doctor let me go into his office and use his phone.

I needed to call someone to pick me up, probably Talon or Ryan. But first, I had to call Melanie and let her know I was all right.

I dialed the number. No response.

"Damn," I said aloud.

I tried again. This time I got a "Hello?"

"Melanie?"

"Jonah! Where are you? Are you all right?"

"I'm okay, sweetheart. It's a long story. I'm at Valleycrest."

"The hospital? What's wrong? Oh my God."

"Baby, calm down. I'll tell you everything."

"I'm here in the city, Jonah. I'll come to you. I can be there quickly."

"What are you doing in the city?"

"It's a long story. I'll tell you when I get there."

★ ★ ★

I was sitting in the waiting area when Melanie shot through the door to the emergency room about fifteen minutes later. She ran straight to me and launched herself into my waiting arms.

"I've been so worried. Where have you been? What happened to you?"

"I'll tell you everything, baby, but first let's get out of here. I want to go home."

After we'd gotten confirmation that Talon and Ryan were fine and were heading back to the ranch, we got on our way as well. Melanie insisted on driving, even though I felt fine. As we drove, I told her what had happened with Wendy Madigan.

"You were right," she said. "You were right to be suspicious of her."

"You don't know how right."

"What else happened?"

"She claimed that she..." How could I even say this? Telling Melanie would somehow make it real.

"She claimed what?"

I sighed. "Melanie, she claimed that she is Ryan's mother."

Melanie dropped her mouth open. "What?"

"I know. It's hard to believe. She's probably lying. But damn, what she said made some sense. I don't want to believe it, but I'll find the truth somehow. I can't tell Ryan until I know for sure."

"I can't imagine that your mother would've allowed your father to raise a bastard son in her home."

"That was my first thought as well, but there's no denying my father was the boss. I've told you before what a sexist my father was. He kept my mother in the house, doing wifely things. She never fought him on anything. No one ever fought him until Marjorie got old enough to help on the ranch. She let him have it, and my father finally relented. She claimed she was as good as any boy, and she was right."

"Still, it's hard to believe that your mother would be willing to raise a child that wasn't hers." Melanie bit her lip. "Besides, didn't Marj and Jade find all of your birth certificates? I assume Ryan's showed the same mother and father as the rest of yours did."

"Yeah, they did. But we already know that my mother's birth certificate has been tampered with, changing her maiden name to Warren, when her real name was Wade. Whoever did that could have easily tampered with Ryan's as well, putting my mother's name on the certificate."

She nodded.

"Somehow, someone hacked into whatever database they needed at the time. I mean, look at what they did just recently. Changing Larry's fingerprints in the attorney database to whoever's fingerprints were on that damned business card we found in Jade's room. These aren't your garden-variety hackers. It's almost as if..."

"What?" she asked.

"I just can't wrap my mind around it. Tom Simpson or Larry Wade or the other one... They can't have that kind of knowledge."

"It's unlikely. But maybe. Or maybe they hired someone to do it for them."

"Hackers of that caliber cost a lot of money, Melanie. Look at Mills and Johnson."

She nodded again. "You don't think..."

"That Mills and Johnson are working for Simpson and Mathias?" I shook my head. "No. I'm pretty sure they aren't. I mean, it was the police who referred us to them."

"That doesn't always mean anything," she said. "Tom Simpson had been a respected man in Snow Creek, and look who he turned out to be."

I raised my eyebrows. Melanie had a point. A good point.

And speaking of Tom Simpson...

I owed Bryce a phone call. Of course, he might not answer. Who could blame him? But at this point, I could back up my claim. I wasn't looking forward to telling my best friend that I now had proof that his father was a psychopathic iceman.

After we arrived home and let Lucy out, my phone buzzed in my back pocket. Speak of the devil. I looked at Melanie. "You mind? It's Bryce."

"Of course not. But are you sure you're up to talking to him right now?"

"I'll be fine. I need to see what he wants." I put the phone to my ear. "Hey, Bryce."

"Hey, Joe." His voice cracked.

"What's up?"

"God... Where to start? I guess I'll just start with this. I'm sorry, man."

"You don't have anything to be sorry about," I said.

"But I do. I got some disturbing news from those PIs I hired. And I have only one question for you."

"What's that?"

"Why the hell didn't you come to me, man? I had to hear this from PIs, when you were directly involved."

I swallowed. "Hey, the way our last conversation went... Plus, I've been a little busy. I was kidnapped by a crazy woman."

Bryce gasped through the phone. "What?"

"I'm good. I'm okay. It's a long fucking story, man."

"Well, when we're both feeling better, let's get together for drinks. For now, though... God, Joe, what the hell am I supposed to tell my mother?"

I sighed. "Just tell her the truth. There's not much else you can do. At least she'll know something so she can stop worrying about where he is."

"It's just so fucking unreal. How could I have lived with this man for the better part of my life and not know who he was? And my mother? How..."

"Look, I hear you. I just found out that my own father probably isn't who I thought he was either. He's dead, so I may never be able to figure it out. People hide things, Bryce. My family was great at it. They hid what happened to Talon. They hid the fact that my mom was related to Larry Wade. And now..." I couldn't form the words. I had been about to spill the beans about Ryan's possible parentage. No way could I do that until I had solid proof. And Ryan would have to be the first to hear it from my lips.

"Have you heard anything about Colin Morse?" Bryce asked. "How is he doing?"

Damn. I had all but forgotten about Jade's ex-fiancé. So much else had been going on. "I haven't checked in on him in a few days, but I will. I'll let you know."

"Did my father...rape him?"

"I can't beat around the bush on this, Bryce. Yes. In all likelihood, your father raped him. I'm pretty sure Theodore Mathias did as well."

"Who's Theodore Mathias?"

"Boy, we do have a lot to catch up on."

"You want to go for that drink now?" Bryce asked.

"I can't. I was drugged, and it's still in my system a little bit. I don't want to add any alcohol."

"Damn, Joe, what the hell is going on?"

"I told you. I was kidnapped."

"By whom?"

"Wendy Madigan."

"The newswoman?"

"Yes. The newswoman. And apparently my father's mistress."

"No way. Your father would never—"

"Stop right there. That's what you told me about your father. Remember?"

"You're right. Maybe neither of our fathers were who we thought they were." He cleared his throat. "Joe, I'm scared. I mean, I've got his psychopathic DNA in my genes."

"That doesn't mean anything."

"Easy for you to say."

"Look, my mother was mentally ill, and God knows who my father was at this point. DNA has nothing to do with who we are."

"How can you say that?"

I stayed silent. How *could* I say that? For all I knew, one day I would snap like my mother had. And Bryce? But I would appease him. At least until I knew what I was talking about. "Look, your dad was involved in this shit when he was way younger than you are now. You're a good man, Bryce. You've got nothing to worry about."

"I hope you're right."

"If it'll make you feel better, go have a psychological evaluation."

I'd be doing that myself. Luckily I had my own live-in psychotherapist standing right next to me.

"Look, man, I need to run. Are you going to be okay?"

"It's just so much to handle," Bryce said.

"It is. But I'm here for you. Always. We'll get together soon enough for that drink. I have a whole shitload of other stuff to tell you."

"Yeah. All right. Take care of yourself, Joe."

"You too, buddy." I ended the call and turned to Melanie. "Go downstairs. Now."

CHAPTER THIRTY-NINE

Melanie

I arched my eyebrows at Jonah. “Are you sure you’re ready for this right now?”

He regarded me sternly, his dark eyes afire. “Don’t question me. I said get downstairs. Now.”

I wanted to please him. More than anything I did. But right now I was still consumed with worry over him, plus I wanted to check in with Ruby. I had left her at Rodney Cates’s house after she assured me she would be fine. She was armed and a trained police officer, but still, I was a bit worried. I hadn’t been able to stick around to hear what Rodney was going to tell her. It had been more important for me to go to Jonah.

I opened my mouth to argue with Jonah again, but his eyes told me he was not about to take no for an answer.

I was determined to please him, and I knew he would never harm me. So I would do as he asked. He needed me, and I would be there for him.

I turned toward the door to the basement.

His deep, dark voice invaded my thoughts. “Be naked when I get down there. Kneeling by the bed.”

Without looking back at him, I nodded and continued toward the door.

I walked down the stairs slowly and flipped on the light

switch in the rec room. Again, slowly, I walked toward the closed door to the dungeon and opened it.

"Oh!"

Lavender buds were spread over the bed, and a plant sat on the table next to the bed. I inhaled the fragrant scent. He had done this for me after our last encounter, to make the room better for me. My God, I loved him so much.

A lavender pillar candle sat on the table next to the bed. Two tapers sat next to it.

My nipples tightened. Was he planning to use the candles on me? The idea of warm wax dribbling over my nipples...

Would it be too hot?

Or would it be warm and sensual?

I secretly hoped it would be a combination of both.

I removed my clothes, remembering his order, and set them on a settee at the foot of the bed. I hid my beige cotton panties under my jeans. He'd told me never to wear them in this room. I hadn't meant to disobey, but I hadn't exactly had the chance to go shopping for new underwear either. He'd said he'd make sure I had plenty of new stuff, but then he had disappeared.

Once naked, I knelt at the side of the bed. I didn't know how long it would take Jonah to come down, but he was clearly in a mood to take control. It made perfect sense. He had just been in a situation where he had no control. Now he needed to exert it.

And I would let him.

I didn't turn when I felt his footsteps jar the floor. He'd told me to kneel, and I would do so until otherwise instructed.

"Do you like the lavender, Melanie?"

I still did not turn. "I love it. Thank you, Jonah."

His fingers tangled in my hair. "You're welcome."

Still, I did not turn.

"Do you have any idea how beautiful you look right now? Kneeling, ready to do whatever I ask of you? Your lovely blond hair flowing down toward the small of your back? Your creamy shoulders, the swell of your hips, the beautiful cleavage of your ass. You're stunning."

I bit my lip. "Thank you."

The word "sir" sat right on my tongue. He had never asked me to call him "sir," but I had done some research on Dominant and submissive relationships. Most Dominants required their subs to address them as "sir" during play. I wasn't sure how I felt about that, but at the moment, saying it felt natural. Still, I would wait until instructed to do so.

"You may rise, Melanie. Turn to face me."

I complied, the soft fibers of the carpet making an indentation on my knees. I turned to face my lover. He had already taken off his shirt, his boots, and socks. He stood, wearing only his jeans, his bronze chest glowing, the musculature of his abdomen a beauty to behold.

"We haven't talked about a safe word yet," he said.

I'd read about safe words. Most people in these types of relationships had them.

"I want you to say 'red' if you want me to stop. Like a red traffic light."

I nodded.

"Say 'yellow' if you're getting a little uncomfortable but you don't want me to stop yet. Like a yellow light. Do you understand?"

"Yes," I said.

"Good." He cupped my cheek, thumbing it lovingly. "Now,

remove my jeans, Melanie. Then kneel and suck my cock."

I looked down and fumbled with his belt.

He touched my forearm. "Look into my eyes. Look into my eyes as you undress me."

Looking into his eyes didn't seem like a submissive thing to do, but he was the boss. I glued my gaze to his, the smoke in his deep, dark eyes heating me. My fingers trembled slightly as I unbuckled his belt and then unzipped his jeans. I slid them over his hips, following with his boxer briefs.

His cock, so large and majestic, jutted out at me, and a pearl of pre-cum glistened on the tip. I licked it off of him, letting the saltiness sit on my tongue. I inhaled. So musky and masculine, so spicy and perfect. I stuck my tongue out again, teasing the head of his cock.

"You're so beautiful, Jonah," I said. And then I gasped. Was I allowed to speak?

He did not berate me. "You're beautiful too, Melanie, but never so beautiful as when those ruby lips are around my cock." He grabbed the back of my head, taking a fistful of my blond hair. "Suck me. Suck me hard."

I had sucked his cock many times before, but his size was always hard to take. Still, I wanted to please him more than anything, so I wrapped my lips over his engorged shaft.

I slid my lips forward until the head of his cock nudged the back of my throat. Still I was only little more than halfway over his length. I would have to get better at this.

But his groans told me I was doing all right.

"Yeah, baby. Suck me. God, this is good."

I slid my lips back, teasing the head once again, and then slid them forward, taking slightly more. I grasped him at the base, moving my fist with my mouth. I sank down upon him again, relishing his moans and groans. His hand was still wrapped in my hair. Still, he was careful not to move my head. I almost wanted him to.

I pulled backward for a moment and then used my tongue and lips to tease the underside, going down to his balls, nibbling and kissing. Again I inhaled his musky fragrance. Such a wonderful masculine scent. I nipped the inside of the thighs, giving him tiny kisses, and then moved back to his cock where I sucked him deeply once again.

This time he did grab my head and pulled me toward him. He was careful, though, and I didn't gag. Above me, he groaned, moaned, urged me on, my name a sweet caress from his lips.

"Melanie... Melanie... Melanie."

His whisper enchanted my ears, spurring me on to take him deeper, ever so deeper, into my throat.

He groaned above me and then pulled my head off of him.

"No, not this way." He pulled me to my feet and slid his fingers between my legs. "Are you wet for me, sweet Melanie?"

I sighed. My nipples were hard little berries, my body coated in perspiration, my clit throbbing, and my pussy itching to be filled.

"Yes." He raised his fingers to his mouth and slid his tongue out to lick off my moisture. "So wet, baby. So fucking wet."

I bit my lip. Was I allowed to speak? I couldn't help myself. "Stick your finger inside me, Jonah. Please."

"All in good time. Your pussy will get satisfied. But tonight I'm going to take you in that sacred place you've saved only for me."

My muscles clenched. He had used an anal plug on me before, and the sensation had been pleasurable. But his cock was so huge. I wasn't sure I could handle it.

"I'm going to lick the cream out of your pussy, and then I'll get your ass ready for me. Get on the bed."

I did as I was told, climbing onto the bed on my hands and knees, hoping I looked seductive. I inhaled the fresh lavender buds. Hopefully they would help me relax, to get ready for what would be a big invasion.

"Good, baby." He gave my ass a quick slap.

The heat from his stinging hand warmed me.

"This ass is mine. Only mine. And I'm going to claim my prize tonight."

CHAPTER FORTY

Jonah

My cock was hard and throbbing between my legs. How I wanted to plunge into that tight little asshole, but I had to wait. I had to get her ready for me first. This was too soon. I knew that in my heart. But I needed her ass tonight. I needed the control so badly. I needed to take what was mine.

I gave her ass another slap, and the pink spread across her creamy skin like a wildfire taking a dried forest. The heat, the sting—I felt every bit of it in my own hand and my own body like boiling honey flowing through me.

I inhaled, and her pussy juice wafted up—sweet pears and Granny Smith apples, sweet musky female. Sweet Melanie.

I spread her ass cheeks and shoved my tongue into her cunt. She squirmed against me, groaning, moaning.

"You like that, baby?" I said against her folds. "You like when I lick that hot pussy of yours?"

"Yes," she moaned. "Lick me, please."

I slid my tongue between her folds again, tasting her, sucking out that succulent cream. Then I slid my tongue up to that sweet little puckered hole that was mine. All mine.

I lubed it up good with my saliva and massaged it with my tongue. She squirmed under me, moaning, groaning, begging for more.

More I would give her. I grabbed a bottle of lube I had set aside and opened it. I poured some into my palm to warm it, and then I rubbed it over her little asshole. Again I massaged her with my finger. "Relax, baby. Relax." I breached the tight muscle with my index finger.

She gasped for a second but then relaxed. Her ass was still pink from the slaps, and although I longed to get in a few more, I decided it was best to concentrate on getting her ready for my dick.

"So tight, baby. So tight around my finger." I moved my finger in and out slowly. "I'm going to add another finger now, okay?"

I stroked her gently...and then eased my middle finger into her tight heat.

The graduated sizes of anal plugs sat next to the bottle of lube. I had given her a small one the last time. My intention had been to ease her in slowly, taking the medium, and then the large. But I couldn't wait. I needed her now. I needed to take her, claim her, have her surrender fully to me.

I grabbed the medium-sized plug.

It would be a stretch for her, but she could do it. I had faith.

"I'm going to use a plug on you, sweetheart. It's a little bigger than the one I used last time, but you can do it."

Already she tensed up. I could see her cheeks clench, feel it in my fingers still inside her ass.

"Don't be scared. I'd never hurt you."

Although I couldn't see her face, I knew she was chewing on her lip. Was I going too far? Should I stop?

No. I needed her. I needed this submission from her, and I needed it tonight. She would tell me if I had to stop. I would, if she told me to. But God, I hoped she let me go where I needed to go.

"Okay, baby?" I said.

"Yes. Okay."

How I loved her. She was so good to me, so ready to give me whatever I needed whenever I needed it. I didn't deserve her, and I couldn't do this to her now.

I removed my fingers.

She turned and looked over her shoulder at me. "Jonah?"

"I'm sorry. I'm not worthy of you, Melanie. I wasn't thinking of you at all. Only myself. You're not ready for this."

She turned and sat, facing me. She cupped my cheek and softly caressed it. "I'm ready for whatever you need, my love, whenever you need it. I am here for you, just like I know you'd be here for me."

I closed my eyes. What a wonderful woman she was. "I can't."

She smiled at me. "You can. I want you to. I know you won't hurt me. I know you'll get me ready. I want to give you this gift, and I want to give it to you now, when you so desperately need it. That is the joy of giving to someone you love."

I placed my hand over hers still on my cheek. Her skin was warm, her touch soothing. "Thank you," I whispered.

She smiled again and returned to her hands and knees. "Take what you need from me, Jonah. I love you, and I'm here for you."

I kissed the small of her back and then reached for the lube. I warmed some in my palm again and massaged it onto her anus. She was already dilated a bit from my fingers, so I went straight for the medium plug. I nudged it against her. "This will be tight, baby. But relax, and you'll be okay."

She inhaled and then exhaled slowly, and upon her

exhale, I pushed the plug inside her. She inhaled quickly and then exhaled again.

"Good. Just like that. You'll get used to it." I eyed the large plug still sitting on the bed. It was a far cry from the circumference of my dick, but I had faith. She knew how large I was, and she wanted to do this for me.

And for that I loved her. Very much.

I owed her so much, and one thing I could do for her while she got used to the medium plug was give her tight little pussy the orgasm she so richly deserved. I turned her over gently, pushed her thighs forward, and dived into her wet heat.

She was so, so wet. I slid my tongue across her folds and lapped up her juice. So sweet and spicy and musky all at once. I nipped at her clit, and she moaned, arching against the lavender-scented bed. She gasped, clawing at the bed covers, the lavender buds jumping around as she gyrated.

I thrust two fingers into her wet channel, and she clamped around them, her climax taking her.

"Jonah, oh my. So good. My ass. I feel it in my ass."

"That's right, baby. It's good. Make it feel good." I continued to suck on her clit as she soared higher. "You're going to have many more orgasms before this night is over."

I turned her back over gently onto her knees. Her scent wafted up at me, making my groin tighten even further. The sight of the plug in her ass made me so hot, I wanted to yank it out and take her there. But I had promised I would make it good for her, and I would.

I gently removed the plug and added more lube. I massaged around the rim with my fingers, murmuring gentle words to her.

And then I picked up the large-sized plug.

"Do what you did again. Breathe in, and then breathe out."

When I heard her exhale, I pushed the large plug into her ass.

This time she gasped.

"Easy, baby. You'll get used to it. And once you do, I'm going to turn you over and suck on your sweet nipples. Would you like that?"

"Yes," she breathed.

"Relax. Unclench. Let it happen."

She let out a soft whisper of a breath. Once her body became less rigid, I turned her over again, pushed her thighs forward so she wouldn't be uncomfortable, and slid between her legs. I took one hard nipple between my lips and tugged on it.

"Yes," she moaned.

I twisted the other nipple between my thumb and forefinger while I sucked on the first. I sucked hard, the way she liked it, and she rewarded me with a groan, arching her back into me.

"Your nipples are so beautiful, baby. So responsive. I could suck on them forever." And that was no lie. Her body was gorgeous to me, the most dazzling thing I'd ever laid eyes on. I wanted nothing more than to worship her all over from dusk until dawn. And part of worshipping her was giving her all pleasures I could extract from her body, including a certain pleasure that was going to be wonderful for both of us.

"Jonah, it feels so...good."

"I love your breasts," I whispered against her soft skin. "I love every part of your body. But most of all I love you."

"I love you too," she whispered. "So much."

"I want to move down to your pussy now, baby. I want to

make you come again. But I want you to twist your nipples for me. Put your fingers on them. Make them feel good for me."

I slid down her soft abdomen, inhaled the musk of her blond curls, and then slid my tongue through her wet folds once more. As I watched, she took her tight buds between her slender fingers and squeezed them, sighing.

"You look so beautiful right now, touching yourself. God, I love you."

She sighed again.

I shoved my tongue into her wet cunt, and then I nibbled on her clit and inserted my fingers once more.

I looked up at her again. She was so beautiful, twisting her nipples, pinching them. Her breasts were red, almost as if I had slapped them. I felt that red heat in my body, and my dick grew harder.

I wanted to be inside her tight asshole, embedded balls deep. I almost came right then and there thinking about it. But no. First I owed her another orgasm.

I rubbed my fingers against the interior wall of her vagina, finding the spot that made her go crazy. The G-spot.

She tightened up as I flicked my tongue over her clit. And then the spasms began.

I finger-fucked her harder, rubbing against her G-spot, and to my surprise, something sprinkled my face.

She had squirted.

Melanie had squirted. I had never made a woman squirt before, and oh my God, I was turned on.

"Baby, that's so hot."

"My God, Jonah. This orgasm... It's like nothing else..."

"You're having a G-spot orgasm. Along with the clitoral orgasm. You're squirting."

"Oh... I'm sorry..."

"No, baby. It's hot." I rubbed against her spongy G-spot furiously. "Come again for me."

And she did. As though she were responding to my command.

I had to have her. Soon. I was tempted to shove my cock inside her wet pussy and relieve myself, but I was determined to have her ass. This climax that was coiling up inside me was going to release inside that tight paradise. I continued to rub her G-spot until she finally started easing down.

"Enough," she said. "I... I can't take..."

I couldn't help a small chuckle. "That's the way I like you, baby. Sated. Unable to take one more ounce of pleasure. But I promise you, more pleasure is yet to come."

CHAPTER FORTY-ONE

Melanie

That pleasure he was talking about... I knew where we were going next, and although I wanted this more than I wanted anything because I knew he needed it, I still couldn't help being a bit apprehensive. The anal plugs had been painful at first, but Jonah had been right. I had stretched to accommodate them.

But the only plug left was...him.

And he was so much bigger and so much longer than any of the plugs.

I understood it would hurt. I understood that the tight ring of muscle was the hardest part to get through and the pain would subside after that.

But still, I trembled.

I raised my head and looked at Jonah. His brow line was saturated with perspiration, his dark hair sticking to his forehead and cheeks. His chin and lips were glistening with my juices, as were his shoulders and neck. How much had I squirted?

His eyes were heavy lidded, smoky.

He was beautiful, yet that word wasn't adequate. He transcended beauty as he looked at me. If only a word existed to adequately describe him. But language was limited. Magnificent wasn't enough. Gorgeous, beautiful, handsome—

none of them were enough.

I hoped he could read what I wanted to say in the look I was giving him, in the love I was feeling as I gazed upon his strong and brilliant form.

"I love you, Melanie," he said, his eyes dark with desire.

"I love you too, Jonah."

"I'm going to turn you over now. I'm going to take what I need from you. If at any time—"

I stopped him with a gesture. "I want this. I want this as much as you do. It's important to me."

He gently turned me over, my ass in the air, the large plug still embedded inside.

"I'm going to take the plug out of you now, baby. I'll give you a little more lube." He sighed. "Do you have any idea how much this means to me? How much *you* mean to me?"

I did know. I knew exactly how much it meant to him, because it meant the same to me. Was it anything I ever thought I would do? No. But I knew in the depths of my soul that I would enjoy it as much as he would, because I was doing it for him.

I would do anything for him.

I felt the tips of his fingers massaging me. I felt the moisture of the lube.

And then the tip of his cock nudged at the entrance to my foreign place.

"Do the same thing, baby. Breathe in and then out."

I complied, and—

A scream ripped from my throat.

His strong hands massaged my cheeks. "Easy. I'm in. All the way. You tell me when I can move."

"I'm sorry." I nodded. "I didn't mean to scream."

"It's okay. I know I'm a lot to take. You will get used to me. I promise you, once you're used to the fullness, this is going to be so much pleasure for you."

I wasn't naïve. I knew people enjoyed anal sex. I enjoyed him fingering me. I had even grown to enjoy the plugs. And I was determined to enjoy this. It was a gift I could only give once, and I was so glad I was giving it to Jonah right now.

He was doing this my way, even though it was something he wanted. He hadn't bound me, and he had only smacked me a few times. He was being purposefully gentle, and while I appreciated it, I didn't want him to feel like he couldn't be himself, couldn't do what he needed to do.

After this first time, I would voice that. But not now.

Right now, I focused on my body, focused on the fullness within me, willed my body to accept the invasion, willed my body to feel the pleasure it was meant to feel.

And once I relaxed, once I accepted that this was Jonah inside me—Jonah, whom I loved more than anything—the invasion began to feel...right.

Wicked, yes. Forbidden, oh yes. But right. Dark and dangerous and right.

Just like life with Jonah would always be.

Dark and dangerous and right.

"You doing okay, baby?" he asked.

I unclenched my teeth from my lip. "Yes. You can move now. I want you to." No truer words had ever left my lips.

Slowly I felt him pull out of me, and then he slowly pushed back in.

The burn. Oh, that glorious burn.

"Again," I said, my voice low. "Please. Again."

He pulled out and shoved back in a little more quickly.

And oh my God, I tingled, my nerves racing throughout every cell in my body and somehow culminating between my legs.

I was feeling it in my pussy. How was that possible? But I was. I was feeling my pussy get wet, I was feeling the need to have it filled, yet I didn't want him to take his cock from my ass.

Meanwhile, he pulled out and thrust back in again.

And before I knew it, I was on the verge of yet another orgasm.

How could this—

"Oh!"

"Good, baby?"

I moaned. "How is this possible? After all those orgasms. How can this be?"

"Because it's you. Because it's me. Thank you. Thank you for this. Ah!"

Drops of sweat, presumably from his forehead, dripped onto my back, each one leaving a tiny bonfire in its wake.

He stayed in me for a few timeless seconds and then withdrew.

Oh, the emptiness.

But I smiled to myself. I knew I wouldn't be empty for long, and in my heart, the most important place, I would never be empty again.

Jonah crawled up next to me on the bed and pulled me into his arms. "Thank you so much for that."

"Thank you," I said back.

"What are you thanking me for?"

"For showing me something new. For wanting to experience this with me."

"You're so amazing," he said. "There's no one in the world

like you."

I couldn't help a chuckle at that. "Girls like me are a dime a dozen."

He pulled my face toward him and gazed straight into my eyes. "You're wrong, Melanie. There is no one else in the world like you. You are worth everything to me."

I saw the truth of his words in his eyes. And I hoped he saw the truth of them back in my own.

I leaned toward him and brushed my lips across his. He was salty from sweat. Both of us were coated in shiny dew. I let out a little chuckle. "I think we're kind of a mess."

He laughed with me. "But a good mess. A very good mess." He stroked my damp hair. "Let's clean up a little, and then I think we need a date in the hot tub."

"Oh?"

"Yes. You might have some soreness, and it will help."

"All right. If you think it's for the best. As long as you promise no one will walk in on us."

That got a big laugh out of Jonah. "Now why on earth would you think that might happen again?"

"Can you name a time when it hasn't happened?"

"No. But this bad luck streak has to break sometime."

★ ★ ★

Jonah had poured us each a glass of water with lemon, and we sat in the hot tub, holding hands. I leaned my head back against the railing and closed my eyes, inhaling the steam rising above us.

I opened my eyes and found him staring at me. "What?" I said.

"Just enjoying the view." He smiled and then took a sip of his water.

I moved toward him, to snuggle into his arms, when–

"Joe?"

The voice came from the deck. I hadn't heard the door open.

I let out a maniacal laugh. At this point, it had become more humorous than embarrassing. Talon, Jade, and Jonah's friend Bryce had all seen me naked.

Jonah turned. "Bryce? What are you doing here?"

"I'm really sorry to interrupt you."

"It's all right," I said, still giggling.

"What is it?" Jonah asked.

"I told my mother tonight, Joe. It didn't go well."

CHAPTER FORTY-TWO

Jonah

I sighed. "Bryce, I'm sorry, man. Can we talk later?"

Melanie stepped out of the hot tub, smiling and not seeming embarrassed. She wrapped herself in a towel. "It's all right. Talk to him. He clearly needs you."

She was so damned wonderful.

"I'm going to take a shower," she continued.

"Actually," Bryce said. "I'd love it if you would stay. I need some...psychological advice."

She smiled again. "I'll be right out. Just let me rinse off. Why don't the two of you have a drink in the family room?"

I got out of the tub, wrapped a towel around myself, and nodded to Bryce. "Let me get some sweats on. Fix us a couple of drinks. I'll only be a minute." I headed into the house and to my bedroom, dried off, and put on some sweats and a T-shirt. I went to the family room. Bryce had pulled a beer out of the bar fridge for himself and was mixing up a CapRock martini for me. Good man.

Bryce was a mess. His silver-blond hair was in disarray, and his flannel western shirt was half untucked. Not that he was into extreme grooming, but he was usually not this unkempt.

"I had to take my mom into the city to see her sister. You know, Luke's mom. She wanted to tell my Aunt Vickie what had gone on, my father's role in Luke's murder." He shook his head. "When we got there, she couldn't even talk, man. I had to take her to the hospital. Aunt Vickie still doesn't know anything, and she's worried sick now about Mom. I brought Henry home so he could sleep in his own crib."

"Who's with him now?"

"Your sister."

"Really?" Marj had never been the babysitting type.

"Yeah. I ran into her at the grocery store when I got back from the city. Henry was out of formula. I told her I needed to talk to you, and she offered to watch Henry for me."

"She knows everything."

"Yeah. I figured she did." He attempted a smile. "Henry took to her right away. I'm sure they're doing fine. He's probably in bed by now."

"Why don't you text her and check on him? That way we can talk free of worries."

"Good idea." Bryce got his phone.

I took a sip of my martini while he was texting. Poor Bryce. Although I was unsure about my own father's involvement in this whole mess, at least I was pretty sure he wasn't as messed up as the other three. The worst he had done so far was befriend a group of degenerates in high school, possibly impregnate a mistress, and sweep his son's abduction and torture under the rug. Not good stuff by any means, but Bryce's father was a child molester, rapist, and murderer.

Damn.

Bryce put his phone away and took a drink of his beer. "Henry's good. Marjorie says he went right to sleep after she fed him."

I guess I didn't know everything about my baby sister.

She'd never struck me as the motherly type.

"Good," I said. "So tell me about Evelyn."

"I hated doing this to her, Joe. It about killed me. Every time I have to think about it, say the words, I die a little bit more all over again. And telling my mother, the woman who raised me, that her husband is... What is he, anyway? What kind of words are there for the man who is my father?"

"I don't know." I shook my head, swirling my martini glass on the wooden bar. "I wish I had some words of wisdom for you, but I just don't."

"I worry, man. I worry what the fuck is in my own DNA. The bastard fathered me."

"Oh. Now I know why you want Melanie to be in on this conversation."

Bryce nodded. "I'm afraid. What the hell is running through my veins, and what the hell have I passed on to my son?"

I nodded. "I've had the same thoughts, like I told you. Look at what I got on my mother's side. She was unstable, and her half brother is as fucked up as your father. And I still don't know about my own father's involvement in all this."

Bryce looked up. "Here she comes."

Melanie was walking down the stairs and into the family room, wearing a pair of old jeans and a tank top, no bra. Her feet were bare, and her red painted toes sank into the plush carpeting.

"Hey, baby," I said. "Bryce is bartending. What'll you have?"

"Just tonic water with a twist. I don't feel like drinking."

Bryce got her drink and slid it across the bar to her.

"I wish I knew what to say to you," she said to Bryce. "If

it's any consolation, I don't care that you saw me naked."

That got a soft chuckle out of my friend. "Seeing you naked is no hardship, Doctor."

"I think you've seen enough of me that we can be on a first name basis."

"Bryce has some questions for you, Melanie."

"Of course. What can I help you with?" She took a sip of her tonic water.

"This is hard for me to get into."

"I understand. Any time you're discussing your psyche, it's always hard. But I'm a professional. I'll answer any questions to the best of my ability."

He smiled. "I feel like I should be paying you."

"Let's just call it a favor between friends."

"Well, you know all about my dad."

She nodded.

"I worry. I'm worried because I have his DNA. My son has his DNA. Obviously, I don't want either one of us to turn out the way he did."

"That's totally understandable," Melanie said. "But you're Jonah's age, right? Thirty-eight?"

"Yeah."

"You've come this far in life without having any problems. No one is perfect. And while research has shown that, yes, psychopathy can be genetic, other factors are also at play, such as environment."

"That's another thing I just don't get. I knew my grandparents. As far as I could tell, they were decent people. How could they have raised my father to be who he is?"

"Again, there are no straight answers here, Bryce. I wish I could tell you for sure that genetics play no role, but there just isn't any research to back that up. I can say this, though. Your genes do not define who you are. Your actions and choices do."

"She's fucking brilliant, isn't she?" I said.

Bryce smiled. "I try to make good choices. Especially now, for Henry's sake."

"Then there's no reason to believe your personality will ever change. Look at Talon, for example. If any man in the world had reason to become a psychopath, it's him. But even before he started healing, he never had any tendencies in that direction. And he comes from the same gene pool Jonah comes from, and their mother and their uncle were both a mess."

"A mess." I couldn't help a smile. "Is that a psychiatric term?"

Melanie chuckled. "You know what I mean."

"Still," Bryce said. "It's freaking me out. How could I have lived with my father my entire childhood, and some of my adult life, and not seen who he was?"

"I know it's hard for you to understand. It's hard for anyone to understand," Melanie said. "But your father is hardly the first person to lead a double life. It happens more frequently than you would think."

"I know that, but this isn't just *any* double life. This isn't a guy who has two wives and neither of them knows. This is a guy who had a wife and kid, was an upstanding member of his community...but was also a child molester and murderer. It's incomprehensible to me."

"I think you have your answer right there," Melanie said. "It *should* be incomprehensible to you. The fact that it is means you will never follow in your father's footsteps. You make your own choices, Bryce, no matter what your genes say. We all do. I understand that these words probably don't make you feel any better right now, but they will. Just trust yourself. You're a good man, a good father. You won't screw up."

"I sure don't want to. Henry's the most important thing in my life. But my mother..."

"Yes," Melanie said. "This will be especially hard on her."

"She has relied on him her whole life. They married young, and she's never worked outside the home. What is she supposed to do now?"

"She may need some help. She may need *your* help."

"Of course, I would do anything for her, but I don't even have a job yet myself. And I've got Henry to think of."

"Is your parents' mortgage paid off?"

"Yeah, I think so."

"Good. Your mother has a house. Your father, once he is caught, will be going to prison for the rest of his life."

"I'll find some work, maybe open a business in town. My mother won't want for money. That's not really my biggest concern. Right now, she's a mess. She just found out that her husband killed her nephew, her sister's son. And God knows how many other people he killed or hurt. She went to her sister's house, but she couldn't tell her the truth. I had to take her to the hospital."

"I'm so sorry. I'll go to the city and see her if you'd like."

"I would appreciate that."

"I'm currently on a leave of absence from practicing, but I'll be happy to visit with her."

"She doesn't deserve this." Bryce shook his head.

"No, she doesn't," Melanie said. "And neither do you. Neither does Talon, or Jonah, or any of us. But we're all involved in this up to our necks at this point. We may never uncover the entire truth, but we're certainly looking."

"I should go," Bryce said, finishing his beer. "Henry needs me. And I need him."

"Children have a way of keeping things in perspective," Melanie said. "When you're feeling like you can't take it anymore, when you think your life is going down one big hole, look at your son. Look at that miracle. That will bring you back."

I stared at Melanie, her green eyes as beautiful as ever. How did she get to be so wise? It wasn't just a psychiatric education. She had wisdom beyond her years.

"Thanks." Bryce stood and held out his hand to Melanie.

She stood, took his hand, and then pulled him into a hug. "It will be all right. Not today and not tomorrow, not even next year maybe. But you *will* get through this."

We walked Bryce to the door and said good-bye.

"I'm going to let Lucy in," I said, "and then, Melanie, let's go to bed. I'm fucking exhausted."

She smiled. "You read my mind."

After Lucy came in, getting pets from both of us, I turned back to Melanie. "I love what you said about Henry. About how a child puts everything in perspective. I'm not a father, and I never thought I wanted to be one, but now, knowing you, having seen what my brother was able to get through, I think I *do* want to be a father. I really do."

Melanie pulled me down for a quick kiss. "I'm so glad to hear you say that, Jonah, because there's something we need to discuss."

CHAPTER FORTY-THREE

Melanie

"What?" he asked.

I looked down. My breasts were tender, more tender than normal. Granted, Jonah had been particularly affectionate with them, but they were tender inside. And when I had gone to take my birth control pill this evening after my shower, something occurred to me.

My period should've started a day or two ago.

This wasn't overly unusual for me, even on the pill. I would go a day or two off schedule every once in a while, but something came to me that hadn't previously. And as I was a physician, it should have, except that my mind had been understandably occupied with other things.

"You know I'm on birth control pills," I said.

"Yeah?"

"Well...if you don't take your pill at the same time every day, or if you miss a day or two, the chances of pregnancy go way up."

"Melanie?"

"Those days I was gone, when I was abducted, I didn't have my pills."

"You mean..."

"I'm a little late. Now this may not mean anything—"

He pulled me to him and crushed his lips to mine.

I opened for him instantly, our tongues twirling in a ferocious yet meaningful kiss. When we finally broke away from each other and inhaled, he cupped my cheek.

"Wow. Just wow."

"I'm not sure yet. I'm sorry this didn't occur to me before. I'm a doctor, for God's sake. But there's been so much going on..."

"Baby, this is the best news ever. No wonder you wanted tonic water tonight."

I smiled. "I actually had a few drinks before this occurred to me, but not enough to matter, and I won't drink again. And it's not really any news yet. I'll go into town tomorrow and get a pregnancy test. Then we'll know for sure."

"The test will be positive. I already know it. All this time, all this new information, not knowing who my father really was... It's all taken its toll. Sometimes I've wondered how we'd get through it all. But now everything is okay. I know everything will be okay."

"Jonah, everything's going to be okay anyway. Look at how much Talon has healed. And now Bryce... We're going through a tough time, but we *will* be okay."

"I know. I know we would've been okay no matter what. But now... A baby. I see the way Bryce looks at Henry. I want that, Melanie, and I want it with you."

I let out a sigh. "You have no idea how happy I am to hear you say that. I was worried about what you might think. That you'd think I subconsciously trapped you because I didn't think about the pills I had missed."

"I would never think that. And it doesn't matter anyway. I'm happy about the news."

"We have to take a test to be sure. And even then, Jonah, I'm not a young woman. Things can go wrong at my age. I'll have a lot of tests and probably an amniocentesis. I'll be considered high risk just because of my age."

"Then you will have the best care money can buy. We'll make sure all the risks are taken care of."

I wrapped my arms around his neck. How I truly hoped the test would be positive tomorrow. Because right now, I wanted to have Jonah's child more than I wanted my next breath of air.

"I'm so glad you're happy about this."

"How could I not be? A baby with you. It will be the most beautiful, wonderful baby in the world."

"So you won't worry about your genetics?"

"My genetics are my genetics. All I know is that we will give any baby of ours a wonderful, happy home."

I felt a vibration.

Jonah reached for his phone in his back pocket. "It's a text. Talon. He wants us to come to breakfast tomorrow. Says he has some great news."

"Great news is always good," I said. "Maybe they got more information from Mills and Johnson."

"I hope so. We need to finally put this thing to rest."

"Remember," I said. "We control our own lives. Whether we ever find out the real truth, we can have a beautiful life."

He took my hand and led me to the bedroom.

★ ★ ★

When we arrived at Talon's house the next morning, I was surprised to see Marjorie holding an adorable child with blond hair and blue eyes.

"Marj, anything you want to tell us?" Jonah said.

She laughed. "I volunteered to take Henry for the day. Bryce wanted to go to the city to see his mother."

"Never thought I'd see you holding a baby like that," Jonah said.

"He's such a good little guy. He's going to be walking before we know it."

"Where's Ryan?" I asked.

"He's running late. Told us to start without him," Talon said.

"Well, then," Jonah said. "What's the news that can't wait?"

Jade held out her hand. On it sparkled a gorgeous solitaire diamond.

I smiled and looked at Talon. "So you finally did it."

"Yeah. She's stuck with me now," Talon said.

"It's absolutely beautiful," I said. But then my heart sank just a little. It hadn't occurred to me the previous evening, but Jonah hadn't said anything about marriage when I told him I might be pregnant. Although he had seemed very happy about the possibility of a baby. Was he planning for us to live together our whole lives and raise our child? I didn't know. Right now I needed to be happy for Talon and Jade. This was a huge step for Talon, one he had been considering taking for a while. I was glad he'd finally done it.

"This is awesome, Tal," Jonah said. "When's the big day?"

"As soon as possible as far as I'm concerned," Talon said. "But of course Jade wants a big wedding."

"No, my *mother* wants a big wedding," Jade said. "I would like to go to Jamaica."

"Wow, Jamaica. That would be amazing," Jonah said. "In fact, the doc and I might just tag along with you."

"We should all go," Jade said. "How long has it been since the two of you had a real vacation?" She looked to Talon.

"Vacation? I'm not sure I know the meaning of the word," Jonah said, laughing. "But with all the things going on—"

"With all that going on," Talon said, "we could all use a goddamned long vacation. I've been taking so much advantage of my men that I feel kind of bad about leaving on vacation. But damn, I could use one."

"Yeah, and one in Jamaica. The beach is..." Jonah sighed. "It's been so long since I've been to a beach."

"Joe loves the water," Talon said to Jade.

"Then it's settled," Jade said. "I don't care what Brooke Bailey wants. We are all going to Jamaica, and you and I will get married there."

Jonah looked at me, his eyes full of love. "How would you feel about a double wedding?"

My heart nearly melted as my skin warmed. Love bubbled through me. I opened my mouth, but I couldn't say anything.

"Damn," Jonah said. "It was never my idea to propose marriage in front of my entire family. That just slipped out."

Was he proposing only because of the baby? That wasn't what I wanted. I touched his arm. "You know I may not be—"

He placed his hand over my lips. "Melanie, it doesn't matter. I'll never love another woman. Will you be my wife?"

I looked around the room. Talon, Jade, and Marjorie were all wide-eyed.

"Are you sure you're ready for this?" I asked.

He smiled at me, his eyes glowing. "More sure than I've ever been about anything, ever."

I smiled ear to ear. "Then yes, Jonah. I would love to marry you."

Marjorie squealed. "Oh my God! This is going to be so much fun. A double wedding in Jamaica!"

"You'll be my maid of honor, of course," Jade said to Marjorie. "Who will you be asking, Melanie?"

A brick hit my stomach. I had no siblings, and I was such a loner. I didn't have very many friends. I smiled shakily. "I don't know. I'll think about it."

"Well, think fast," Marj said, "because let's get this thing moving. We all need a vacation."

I couldn't fault Marj's observation. The vacation would be good for every person sitting at this table. But if they were planning to get this moving quickly, I'd have to do some thinking.

How had I gotten to be a forty-year-old woman with no friends? I had been depending on myself for so long it never even occurred to me to have a girlfriend. I had never been lonely. I always enjoyed my own company. About the closest thing I had to a friend right now was Ruby Lee. Maybe she could use a vacation.

"And you'll be my best man, Joe," Talon said.

"What about Ryan?"

"He can be yours."

"Are you okay with that?" Jonah asked.

"Of course I am. Why else would I have suggested it?"

"I mean, you really want me? If I had gone with you that day..."

"Damn it, Joe, we've put all that behind us, remember? We're going to be happy now. If I were holding any kind of grudge against you, I wouldn't want you as my best man. You're my big brother, and that's why I want you."

"Wait a minute," Marjorie said. "Can Joe be a groom and a best man? It won't work. We won't have the right amount of people."

"Marj, who cares?" Talon said. "This is our wedding, and we're going to do what we want to."

Marj huffed. "Fine, then. We'll be one guy short, but no matter."

"I'll ask Bryce to come along. God knows he could use a vacation. He can stand up for me as well," Jonah said.

"There you go, Marj," Talon said. "It's all settled."

"So now we just need a date," Jade said. "Life is crazy at my office right now. Only one city attorney—me—and no mayor."

"All the more reason you need a vacation," Marjorie said.

"True." Jade nodded. "And as far as I'm concerned, the sooner the better."

"How about in two weeks?" Talon said.

"Let me text Dolores," Jonah said.

"We all know I'm free," I said.

"Still no word on your medical board issue?" Talon said.

I shook my head. "I've been meaning to get in touch with Miles Bennett at the hospital, but things have been...a little busy around here."

"You can say that again," Jonah said. "We're going to get this all taken care of. You need to get back to practicing. Your patients need you."

So much had been going on that I'd had a hard time giving my patients a thought during the last couple of weeks. But I missed them, and I missed working. Talking to Bryce the previous evening had proved that. I'd nearly forgotten the joy I got from my work, from helping people.

"Dolores says she can make the vacation work for me in two weeks," Jonah said. "So it's settled, then?"

"Sounds like it is," Talon said.

"Perfect," Marjorie said. "You just leave this all to me. I'll plan the best wedding ever."

"Good," Jade said. "Honestly, I don't have any time to help you."

"Don't you worry. Your maid of honor is on the job." Henry had fallen asleep in her arms. "I'm going to go put him to bed, and then I'll get started on it."

Jonah and Talon exchanged wary glances. "This is going to cost a lot," Jonah chuckled.

I shuddered. "I don't want you to go to any expense."

"Doc," Talon said, "it's all on us. Don't worry."

"Melanie," Jonah said, "we all deserve a vacation, and this is our wedding. Let me treat you. Please."

"All right." I smiled. "I don't know how I got lucky enough to get involved with this great family."

"Doc," Talon said, "we're the lucky ones."

"Agreed," Jade said.

"Agreed a hundredfold," Jonah said, taking my hand and laying a light kiss on it. "We are the lucky ones." Then he stood. "If you'll excuse us, Melanie and I have an errand to run." He squeezed my hand. "I think our little sister has all of this under control, so we're not needed here."

"Before you go, Joe," Talon said, "I've been thinking..."

"Yeah? What is it?"

"When are you going to see Larry Wade again?"

"As soon as I can get away," Jonah said. "I have a lot more questions for him, after my ordeal with Wendy Madigan."

"I think"—Talon rubbed his forehead—"I'd like to go with

you."

"Are you sure?"

"Yes. I'm sure."

CHAPTER FORTY-FOUR

Jonah

Melanie had insisted on going home before taking the pregnancy test. I wanted her to use the bathroom at the drugstore, but she wouldn't hear of that. Now, as I sat on my bed, wringing my hands and waiting for her to come out of the bathroom, my heart raced.

I wanted a positive result so much.

I kept telling myself it would be okay no matter what. That we would have more chances to have a baby. But Melanie was right about one thing. Neither she nor I were getting any younger.

I rubbed Lucy's soft head as I glanced at my watch. Melanie had said it would only take a minute.

This was the longest minute in the history of the universe.

Finally, Melanie strode out of the bathroom, the expression on her face unreadable.

I arched my eyebrows.

She came and sat down on my lap. Still no smile.

"Baby," I said. "Whatever it is, it's okay."

"Well," she said, "there will be other times."

My heart sank, but I had to be strong for her. "Yes, sweetheart. We'll have lots of babies. As many as you want."

She bit her lip. "I think I'd like one." Then she beamed.

"After this one."

Her words took a moment to sink in. Then I smiled at her.

"Positive." She held out the test stick showing two blue lines.

I stood with her in my arms and spun around the room. "This is the most wonderful news." Then I sat down. "I'm so sorry. That can't be good for the baby."

"Don't worry. I'll be fine."

"Damned right you will be. We'll get the best prenatal care for you. I'll have the best doctors in Denver flown in."

She laughed. "There are many perfectly good obstetricians in Grand Junction."

"This is so amazing, Melanie. I love you so much."

She cupped my cheek. "I love you too, so much."

★ ★ ★

A few days later, I sat with Talon in the visitation room at the prison, waiting for the guard to bring Larry Wade out to us. Talon was rigid, his face pale. I had told him on the way over that he didn't have to do this, that if he found he couldn't, it didn't show any weakness on his part. But he was determined.

I opened my mouth to repeat my earlier words but then thought better of it. He clearly wanted to do this, no matter how difficult it was going to be for him.

He had seen photos of Larry but had never seen his face in person. Larry had always worn a mask during the time Talon was held prisoner.

I cleared my throat. The guard was bringing Larry toward us. "Here he comes, Tal."

Talon nodded. No words. Not that I expected any.

Larry sat down with a plunk. "What do you want today, Steel?" He looked at Talon. "I see you've brought company. Who's—" He stopped abruptly, eyeing Talon.

"This is my brother. Talon."

Larry showed no emotion. Nothing at all. And I'd thought Simpson was the iceman.

"I'll be right over there." The guard gestured.

I nodded. I looked toward Talon, but he didn't look like he had anything to say, at least not yet.

"You have anything to say?" I asked Larry.

"Why should I?"

"Just so we're clear, you don't talk to him," I said to Larry. "He'll talk if he wants to. If he doesn't want to, he won't."

Talon was tense next to me. I squeezed his shoulder and then turned back toward Larry.

"I have a lot of questions for you today, Uncle Larry."

"I'm sure I won't have any answers for you."

Talon stood abruptly and walked toward the door to the visiting area.

"Shit," I said under my breath. I looked at Larry. "I'll be right back."

I followed Talon out the door. "Tal?"

He shook his head. "I'm sorry, Joe. I tried. I guess I'm not ready."

"It's okay. We'll go."

"No. We came all the way out here. You have questions you need to ask. Take as long as you need. I'll be outside getting some fresh air."

"Are you sure?"

"Yeah, I just need some air." He shook his head. "Your strength, Joe. It's humbling."

"What?" I had no idea what he was talking about.

"The way you deal with him. You own that room, that table. You own *him*. You've always been that way. You're not scared of anything. You never have been."

Wow. This was what my brother thought of me? Unbelievable.

"I'm scared of a lot of things, Tal."

"You sure as hell never show it. You faced off Tom Simpson and Theodore Mathias unarmed. Twice." He shook his head. "Fucking amazing. I've always looked up to you. Always. You're a good man, Joe. A strong man who always tries to do the right thing. That's why I want you for my best man. You're the kind of man I want to be." He cleared his throat. "Now go on back in there and get the information you need. I'll be fine. I'll text you if I go anywhere."

He walked off before I could answer. Was that really how Talon thought of me? After I'd let him down twenty-five years ago? I wasn't worthy of his praise. But I'd deal with feeling unworthy later. I walked back into the prison and into the visiting room. Larry still sat at the table. I sat back down.

"Your brother doesn't seem to have a lot of guts," Larry said.

"If you mention my brother again, I will have your throat slit in your sleep tonight."

That sobered him up a little. "What is it that you want now, Steel?"

"Information, Larry. The usual."

"I don't know where Simpson and Mathias are."

"Funny enough, I actually believe you. My questions concern someone else. Wendy Madigan."

"I don't know anything about Wendy Madigan."

"You were in the future lawmakers club with her."

"So?"

"I have a lot of questions about that club and what you did there. But I won't go there yet. You told me once that Wendy wasn't who she seemed to be. I need you to elaborate."

"Figure it out yourself."

"I'm serious, Uncle. I *will* have your throat slit tonight. I can pay those guards off to do anything, and if they don't want to do it, they'll have one of your fellow prisoners do it."

Larry sighed. "Might make my life a whole lot easier, to tell you the truth."

Time for a different tactic. I needed Larry alive. If his impending death no longer scared him, I needed to find something that would.

"I can smoke Simpson and Mathias out. They'll make your life miserable."

Yup, that got him. He paled and clenched his hands onto the sides of the table, his knuckles whitening.

"Look, just answer one question for me. What the hell was the relationship between Wendy Madigan and my father?"

"They were lovers. You already know that."

"Was my father in love with her?"

"At one time."

Not surprising, though my stomach clenched. "Was my father in love with my mother?"

"Yes. I believe he was. But I didn't really have anything to do with your father. Or my sister, for that matter."

"Were Wendy and my father having an affair while he was married to my mother?"

"Only Wendy and your father know the truth."

"Tell me why Talon was taken."

"Talon was never supposed to be taken. I've told you that."

"I know that. And you know as well that Wendy told me something entirely different. I had the opportunity to talk to her recently."

"She's lying."

"I haven't even told you what she said yet."

"The bitch is a liar. She'll say anything to get what she wants. She'll shatter your world if it will get her closer to her ultimate goal."

"What's her ultimate goal?"

"Surely you've figured that out by now."

I let out a breath. "My father."

"Your father."

"But he's dead."

"Is he?"

Yes, he was. I knew that as fact, but still, a chill coursed through my body. Was Larry suggesting that Bradford Steel was alive? "His body was cremated. Yes, he's dead. Wendy knows that."

"Maybe he's dead, and maybe he isn't. It doesn't matter. Reality was never a concern of Wendy's."

How well I knew the truth of that. But I'd play along. "What makes you say that?"

"I've told you before. She isn't what she seems."

"Yes. And I've told you before that I need you to elaborate."

Larry shook his head. "She's a smart woman. Very smart. A genius. Cunning. She'll do anything, and I mean *anything*, to achieve her ultimate goal. She doesn't care who she hurts."

"Did she have anything to do with Talon's abduction?"

"Is that what she's claiming now?"

"I have reason to believe that, yes."

"I've told you before. Talon wasn't meant to be taken. He was at the wrong place at the wrong time. The others didn't know who he was when they took him."

"I can't believe that. They both knew my father. They would know who his sons were."

"If they took him on purpose, they didn't tell me about it. I've told you before. I advised them to return him unharmed. They wouldn't listen."

I cleared my throat. "Wendy is claiming that Talon was taken as a way for her to punish my father."

"For what?"

Just how honest could I be with Larry? What the hell? Why not go all out? "I'm not exactly sure, but I think it has something to do with my youngest brother, Ryan."

"Shit. That bitch is worse than I thought."

"Give it up, Larry. Tell me what you know."

"I've warned you before about the truth, Steel. It's a dark room with no escape. You sure you want to go there?"

Did I? Or did I want to go home and start my life with Melanie and my child? The latter sounded much better. I could walk out of here and leave the past behind. Let Uncle Larry rot in his cell until his trial. Let Tom Simpson and Theodore Mathias stay on the run. Mills and Johnson would find them eventually. Let Wendy Madigan rot in the psych ward at the detention center where she was now being held, no doubt knee-deep in her delusions about me and my father and my brother. Let Ryan live out his life as the third son of Brad and Daphne Steel, not Wendy Madigan's bastard.

It would be so easy to walk away, to live my life. To let it all go.

I breathed in and exhaled slowly, looking my uncle

straight in his blue eyes.

"Yes. I want to go there."

CHAPTER FORTY-FIVE

Melanie

I smiled as I walked out of the doctor's office. I'd gotten a clean bill of health and another positive pregnancy test. No heartbeat for the baby yet, but I was only about five weeks pregnant. Armed with a prescription for prenatal vitamins and a copy of *What to Expect When You're Expecting,* I headed toward my car.

"Melanie!"

I turned. Oliver Nichols walked toward me. I hadn't seen or heard from him since Jonah had basically kicked him out of my office several weeks ago.

Seemed like a lifetime ago.

He looked good, his auburn hair blowing slightly in the breeze. "Oliver. How are you?"

"I'm good. I stopped by your office a couple of times, but no one was there."

"Oh." I cleared my throat. "I'm on a leave of absence."

"Really? Is everything okay?"

"Yes." I really didn't want to go into it, so I lied. "Just taking a much-needed vacation."

"Oh. Where are you headed now? Do you have time for a quick lunch?"

I looked at my watch. I didn't want to be rude to Oliver,

but Jonah would not react well to my having lunch with him, even if it was just a friendly lunch. He'd caught Oliver kissing me in my office, and that hadn't gone well.

"Look, Oliver—"

He shushed me with a gesture. "Melanie, I'm interested, okay? I know that Steel guy made it pretty clear you belonged to him, but from where I was standing, I never heard you say so."

I felt my cheeks burning. "It's just..."

"What?"

"Well, to be honest, I'm...pregnant. Jonah and I are getting married."

"Oh." He smiled. "I won't say I'm not disappointed. I was hoping something might spark between us."

"It would have been fun." And I meant it. He and I had engaged in a hot one-nighter after medical school graduation. Then we hadn't talked until... Well, until we'd run into each other at the coffee shop by my office several weeks ago.

"I do owe you a meal, though," Oliver said.

"I suppose—" My phone interrupted me. I pulled it out of my purse. Talon.

Talon would never call me unless it was important.

"I'm sorry. I have to take this."

Oliver nodded.

"Talon?" I said into the phone.

"Doc, are you still in the city?"

"Yeah. Just finished at the doctor's. What's up?"

"I need to see you."

★ ★ ★

Talon sat in my office. I'd opened it up for him, even though I technically wasn't supposed to. I'd said a quick good-bye to Oliver, promising to call him.

But I wouldn't call him. I knew that.

"It was a weird sensation," Talon was saying. "Actually seeing the face of one of the men who... God, it's still so hard to form the words. Who raped me, Doc. One of the men who raped me."

"What do you mean by 'weird?'" I asked.

"I wasn't frightened, exactly. I just kind of froze."

"Sounds like a completely normal reaction."

"I really thought I was ready to face him."

"And you did."

"But I ran away like a little pussy. Just like they always called me back then."

"Look, don't let the head games they played with you when you were a little boy affect you now. I know it's hard, but you're a strong, capable man now, Talon. You know that. Larry Wade can't hurt you anymore. Neither can the other two."

"Well, they can. They haven't been caught yet."

"No, they can't. You won't let them."

"Just when everything was going so great. Jade and I are getting married. I thought I was ready. I really thought I was."

"You *were* ready. You just didn't stay long. Please don't beat yourself up about this, Talon. You've come so far. Facing an attacker is not an easy thing for anyone, even someone as strong as you are."

"I don't feel very strong at the moment."

I smiled. "Of course you are. Look how far you've come."

He shook his head. "But I'm not. Not compared to Joe. He has stared down the barrel of a gun twice now. I swear he could look into the eyes of a lion attacking him and keep his cool."

"Jonah is an amazing man. You won't get me to disagree with that. But Talon, you're just as amazing. Remember, your brother didn't go through what you went through at these men's hands."

"He went through it in his own way."

"He did. But not the way you went through it. Don't try to equate the two situations because they're very different."

"I just wanted to..." He raked his hands through his hair. "I wanted to be strong. To face Larry. I needed to prove to myself that I was ready. Ready to marry Jade and to be...normal."

I smiled and patted his hand. "What you're feeling *is* normal, Talon. So very normal."

"You know what I mean, Doc."

"Yes. I do. But what is normal? You're happy. You're healthy. You're in love. That's pretty normal."

That got a laugh out of him. "You always make everything so clear."

"That's my job." I smiled.

"Sorry to interrupt your day. I should text Joe and let him know where I am. Do you have anything you need to be doing?"

I looked at my watch. "Yeah. I'm meeting Detective Lee for a drink in a half hour. She and I need to talk about what she found out from Rodney Cates. I had to leave in the middle of our conversation with him when I heard from Jonah. You want to tag along?"

"Nah, that's okay. I'll see if Joe's still in town. If not, I'll take a cab home."

"A cab all the way to Snow Creek? That's expensive."

He let out a guffaw. "One day you'll understand Steel money, Doc."

I smiled timidly. "Maybe. I've always been so frugal. And you know, just because you have money doesn't mean you should waste it."

"Getting a ride home is hardly a waste of money, Doc. See you back at the ranch."

* * *

Ruby sat across from me at a local bar, dressed as usual, though this time her Dockers were black, not khaki. Still the same white Oxford shirt, with only one button undone. Hair pulled back severely. Not a touch of makeup.

She was a naturally pretty woman with a wonderful figure. Better boobs than I had and curvier around the butt too. Plus a few inches shorter than I. Not nearly as gawky.

"Were you able to find out anything about the future lawmakers club?" I took a sip of my mineral water.

"He clammed up like you wouldn't believe," Ruby said. "Actually cried. Said they'd kill him if he said anything. Said they were into some nasty shit, but I couldn't get him to give me any details. But I did find out one thing."

"Yeah?"

"They had a financier. A backer. A fellow member of the club."

My heart sank. A member of the club who had the kind of money to back their activities. Who else? "Bradford Steel."

CHAPTER FORTY-SIX

Jonah

The guard approached us. “Time’s up.”

“Are you fucking kidding me?” I stood. “Can we have a few more minutes? I was just getting him to talk.”

Larry stood. “Just as well. I need to keep my big mouth shut.”

The guard led him away just as my phone buzzed. Talon. “Hey, Tal.”

“You still in town?”

“Yeah, just finishing up with Larry.”

“Good. I need a ride home.”

But I wasn’t going home. I wasn’t going anywhere without some new information. “Can you wait an hour or so? I want to make one more stop.”

★ ★ ★

Wendy Madigan looked old and tired as she sat across from Talon and me. She was flanked by two orderlies who would be privy to our conversation, and an armed guard stood to the right. Wendy’s short hair was greasy and slicked back on her head. She looked very different than she had mere days ago.

“Hello, Joe,” she said.

At least she was in her right mind today.

"Hello, Talon."

"Hello, Wendy," Talon said.

"What brings you two here?" she asked.

"Information," I said. "We need information."

She sighed. "I've told you all I can."

"The future lawmakers club. What was it about?"

"You know, you look so much like Brad, Joe."

"So you've told me."

She turned to Talon. "And you... You resemble your father, but not quite as much. It's such a shame what happened to you."

"Wendy, you told me that Talon was taken to punish my father. I need to know the details." I drummed my fingers on the table.

"I shouldn't have said that."

"Well, you did."

"That sounds like something I would have said to your father."

"You did. When you thought I was him."

She laughed. "Don't be silly. I know who you are. Though you do look just like him."

I heaved a sigh. "Wendy, are you saying you don't remember holding me hostage?"

"Why would I do that?"

"It's the reason why you're here," I said. "For God's sake."

One of the orderlies eyed me.

"Wendy," Talon said. "We need the truth. If you can't talk about the future lawmakers club, you need to tell us about our brother."

"Ryan." She closed her eyes dreamily.

"You said he's your son," I said. "I was six when Ryan was

born. I remember our mother being pregnant. Having a big belly."

"Those were pillows. Brad's idea."

"What happened? If you're Ryan's mother, why did you give him up?"

"Because I would do anything for Brad, and he asked me to."

"Why didn't you tell us about this before now?"

"I promised Brad I wouldn't. And I'd do anything for him. How did you find out?"

"You told me. When you thought I was my father."

"Why do you keep saying that?"

"I just need to know if it's true. Is Ryan your son?"

"Yes. He's my son. My beautiful son."

"We'll need to get a DNA test," Talon said.

"We need to tell Ryan first."

"I should tell him," Wendy said. "I'm his mother."

"You don't go near him," I said through clenched teeth. "We'll take care of it." I turned to the orderlies. "Please make sure she doesn't contact our brother."

"Don't worry. She doesn't have access to a phone."

I sighed with relief.

"Haven't you ever wondered where he got his creativity? From me, of course."

"From you? You were a journalist, not an artist," I said.

"Ah, but I could have been. I used to love to paint. They let me paint here. Would you like to see some of my work? The doctors say it's remarkable. Genius, even."

Ryan wasn't a painter, but he was a master winemaker. Creative in his own right. A creative genius.

Genius.

Larry had said Wendy was a genius.

Oh, God...

"You're telling the truth, aren't you?" I said to her. "About Ryan?"

"Of course. I can't lie anymore."

Talon spoke up. "You said I was held for ransom. By some enemy of my father. Who was that enemy?"

"Oh, it could have been any of a number of people."

"Tom Simpson and Theodore Mathias?"

"They had reason to hate your father," Wendy said. "But neither of them was the enemy who held Talon for ransom."

"Then who did?"

Her eyes narrowed. "*I* did."

I gulped. Next to me, Talon paled and clutched at the table. I gripped his shoulder in what I hoped was a soothing gesture.

"Did you take the payment of five million dollars?"

"It was no more than I deserved. I gave your father my only child!"

Talon stood. "You bitch!"

"Easy, Tal," I said.

He sat back down.

"You told us before, Wendy, that you didn't know where the five-million-dollar withdrawal had gone. Why did you lie to us? Or are you lying now?"

She giggled. "It was a secret. I couldn't tell you."

"Why now, then?"

"Because I want to see my son."

"You stay away from Ryan," Talon said through gritted teeth.

"She's locked up here," I said. "She can't get to him."

"She'd better not," Talon said. Then, to Wendy, "You're something, aren't you? You got Jade to believe you. You got me to believe you. Only Joe here was skeptical, and turns out he was right." He turned to me. "You were right, Joe."

I shook my head. "I take no pleasure in being right. This is going to kill Ryan."

"I'd never hurt my son," Wendy said. "Why do you think I stayed quiet and away all these years? I didn't want to screw up his life. But he's a very special man. He's a child conceived in love between two people who should have been together. He's perfect in every way."

Talon was still gripping the table, his knuckles white. "How could you? I was a fucking kid. Do you have any idea what they did to me? What they did to Luke Walker? And all for what? Because you told them to?"

"I had nothing to do with any of the other ones," she said. "That was all them."

"You fucking bitch!" Talon pounded his fist on the table.

As angry as I was, I needed to keep Wendy talking to get as much information as I could. "Tal, why don't you wait outside for a while? Cool down a little. This isn't helping."

"No." He sat down. "Not only no, but hell, no. This has as much to do with me as it does with anyone else."

I sighed and nodded. He was right about that. "All right."

Wendy yawned. "I'm tired. I don't think I want to talk anymore right now anyway."

"Oh, you're going to keep talking, bitch," Talon bit out.

She smiled—an eerie smile, like a clown in a horror movie. "I'm done. Take me back to my room, please," she said to the orderlies.

"Sorry, guys," one of the orderlies said. "Looks like she's

had enough."

I rolled my eyes. "Let's go," I said to Talon. I stood, walked around to where Wendy was still sitting, and, as stealthily as I could, plucked a few hairs from her head.

"Ow!"

"Sorry," I said. "My watch got caught." I flicked my wrist to show the guard standing to the right.

The orderlies led Wendy away.

Talon stood, his eyes glassy. "Jesus, Joe. What are we going to tell Ryan?"

"Nothing," I said. "Nothing until we have solid proof. He's gone thirty-two years without knowing. A little longer won't hurt him. She can't contact him, so we're safe. And hopefully we'll find out that the bitch is lying."

"How?"

I showed him the fine hairs in my hand. "We're going to get a lock of Ryan's hair and have a DNA test done. If it's negative, he never has to know."

CHAPTER FORTY-SEVEN

Melanie

Bradford Steel had been the financial backer for the future lawmakers' misdeeds. This was going to kill Jonah.

"The most I could get out of Rodney is that the future lawmakers club was founded by my father, and it started out as a legitimate business idea," Ruby said, "though he wouldn't elaborate on what the idea was. Then things went wrong."

"Meaning?"

"I wish I could tell you. Rodney says the three of them—my father, Simpson, and Wade—got greedy. They decided to push the law a little. Steel didn't realize what they were doing at first and continued to back them. When he pulled out, they never forgave him. Always felt he owed them."

"Which could have led to their abduction of Talon."

Ruby shook her head. "I don't think so. Those three are a lot of things, but stupid isn't one of them. They would have known better than to take one of Steel's sons."

"That corroborates what Larry says," I said. "But Wendy Madigan says differently."

"From what you've told me, Wendy Madigan is crazy," Ruby said. "Of course, Larry is a sociopath. So who knows which one to believe?"

"As a psychotherapist, I should have an idea." I shook my

head. "But I'm at a loss. I've met Larry but not Wendy. They're both crazy."

Ruby took a sip of her drink. "It's a crazy situation from all angles. We already know that the three of them are pedophiles and rapists. I'm not sure how they figured all of that out and decided to act on it, but I'm betting it began with money."

"Money?"

She nodded. "While I couldn't get much out of my uncle, what I did glean from him was the greediness of my father, Simpson, and Wade. They didn't grow up rich like Brad Steel did, and when he was backing them, they got used to having a windfall of cash to do what they wanted. When he cut them off, they didn't take it well."

"So they found another way to make money."

"Right."

"By sexually molesting kids?"

She shook her head. "I have a working theory."

"Yeah?"

"There isn't much money in molesting kids," Ruby said. "That part of it was just for their own fucked-up amusement. But there *is* money in selling kids."

My stomach clenched as nausea overwhelmed me. "Selling kids?"

"Slavery," she said. "Nice little American girls and boys to be used and abused."

"But they killed Luke Walker..."

"True. So there's a glitch in my theory. But like I said. It's only a theory."

"The others were never found..." I said, more to myself than to Ruby.

"Right. And I've pulled up the news from that time. Huge

investigations were done. I mean, these were missing kids. No trace of any of them was ever found. Talon was the only one."

"And Larry let him go..."

"Right."

"Oh, God..."

"I've been thinking back to the short time I lived with my father. He was nice at first, indoctrinating me, so to speak. Then, when he tried to rape me, I ran. But I'm wondering..."

"Yeah?"

"I'm wondering if he had plans to sell me as well. I was an early bloomer. I had the same body at fourteen that I have today."

"Oh my God... What if Gina..."

"Is still alive somewhere?" Ruby cleared her throat. "I've thought of that. But Rodney claims they found her body in the garage and had her cremated."

"Could he be lying?"

"I've thought about that too." She shook her head. "I don't want to believe any of this. I really don't. But what other financial benefit would there be to molesting kids?"

"And Gina was no longer a kid. At least not when she died. Or disappeared."

"True. But there's lots of money in women too, and Gina was beautiful."

She was. Olive skin, long dark hair, deep-brown eyes... She looked a lot like her mother. I cringed. And her uncle.

"I could be completely off base," Ruby continued. "Just a working theory. We need more information. And the people we can get it from right now are Rodney, Larry Wade, and Wendy Madigan. But...Larry and Wendy can't be trusted, and Rodney's not talking."

"Hmm..."

"What?"

I was hesitant to voice this, as Jonah's money was not my money. But when we had visited Frederick Jolly, the registered agent for the corporation that owned the house I was held captive in, Jonah had said he could "pay him to talk."

"How loyal do you think your uncle is to those three?"

"My father and the rest? Like I said, he cried, Melanie. I couldn't believe it. He's scared shitless. If I had to guess, it's not loyalty so much as fear."

"You say those three are greedy. What about Rodney?"

"I couldn't say, but everyone likes money."

"Would money make him talk?"

She laughed. "You don't have that kind of money, and neither do I."

"My fiancé does, and believe me, he wants to get to the bottom of this just as much as you and I do. Maybe even more."

CHAPTER FORTY-EIGHT

Jonah

The next day, I had to be out in the pastures early. After I finished my work, I came home to have lunch with Melanie. She looked radiant. Pregnancy agreed with her. With all the shit going down right now, she was the calm amid a stormy sea. We had discussed what we'd both found out the previous evening when we returned home. I'd had a voicemail from Mills that the house where Simpson had been holed up, where Colin Morse had been raped and tortured, was owned by the elusive Fleming Corporation, the same corporation that owned the house where Melanie had been kept.

Today, I was still in shock about my father having been the financial backer for whatever horrible things the future lawmakers club had been involved in. Tom had said, when I was imprisoned at Wendy's house, that my father owed him, that there was something in his will that we didn't know about.

I shook my head. None of that made any sense.

Or did it?

My father, whom I'd always looked up to as a pillar of strength, was now an enigma to me. I'd never been able to figure out why he swept what had happened to Talon under the rug, why he'd never let us deal with it as we needed to...

I had to face the truth.

I had to face the truth that my father might not have been the man I'd thought he was. He might have impregnated another woman and raised the child as my mother's.

He might have contributed to my mother's suicide. Maybe even to my brother's abduction.

"Jonah?" Melanie touched my arm.

I turned to face her. She was so beautiful, and she represented all that was good in the world.

Thank God for her.

"I'm all right." And I was. As long as I had her.

"I know this is hard," she said. "But we'll get through it. And we'll find the truth if it's out there."

I smiled, brought her fingers to my lips, and kissed them.

And then my phone buzzed.

★ ★ ★

Melanie had begged me not to go, but I'd promised her I'd return. As I looked down at my ankle, my holster hidden, while pulling into the driveway at the Simpsons' house in town, I hoped I'd be able to keep that promise.

Mills and Johnson had found Simpson, ironically at his own home. Why had he been so stupid as to return? I couldn't say. But because I knew Bryce was in Grand Junction with his mother and Henry was safe at Talon's with Marj, I had to try.

I wasn't alone this time. I eyed my phone. I'd just called the police. They wouldn't be far behind me. This time, Tom Simpson wasn't getting away.

I exited my truck and walked stealthily to the front door. I turned the knob, and oddly, it was unlocked. I unstrapped my Glock and entered. "Tom? I know you're here."

I inhaled. He was cooking something. Odd. It smelled kind of like refried beans.

I walked toward the kitchen—

Something hard hit the back of my head.

"Drop your gun, Joe."

I gulped. I'd stared down a gun twice, and now twice someone had held a gun to the back of my head.

As much as I hated to do it, I laid my gun down carefully on a table to the side of me, my nerves skittering.

"Now turn around."

I complied.

Tom stood there, his dyed hair greasy and unkempt, his blue eyes eerily calm. "This is the third time, Joe. The third time we've come face-to-face since I left. And this time, you're not going to get out alive. You've cost me my wife, my son, my grandson."

"You cost yourself those people," I said. "Your actions caused this, not mine. I simply shed light on who you really are."

"Who were you to do that? My family and I were happy."

"Your family and you were living a lie. You'll never see your son or grandson again. I can guarantee you that."

"You're wrong. I *will* get my family back."

"Not if you kill me."

"Evelyn loves me. So does Bryce. So does that baby. They will take me back."

I shattered inside. This time he truly meant to kill me. I felt it in the marrow of my bones.

Melanie, I said in my mind. *I love you. I will never stop loving you. Teach our child about me. Tell him how much I love him.*

The thought of never seeing my child killed me.

And now... It would fall to Melanie and Talon to get the DNA test and tell Ryan the truth.

They were strong. They would handle it. Melanie would have our baby, and she would be a wonderful mother, even without my help.

"I'm so sorry," I said aloud.

"Your apology won't get you anywhere now, Joe."

I jerked back to reality. "I wasn't talking to you."

Then a shrill sound met my ears.

Tom nearly jumped out of his skin, and I took advantage and rammed my body into his, knocking the gun loose from his grip. It landed with a thud on the carpeting.

I inhaled. Smoke. The sound was coming from one of the fire detectors. In the kitchen. The refried beans were burning. While Tom was still disoriented, I grabbed the gun and pointed it at his head.

"Looks like the game has changed," I said through clenched teeth.

"You can't kill me, Joe. You don't have it in you."

I gripped the handle of the gun. "Try me."

"You won't do it."

"You kidnapped, tortured, and raped my brother. You killed your own nephew. You tortured and raped Colin Morse, and God only knows what other heinous acts you've committed. Why shouldn't I kill you?"

I glared at him, my body hot with rage. Redness pulsed around me. It would be so easy to put a bullet in his brain, to end the life of someone who no longer deserved to walk the streets alive.

"Think of Bryce. Your best friend. My son. I'm begging

you now, Joe. Have mercy on an old man."

I cocked the gun. "My mercy ran out long ago."

Sirens blared in the distance. Tom looked around frantically.

"Hear that?" I said. "The cops are coming for you, Tom. Everyone knows about it now. What a degenerate you are. I don't have to kill you. You'll get the punishment you deserve. The torture you deserve. You know what they do to child molesters in prison? Have you visited Larry lately?"

Tom gulped audibly.

Seconds later, three armed officers burst into the house.

"You can put the gun down now, Joe," Steve Dugan said. "We've got him."

I lowered my arm, but Tom acted quickly.

He grabbed the gun out of my hand, and as I braced myself to be shot, a boom rang out into the room.

Tom lay on the floor of the kitchen, blood pouring out of his head, scarlet brain flesh glopped on the linoleum.

I gulped down acid. The bastard had killed himself.

"Shit." Dugan motioned to one of the others. "Check him out. Make sure he's gone."

An officer knelt down by Tom and felt his neck. "No pulse."

"Good enough," Dugan said. "I'll notify the coroner."

I backed away from the scene unfolding before me, my heart slowing, my skin prickling. It was as if I were an outsider looking in, as if a scene on television were climaxing.

Tom had killed himself, rather than face the music.

In the end, after everything he'd done, after everything he'd put my family through, he was nothing more than a coward.

One of the officers, a female, approached me. "Mr. Steel? Are you all right?"

Her voice was tinny, as if it were being filtered through a cheap walkie-talkie like Bryce and I had played with when we were kids.

I nodded.

I was fine. I would get through this. I would see my child born, and I would have a life with the woman I loved. I longed to put all of this behind me, to focus on the life I had with Melanie and our child. To embrace my family. To maybe have more children and to watch my nieces and nephews born to Talon and Jade. Ryan and Marjorie would each eventually marry as well, and our family would expand into one giant crowd of Steels.

The thought almost made me smile.

Almost.

I couldn't yet smile, because this wasn't over.

If my suspicions were correct, once I had the necessary proof, I would have to tell my brother the devastating truth of his parentage.

But that wasn't all.

One man was still out there. The most dangerous one.

The one who had been untouchable so far.

Theodore Mathias. Alias Nico Kostas, Milo Sanchez, and a host of other names. The one who had founded the infamous future lawmakers club. The one who had orchestrated the abduction, torture, and rape of my brother. The one who had raped his niece and attempted to rape his own daughter. The one who most likely had killed Jordan Hayes.

If degrees of evil existed, he was the most evil of the three.

None of us would be truly safe until he had been caught.

CHAPTER FORTY-NINE

Melanie

Several days later...

Jonah pushed a gift bag into my hand. “Go downstairs,” he said softly. “Put the contents of this bag on, and wait for me. On your knees.”

I smiled. I’d missed him. We hadn’t made love in a few days. Too much had been going on.

But he shook his head. “That’s not what this is about. I don’t want to take any chances until the baby is born. We have to be careful.”

“I’m a physician, Jonah. Sex is perfectly safe during pregnancy.”

“I’m not saying no sex. I could never keep my hands off you for that long. But I worry. I don’t want to be too rough with you.”

“What if that’s what I want?”

He smiled. “We’ll both get what we want. I promise. But right now is about something else.”

I nodded, biting my lip. I took the bag and headed downstairs. I opened the door to the dungeon and walked in. I smiled. The bed was covered in lavender buds and rose petals.

Jonah was so wonderful.

I opened the bag and gasped.

It was a gorgeous bra and panty set in purple silk and lace. The Midnight Reverie set from the lingerie shop near my office.

It would clash terribly with my green eyes. As much as I loved purple, I never wore it. But, oh, I longed to put it on. I longed to feel the soft fabric against my skin.

I would. After all, Jonah had told me to wear it. I wanted to please him more than anything.

I undressed, folding my clothes and piling them on the settee at the foot of the bed. I smiled when I removed my pink satin panties. Jonah had said never to wear cotton underwear in this room. I had stopped wearing it altogether, so I'd never be caught off guard.

Slowly I dressed in the violet lace, letting its softness caress my skin. I regarded myself in the mirror on the ceiling above the bed.

Not bad. Even with my green eyes.

I knelt at the side of the bed and waited for Jonah.

A few minutes later, I heard the doorknob.

"Beautiful," he said in a low voice behind me. "You are simply stunning."

I stayed put while he padded across the soft carpeting and took a seat in the leather Master's chair.

"Come here," he said. "Kneel at my feet, Melanie. Kneel and surrender to me completely."

I smiled as I rose and went to him. I knelt in front of him.

"You're so beautiful, with your blond waves teasing your shoulders. That lingerie doesn't do you justice."

I opened my mouth to speak, but he stopped me.

"I love you. I love you, Melanie." He touched my hair, twisted a few strands through his fingers. "There will always be a darkness in me, but only because I want it there now. Because we both need it and enjoy it." He cupped my cheek. "You've banished the bad part. You and your love. I thank you for that."

"I love you," I said.

Jonah pulled a small velvet box out of his front pocket and opened it. "I'm so happy about our baby, but I don't want you to think for one second that he's the reason I'm offering you this. That he's the reason I want a life with you." He pulled a ring out of the box.

I gasped. It was large. Larger than Jade's. And it wasn't clear. It was the lightest shade of purple. Lavender. Was it a light amethyst?

As if reading my mind, he said, "It's a diamond. A mauve diamond. Very rare, just like you are."

"It's perfect," I breathed.

He took my left hand and placed the gorgeous ring on my finger. "Then wear it. Forever. Show the world that you're mine. Marry me, Melanie, and make me the happiest man in the world."

I sighed and laid my cheek on his knee. "I love you, Jonah. I will be honored to marry you. And in this room, I surrender to you. Completely."

EPILOGUE

Ryan

The last barrel of wine had been sent to bottling, and my busy season was finally over. I knew I had been neglecting my family, and it wasn't fair to them, with both Talon and Jonah going through so much.

Now that Jonah was back, the woman who had been stalking him was safely behind bars in a mental institution, and two of Talon's abductors had been taken care of, life was finally getting good for my family.

Jade and Talon and Jonah and Melanie were planning weddings. Actually, Marjorie was planning everything. Soon we'd all be en route to Jamaica for the celebration. And Melanie was pregnant. I would be an uncle in several months. I couldn't help smiling. It would be good for Joe. That man was a born father. He had taken good care of us when we were little, though of course he would deny that. But Melanie had been so good for him. Finally, he was letting go of the guilt that had consumed him for so long. He had been through so much during the last month. He deserved all the happiness in the world. He and Talon both did.

I was heading over to the main house now, to have dinner with my family. From now on, I was going to take an active role in finding Talon's last abductor. We had a name and several aliases. We would find him. My brothers and I were that determined. But first, I was going to get my two brothers married off.

As I stepped into my truck, my cell phone buzzed in my pocket. It was a number from Grand Junction I didn't recognize.

"Ryan Steel," I said.

"Ryan Steel? Ryan Warren Steel?"

"Yep, you got him. Who is this, please?"

A soft whimper came through the phone.

"Hello?" I said.

"Ryan," the female voice said. "Ryan, my darling. This is your mother."

Continue The Steel Brothers Saga with Book Seven

Shattered

Coming August 29th, 2017

MESSAGE FROM HELEN HARDT

Dear Reader,

Thank you for reading *Surrender.* If you want to find out about my current backlist and future releases, please like my Facebook page: **www.facebook.com/HelenHardt** and join my mailing list: **www.helenhardt.com/signup**/. I often do giveaways. If you're a fan and would like to join my street team to help spread the word about my books, you can do so here: **www.facebook.com/groups/hardtandsoul**/. I regularly do awesome giveaways for my street team members.

If you enjoyed the story, please take the time to leave a review on a site like Amazon or Goodreads. I welcome all feedback.

I wish you all the best!

Helen

ALSO BY HELEN HARDT

The Sex and the Season Series:

Lily and the Duke

Rose in Bloom

Lady Alexandra's Lover

Sophie's Voice

The Perils of Patricia (Coming Soon)

The Temptation Saga:

Tempting Dusty

Teasing Annie

Taking Catie

Taming Angelina

Treasuring Amber

Trusting Sydney

Tantalizing Maria

The Steel Brothers Saga:

Craving

Obsession

Possession

Melt

Burn

Surrender

Shattered (Coming August 29th, 2017)

Twisted (December 26th, 2017)

Daughters of the Prairie:

The Outlaw's Angel

Lessons of the Heart

Song of the Raven

DISCUSSION QUESTIONS

1. The theme of a story is its central idea or ideas. To put it simply, it's what the story *means*. How would you characterize the theme of *Surrender*?

2. What new things are revealed about Jonah in this book? About Melanie?

3. A lot is revealed about Wendy Madigan in this story. Did you see this coming? Why or why not? Do you think she's telling the truth?

4. Discuss what you know so far about Jonah and Talon's father, Bradford Steel. What might have motivated him to act the way he did? Do the things he did? What kind of man was he? What might be revealed about him next?

5. Do you think Jonah suffers from depression? Why or why not?

6. Discuss Jonah's dungeon. Do you think his brothers know the extent of his involvement in the BDSM lifestyle? Why did he keep the dungeon? Why didn't he get his key back from Kerry?

7. Do you still think Gina killed herself? Or was she murdered? Who might have murdered her? Is there a chance she's still alive?

8. How do you feel about Melanie's initial decision to shred Gina's letter?

9. If Jonah hadn't received Melanie's text, what might he have done when he went back to the hospital to confront Colin's accusation?

10. Discuss the character of Ruby Lee. What characteristics does she possess? What will her role be in the next story?

11. Discuss the future lawmakers club. Why did Theodore Mathias (alias Nico Kostas) found the club? What do you think the original goal of the club was?

12. How do you feel about Melanie's pregnancy? Will she and Jonah be good parents?

13. Discuss Tom Simpson, the iceman. Why does Jonah call him an iceman? Why does he commit suicide rather than face what he's done?

14. How will Bryce and his mother deal with Tom's death?

15. How do you feel about Melanie and Jonah's sexual relationship and the turns it took in *Surrender*? Will it make both of them happy?

ACKNOWLEDGEMENTS

Surrender marks the end of Jonah and Melanie's journey, at least as far as their relationship is concerned. Like Talon and Jade, they will reappear in the coming books, but the focus will be on Ryan. It's always sad to say good-bye to a couple, but I'm excited to share Ryan's story with all of you.

Thanks so much to my amazing editors, Celina Summers and Michele Hamner Moore. Your guidance and suggestions were, as always, invaluable. Thank you to my line editor, Scott Saunders, and my proofreaders, Jenny Rarden, Lia Fairchild, Amy Grishman, and Chrissie Saunders. Thank you to all the great people at Waterhouse Press—Meredith, David, Kurt, Shayla, Jon, Yvonne, Jeanne, and Robyn. The cover art for this series is beyond perfect, thanks to Meredith and Yvonne.

Special thanks to David, Jon, and Meredith for your unwavering belief in me and my work. Hitting #1 on the *New York Times* list is every author's dream, and you made it come true for me. Words cannot express my appreciation.

Many thanks to my assistant, Amy Denim, for keeping my social media alive while I was in the writing cave. I couldn't do it without you!

Thank you to the members of my street team, Hardt and Soul. HS members got the first look at *Surrender*, and I appreciate all your support, reviews, and general good vibes. You all mean more to me than you can possibly know.

Thanks to my always supportive family and friends and

to all of the fans who eagerly waited for *Surrender*. I hope you love it.

Thanks to my local writing groups, Colorado Romance Writers and Heart of Denver Romance Writers, for their love and support.

I hope you're all as excited as I am to begin Ryan's journey!

ABOUT THE AUTHOR

#1 *New York Times* and *USA Today* Bestselling author Helen Hardt's passion for the written word began with the books her mother read to her at bedtime. She wrote her first story at age six and hasn't stopped since. In addition to being an award winning author of contemporary and historical romance and erotica, she's a mother, a black belt in Taekwondo, a grammar geek, an appreciator of fine red wine, and a lover of Ben and Jerry's ice cream. She writes from her home in Colorado, where she lives with her family. Helen loves to hear from readers.

Visit her here:
www.facebook.com/HelenHardt

MISADVENTURES
OF A
GOOD WIFE
#1 NEW YORK TIMES BESTSELLING AUTHOR
MEREDITH WILD
#1 NEW YORK TIMES BESTSELLING AUTHOR
HELEN HARDT

island—Kate agrees. At a villa as secluded as the island, they're the only people in sight, until Kate sees a ghost walking toward them on the beach. Price is alive.

Their reunion is anything but picture perfect. Kate has been loyal to the husband she thought was dead, but she needs answers. What she gets instead is a cryptic proposal—go back home in three weeks, or disappear with Price...forever.

Emotions run high, passions burn bright, and Kate faces an impossible choice. Can Price win back his wife? Or will his secrets tear them apart?

ALSO AVAILABLE FROM

HELEN HARDT

Keep reading for an excerpt!

CHAPTER ONE

Seventeen years later

"He doesn't look so tough," Dusty said to Sam as she eyed El Diablo, the stud bull penned up outside the Western Stock Show grounds in Denver. She winced at the pungent aroma of dust and animals.

"No man's been able to stay on him more than two seconds, Dust," her brother said.

"He just needs a woman's touch." Dusty looked into the bull's menacing eyes. Oh, he was mad all right, but she had no doubt she could calm him. The ranchers in Montana didn't call her the Bull Whisperer for nothing.

"I don't know. I'm not sure you should try it. Papa wouldn't like it."

"Papa's dead, Sam, and you can't tell me what to do." She pierced her brother's dark gaze with her own. "Besides, the purse for riding him would save our ranch, and you know it."

"Hell, Dusty." Sam shoved his hands in his denim pockets. "I plan to win a few purses bronc busting. You don't need to worry about making money."

"I want to make the money, Sam."

"That's silly."

"No, it's not."

"Look, you don't need to feel any obligation. What happened couldn't be helped. It wasn't your fault. You know that."

"Whatever." She shrugged her shoulders and turned back to the bull. "Besides, if I ride old Diablo here, I can make five hundred thousand dollars in eight seconds. That's"—she did some rapid calculations in her head—"two hundred and twenty-five million dollars an hour. Can you beat that?" She grinned, raising her eyebrows.

"Your math wizardry is annoying, Dust. Always has been. And yeah, I might be able to come away from this rodeo with half a mill, though I won't do it in eight seconds. Besides, Diablo's owner will never let a woman ride him."

"Who's his owner? I haven't had a chance to look through the program yet."

"Zach McCray."

"No fooling?" Dusty smiled as she remembered the lanky teenager with the odd-colored eyes. Yes, he had tormented her, but he had been kind that last day when the O'Donovans left for Montana. At thirteen, Zach had no doubt understood the magnitude of Mollie's illness much better than Dusty. "I figured the McCrays would be here. Think they'll remember us?"

"Sure. Chad and I are blood brothers." Sam held up his palm. "Seriously, though, they may not. Ranch hands come and go all the time around a place as big as McCray Landing."

"It's Sam O'Donovan!"

Dusty turned toward the deep, resonating voice. A tall broad man with a tousled shock of brown hair ambled toward them.

"Chad? I'll be damned. It *is* you." Sam held out his hand. "We were just talking about you, wondering if you'd remember us."

"A man doesn't forget his first and only blood brother."

Chad slapped Sam on the back. "And is this the little twerp?"

"Yeah, it's me, Chad." Dusty held out her hand.

Chad grabbed it and pulled her toward him in a big bear hug. "You sure turned out to be a pretty thing. " He turned back to Sam. "I bet you got your work cut out for you, keeping the flies out of the honey."

"Yeah, so don't get any ideas," Sam said.

Chad held up his hands in mock surrender. "Wouldn't dream of it, bro. So how are you all? I'd heard you might be back in town. I was sorry to hear about your pa."

"I didn't know the news made it down here," Sam said.

"Yeah, there was a write up in the Bakersville Gazette. The old lady who runs it always kept a list of the hands hired at the nearby ranches. Once she discovered the Internet five years ago, there was no stopping her." Chad grinned. "She found every one of them. Needs a new hobby, I guess. So what are you all up to?"

"Here for the rodeo. Dusty and I are competing."

"No kidding?"

"Yep. I'm bronc busting, and Dusty's a barrel racer. And..." Sam chuckled softly.

"And what?"

"She thinks she's gonna take Diablo here for a ride."

Chad's eyes widened as he stared at Dusty. Warmth crept up her neck. Clearly her five-feet-five-inch frame didn't inspire his confidence.

"You ride bulls?"

Her facial muscles tightened. "You bet I do."

Chad let out a breathy chortle. "Good joke."

"No joke, Chad," Sam said. "She's pretty good, actually. But she's never ridden a bull as big as Diablo. She's tamed some pretty nasty studs in Montana, though never during competition."

"I hate to tell you this, Gold Dust, but this rodeo doesn't allow female bull riding."

"I'll just have to get them to change their minds then," Dusty said.

"Good luck with that," Chad said. "In fact, can I go with you? I think the whole affair might be funny."

"Fine, come along then. Who do I speak to?"

"Honey, why don't you stick to female riding? I'm sure the WPRA will be happy to hear your pleas. But this here's a *man's* rodeo."

Dusty's nostrils flared as anger seethed in her chest. "I'm as good a bull rider as any man. Tell him, Sam."

"I already told him you're good."

"But tell him what they call me back home."

"Dust–"

"Tell him, or I will!"

"They call her the Bull Whisperer. She's good, I tell you."

"Bull Whisperer?" Chad scoffed. "So you're the Cesar Millan of cattle, huh? Ain't no whisper gonna calm Diablo. Even Zach hasn't been able to ride him, and he's the best."

"Yeah, well, he hasn't seen me yet." Dusty stood with her hands on her hips, wishing her presence were more imposing. Both her brother and Chad were nearly a foot taller than she was. "I'm going to ride that bull and win that purse!"

"Seriously, Dusty," Chad said, "I was teasing you. But you can't try to ride Diablo. He'll kill you. Trust me, I know. He damn near killed me. I was out all last season recovering from injuries I got from him."

"I have a way with animals," Dusty said.

"So do I, honey."

Sam rolled his eyes, laughing. "Whatever you say, McCray."

"Hey, dogs love me," Chad said.

"I'm not surprised," Dusty said, smiling sardonically. "I'm sure you make a nice tall fire hydrant. Now tell me, who do I need to talk to about riding the bull?"

"You need to talk to me, darlin'."

Dusty shuddered at the sexy western drawl, the hot whisper of breath against the back of her neck.

"And there ain't a woman alive who can ride that bull."

Continue Reading in Tempting Dusty

Visit www.helenhardt.com for more info!